Calamity Rayne Knocked Up

CALAMITY RAYNE
BOOK FIVE

LYDIA MICHAELS

CALAMITY RAYNE KNOCKED UP
CALAMITY RAYNE 5
© 2024 Lydia Michaels Books, LLC

Romantic Comedy
Horny Unicorn Press

USA | CANADA | SPAIN | EUROPE | NEW ZEALAND |AUSTRALIA | ASIA

*For my mom,
a woman who dedicated her entire life
to raising a family and making our house a
home.*

Listen to the Calamity Rayne Playlist on Spotify!
Click Here to Listen!

Working in the Coal Mine by Lee Dorsey
Doctor Doctor by Thompson Twins
Rumors by Lizzo (feat. Cardi B)
The Imperial March by John Williams
Baby Love by The Supremes
Always Be My Baby by Mariah Carey
Baby Got Back by Sir Mix-a-Lot
The Thanksgiving Song by Adam Sandler
Jingle Bell Rock by Bobby Helms
Have Yourself a Merry Little Christmas by Judy Garland
Flight of the Valkyries by Richard Wagner
Auld Lang Syne by Susan Boyle
ABCDEFU by GAYLE
Wings (acoustic) by Birdy
And more...

You Can't Make a Baby That Way

My knees pressed into the carpet as my throat relaxed, allowing him to slide deeper.

"That's it, baby." Hale's hand fisted my hair, angling my head back as he took complete control. "God, your mouth feels incredible," he growled, hips pistoning faster and faster as I moaned around his thick cock. "Fuck, Rayne, I'm going to come."

Alarm bells roared in my head, and my eyes went wide. I shoved back at his thrusting hips, but his fingers knotted tighter in my hair.

"That's it. Take it like a fucking good girl. *My* good girl."

"*Granlgeh*!" A garbled sound of distress escaped my throat, but the swollen head of his cock shoved it back down, so I pinched him.

"Ow!" He stiffened and stilled. "What the hell was that for?"

Ripping my mouth free, I bolted to my feet and shoved him onto the bed. Hale's naked body sprawled across the rumpled covers like a work of art, and I climbed his body like a squirrel racing to its nest—my main goal to get that nut.

"Don't come!"

"Jesus, Rayne! I think your teeth cut my dick—*whoa*—take it easy!"

"No time." I straddled him faster than an old Hollywood western, aligning our bodies and taking him to the hilt. "Go ahead."

His face contorted in a twist of pain and pleasure and he grunted.

"We're good now." When he just looked up at me with the confused face of a battered husband who had just been denied an orgasm and tackled to his back and mounted like a mechanical bull, I realized I could have been a tad more tactful, so I softened my smile and angled my body in a more feminine position —tits out and whatnot. "Hale, I'm ready now."

"I..." His enthusiasm flagged. "What just happened?"

"You were going to come." Planting a hand on his chest, I started to ride him so he didn't lose his erection. "You can do it now." His brow creased when I directed his hand to my crotch. "The success rates are higher if the woman comes, so...get busy."

"Get *busy*?"

"Yes. Start rubbing." Sex was the extent of my cardio, and I was already panting while Hale was just lying there. "Hale, a little help, please."

"Give me a second to find my bearings, Rayne. Two seconds ago, I was enjoying a blowjob, and now—"

"The books say there's a higher chance of conception if the woman comes." My legs were already tired, and I was ready to wrap this up. "Blowjobs don't make babies." Gah! Being on top was too much work. "I thought you had to come."

"This is a lot of pressure."

"Seriously?" I rode him like a jockey on Sea Biscuit. "I'm the one in a sweat. Feel free to jump in the game at any time."

"Rayne, this isn't exactly what I had in mind when we discussed trying."

"Speaking of trying, could you?" I waved a hand at the front of my body. He could at least grab my boobs.

He dropped his head back. "You seem to have everything under control."

"Hale!"

"*What?*"

"Do something before I get a charley horse, and this ride ends."

"You can't just bark out orders in bed, Rayne. It doesn't work that way."

"Why not?" My leg was starting to cramp. "You're always barking them at me." I impersonated his bedroom voice, "Deeper, Rayne. That's it, baby, open wide for me. That's a good little wife. Take it all the way down. It's your turn to be a good little husband and put a baby in me."

Rolling his eyes, he toppled me off of him. I yelped in surprise as he pinned me to the bed, his large hands capturing my wrists over my head. "*Little* is never the word to describe your husband, Mrs. Davenport." He shoved his length deep and I gasped. "I call the shots. I'm in control."

I nodded quickly, recognizing that possessive gleam in his gunmetal eyes. "Yes, sir."

He thrust again and we both moaned but then he was gone, pulling out of my body as his weight vanished. "Don't move."

"Wait. Where are you—"

"What did the doctor say about too much pressure?"

"Not to use water-based lube?"

His mouth firmed into a flat line. "Not that kind of pressure."

I sighed. "He said it'll happen when we're both relaxed."

"And do you feel relaxed?"

I took a quick inventory of my body. "Sort of?"

"You have to stop thinking about conception, Rayne. Just enjoy it."

I never expected this much tension between us, but making a baby was a lot more complicated than I thought. Girls in high school got knocked up left and right without trying. I honestly thought this would be the easiest part of parenting, but boy was I wrong.

He brushed the back of his knuckles down my cheek. "Baby, you need to relax."

Relaxed seemed too close to lazy, and when I got lazy, I tended to procrastinate. It had already been thirteen months since we started trying. We needed to throw some fuel on this fire and start cooking, but first, we needed to get an actual bun in the oven.

My gaze drifted to his cock, which appeared to be softening. *Oh my God, I was killing his penis!*

"Rayne. Eyes on me."

My gaze snapped to his. "Fine, I'm not relaxed, but you're not even turned on."

He caught my jaw. "Is that what you think?"

My breath quickened. When he used that commanding tone, my insides melted like butter. "I don't know."

His large hand slid down the column of my throat with a sense of total ownership. His stare remained locked with mine as his fingers trailed down my chest and fondled my nipple. "Tell me again that you think I'm not turned on."

My gaze darted to his swollen cock. *Well, that sure recovered quickly.* "My mistake."

"Yes, your mistake. When it comes to being turned on by you, it only takes one thought and I'm there, baby." His hand slid lower, and he wrenched my knees apart, dragging his hand right to my bajingo. "Understand?"

"Yes." He sank a finger inside of my heat and I sighed.

Hale's touch always unraveled me. When his thumb grazed my clit, my hips tipped forward, begging for more.

"That's a good girl." He pumped his fingers in and out, drawing me back into the moment and closer to that pesky orgasm I'd been chasing. "Now, isn't this better? When I'm in control, you're always satisfied."

"True," I breathed, my body coiling tighter and tighter as the pressure built. What he was doing felt really good, but... "Hale..." I panted, getting closer. "I'm supposed to come with you *inside* of me."

He wedged two fingers deep and teased that secret spot that made me lose control. "Feels like I'm inside of you now."

"Yeah, but..." Damn, his fingers were getting it done. "But...We gotta grab the bull by the horns—"

His touch disappeared, and his lips pressed to my mouth, silencing me with a bruising kiss. "Listen to me, you beautiful hurricane." His fingers cupped my jaw and I could scent my arousal on his touch. "There will be no grabbing of horns. There will be no talk of ovulation. There will be no references to implantation, sperm, or uterine lining while we are in this bed. Do you understand?"

I nodded. "But if we want—*umph.*"

He covered my mouth. "I'm not finished. There *will* still be blowjobs. I will eat your pretty pussy whenever I'm hungry for it. And you will *not* micro-manage which way I get to make you come. Is that clear?"

This was probably why we still weren't pregnant. "I guess."

"You're *not* going to use my dick like a lab tool, Rayne. Sex is meant to be fun, not stressful."

I dropped my chin to my chest and pouted. "Fine."

"Good girl." He kissed me again, this time much softer. "Now," he whispered, his nose nuzzling that sensitive spot below my ear. "Let's try this again."

As he traced kisses down my body, I tried to relax, but my thoughts spun on the same broken record. We only had a few more hours left before that fertile window closed. Temperatures were right. My eggs were in place. I couldn't bear the thought of one more negative test, one more period, and one more conversation where we each go to bed with our hearts full of disappointment.

"You're not relaxing, Rayne." He settled between my legs and pressed a kiss on my clit. "Let me help you."

I sighed as if his solution were some sort of burden, which it absolutely was not. But I had no patience when I wanted something, and what I wanted was his dick pumping inside of me until a million little Hales came rushing toward my eggs, and one of those little suckers fertilized me. I just needed one.

"Rayne."

"Ah! Did you just pinch my clit?"

"Were you relaxing?"

I pursed my lips, refusing to answer. He knew I wasn't. Telling me to relax was like telling a zebra not to be striped.

Looking up at the ceiling, I tried to clear my mind so I could focus on the pleasure, but I only pictured calendars and pages from my appointment book where I'd marked dates and appointments. I had to see the gyno again next week. By now I was sure there was something wrong.

"Mother-humper!" I gasped when pain

shot through the fleshy part of my inner thigh. "Did you just bite me?"

"Yes. Am I boring you?"

I rolled my eyes and scoffed. "No."

"Sure seemed like it."

"Well, you weren't."

His eyes narrowed and he got back to work. I did some period math in my head to calculate how long I'd have to wait until the next fertile day of my cycle.

"That's it." He snapped, flipping me to my stomach.

"What? No! Wait!"

"Too late." He landed a hard smack on my ass.

"Hale!"

"I tried being patient with you, Rayne." The drawer opened, and he tossed something on the bed.

Lube? "Hold on!"

"The time for excuses is over. Don't move off this bed." Cool air teased my spine as he disappeared into the closet and returned a moment later with a long silk tie dangling from his fist. "Give me your wrists."

I dutifully placed my hands over my head, knowing exactly how this would go. Hale generally accepted my neurotic behavior, but every once in a while, he needed to reel me in, and the fastest way to do that was to take complete control.

The silk tie cinched around my wrists, and a giddy wave of excitement surged through my belly. My NASA-grade period math would have to wait.

Once he had the tie knotted to the headboard and my hands where he wanted them, he dragged his hand down my spine. "Ass up." He hitched my body into position and pushed my head down on the pillow.

Resting on my cheek, I noticed the lube was gone. *Click.* And there went the cap. "Um...I'm pretty wet."

"Not where I'm going."

My heart raced. I hadn't prepared for that. A girl needed a bit of notice when company wanted a tour of the basement. Plus, we *definitely* weren't making a baby *that way.* Oh fuck! Oil drizzled down my ass crack.

"That's cold!" My cow pose reflexively shot into a cat pose.

"You'll be hot in no time. Sex is meant to be fun, Rayne. It's a stress reliever, not a stress inducer." He gripped my hips and the oil warmed as he massaged it between my cheeks.

"You, uh, seem to be rubbing the wrong hole, dear."

"No, this is the right hole."

"Really? Because in health class, they taught us otherwise."

"This isn't health class." His finger teased the tight ring of muscle and my eyes widened.

"*Zoinks!*" I lunged forward like a German shorthair pointer. His finger was in the trust hole.

"Now, let's set some new ground rules, shall we?" His knuckles pressed firmly into my ass cheek as he held his finger deep inside of me. "We're going back to the way things used to be."

"Hale..."

"What?"

I was very aware of his every move, and his stillness was absolute torture. "Please... I'll behave."

His finger twisted, pumping slowly in and out so that I could relax a smidge. I sighed and my posture softened, my tethered upper body sinking more into the pillows. I remembered how good this could be and how much I loved his absolute domination. My orgasm started creeping closer until the pressure increased and it skittered away.

I moaned, because two fingers was a lot for my little asshole.

More oil drizzled down my crack as he slowly scissored his fingers inside of me. I couldn't concentrate, which was probably his goal.

"Feels good, doesn't it, baby?"

The back of my knees started to sweat. "Mmm-hm." I closed my eyes. It was the only way I could tolerate the pressure. The more he stretched me, the more that hint of pain transcended into pleasure.

"Who's in charge?"

"You."

"That's right. And you like when I'm in charge, don't you, baby?"

"Yes."

"Such a good wife. I wish you could see how sexy you look right now with your hands tied and my fingers stuffed in your ass. Imagine how good it's going to feel when my cock's buried deep inside of you."

I trembled at the thought. Hale's cock was beyond average.

"Here's how it's going to work, darling wife of mine." He leaned over me so I could feel the weight of his engorged erection resting on my back as he whispered in my ear.

"We're throwing away the basal thermometers. We're done calculating ovulation days.
There will be no more weird teas, no fertility
diets, and no more self-diagnosing or trolling
medical websites." His fingers pulled out.
"You're ready for me."

"But—"

His hand pressed between my shoulders,
lowering my chest to the bed. "This part always makes you a little nervous, baby, but
then you love it." The blunt head of his cock
pressed to my slick opening. "Do you remember what to do?"

I sucked in a breath, shut my eyes, and
nodded. As soon as he pressed forward, I
leaned into the pressure and he breached my
opening. No matter how many times we did
this, it always took a moment to adjust.

"Beautiful." He caressed my back and
his praise penetrated my soul, fulfilling me
in a way only Hale could. "How does that
feel?"

Hale wasn't necessarily a large man, but
his cock was mammoth. Not just long, but
thick. The first time we slept together, I
feared he might shatter my *hoo-ha*. And yes, I
was working with the sexual maturity level of
someone who found words like hoo-ha, ba-

jingo, and tinkle flower completely acceptable -- both then and now.

"Feels like I have a massive cock up my ass, Hale." I also wasn't one to beat around the bush. And if I didn't have a dick up my ass, I'd probably make a joke about Hale beating around *my* bush, but I was a bit pre-occupied at the moment.

His nails scraped over my ass cheek where he'd landed that spank earlier, and I shivered. "Sex between us will never be a means to an end, Rayne." His hips flexed, and he thrust forward until it felt as if he were pushing into my lungs. "When I'm with you, I exist only for you." He dragged back slowly and intentionally punctuated his words with deliberate thrusts. "Mind. Body. Soul. You get all of me, Rayne. Don't I deserve the same?"

"Yes," I moaned, the mixture of pleasure, pressure, and dominance an intoxicating drug that numbed my senses to all else. I was his. He had total possession of my body, and he knew it.

I knew it.

When he took me so completely, my scattered thoughts silenced and he owned me down to my soul.

"I love fucking you for the simple joy of

it." He thrust harder. "It's not about the outcome." He withdrew with agonizing slowness, dragging his body back then plunging forward hard enough to nudge my body.

I lay pinned beneath him with my arms tied to the bed as he held me exactly as he wanted me. I didn't have to think or move or even try to be sexy. He was calling all the shots.

"So if I want to come in your mouth or on your tits or in your ass, that's exactly what I'll do, Rayne."

His words were an aphrodisiac that added to my pleasure.

"You like it when I do what I want with your body, don't you, baby?"

"Yes."

Honestly, I lived for this sort of possession. He took the stress of thinking completely out of sex. And, for me, stress was once a very stressful topic, but Hale changed that. There was nothing hotter than knowing I could have this effect on a man like Hale.

"Such a good wife," he crooned, reaching under me to fondle my breasts. He pinched my nipple hard enough to make my pussy clench. "I'm going to come all over your hot little ass."

I panted as his hips rocked into me with intense purpose. He wanted me to submit to his possession and I had. There was no point fighting it when he got like this. Hale liked control and I loved when he took it. End of story.

"It's going to be dripping off of you, Rayne. Down your thighs..." Thrust. "From your pretty tits..." His touch rode up my chest, over my throat, and cupped my jaw. "Out of this sexy mouth..."

I moaned, my eyes rolling back in my head. "Yes, please."

My hands balled into fists as my arms stretched over head, the silk tie softly chafing my wrists as the slack disappeared. My eyes opened and I saw the way he tightened the knot to the headboard.

"Do you like when I fuck you like this, Rayne?"

"Yes."

"When I use your body however it pleases me?"

"Yes, Hale..."

"Do you know how fucking hot you are to me? How much it's killing me to hold back my release?"

My breath quickened as he rotated his

hips, drilling his cock deeper. "I want you to come, baby." I gasped, my voice a sultry whisp of smoke.

"When you give me control, you get all my attention. It feels good, doesn't it, baby? Tell me how good my cock feels when it's stuffed inside of you."

Lungs tight, I could only draw in a shallow breath, but I wanted to tell him that I loved every dark, devious thing he was doing to me. His fingers delved between my thighs, teasing my drenched folds, and I twitched as he grazed my over-sensitized clit.

He chuckled, the sound dark and dangerous. "Tell me, Rayne."

"It feels amazing."

"That's right. And if your hands weren't tied right now, I'd make you feel how soaked you are."

He sank two fingers inside of me and I whimpered, my body stretched to the max.

His lips pressed softly to my shoulder. "I can feel your heart beating when I'm inside you like this." He strummed my clit. "Especially here."

Shallow breaths spiked in and out of my lungs as the pleasure seemed to howl out of me.

He groaned. "I love when you make noises like that. No inhibitions holding you back. No filter. Just raw."

Pressure built quickly. I trembled dangerously close to the edge waiting for Hale to pull me back but instead he just pushed me on.

"Let go, Rayne. Give in."

My body shook until I shattered, raspy cries spilling from my lips as he fingered me hard while he fucked my ass. I no longer cared about making a baby or being somebody's mom. I only wanted to be Hale's slutty little wife, his fuck toy, his dirty little fantasy.

My jumbled thoughts became a mess of profanity, prayer, and gibberish. He held still, waiting for me to say the magic words. To beg. It didn't take long.

As soon as my orgasm waned, I yelled out, "Fuck me harder, Hale, please!" And he did.

His body slammed into mine as his fingers worked their magic. My body pulsed, so weak with pleasure I could only fall to my stomach, but that didn't stop Hale. He pounded into me, shaking the tension from my bones. He tamed the storm inside of me until I was soft and passively his.

All his.

I might never care about self-possession or independence ever again. Why did I need to worry about such things when Hale could fuck all my worries away? That's all I wanted in that moment. I wanted him to fuck me until he broke me because when I shattered like this, it wasn't ugly at all. It was peaceful and beautiful, like a galaxy exploding into a billion little stars, and all my neurotic tendencies disappeared into stardust too small to see.

He carefully turned me to my back and traced a finger down my cheek. "There's my baby." The way his possession could effortlessly shift from aggressive to gentle filled me with a sense of security and trust. "I knew I'd find you eventually."

He bent to kiss me softly, and I felt his love pouring into my soul. A divine sense of adoration washed over me, and I chased his lips, always wanting more.

He chuckled, the sound deep and oh-so-sexy. "Don't worry. I'm not finished yet." My drenched thighs fell open as he rearranged our bodies. "Look at me, Rayne."

My bleary eyes opened. God, he was beautiful.

He kissed me again with absolute tenderness. "I love you, baby."

My mouth formed a lopsided smile. "Love you, too."

He still made sure I said it every time. Words of affirmation mattered to Hale. He not only wanted to hear that I loved him, he needed to make sure I knew he loved me. I was his world and he was mine. It was us, and Elara—a family. We were happy, so it made perfect sense that I wanted to add to that happiness with another baby, but Hale never wanted me to feel like anything was missing if that wasn't in the cards for us.

"I'm sorry I get so crazy sometimes."

"I'm used to your crazy, Rayne. It's what made me fall in love with you." Loosening the silk tie, he pulled my weak fingers to his lips, kissing my knuckles as he rubbed feeling back into my arms.

I sighed, my heart full of gratitude that I found this incredible man and somehow managed to marry him. "Are you going to finish?"

He cocked a brow. "I thought you might have had enough."

"I'll never have enough of this." My alone time with Hale was what kept me sane on most days. "Go ahead."

"You're so fucking good to me, baby." He

pushed inside of me again and groaned. Pumping slowly, I could tell he was close.

As his teeth scraped over my shoulder his body shivered and his cock pulsed. His grip on my hips tightened, and he sighed. His weight blanketed me as he slowly pulled out, and I lovingly ran my fingers through his blond hair. Only I got to see him this vulnerable.

I did this to him. *Me.*

My body trembled in the gentle aftermath of my prior climax. He was exhausted and I was more than content to hold him for a while. It was now my turn to take care of him, and I loved that we had this sort of give-and-take together.

Yeah, yeah, yeah, we totally misunderstood the assignment, but so-fucking-what? My husband was hotter than Lucifer's wettest dream, and he loved me in a way I once thought nobody could. We could try for a baby next month. Right now, this was precisely what we both seemed to need.

Rolling to his side, he sighed. "You okay?"

Words were hard, but I managed to slur, "I'm wonderful."

As always, he rose from the bed and disappeared into the bathroom. A moment later he returned with a warm, damp washcloth and pressed it between my thighs. "I don't want you to be sore."

There would be no avoiding that. "It was worth it."

He kissed my clit and stretched out beside me, his fingers lacing with mine. "We needed that."

No matter how much he projected nonchalance, this pregnancy thing was killing him. We both knew it would take some time, but we had no idea it would take this long or be this emotionally draining.

Hale didn't like to fail. And I didn't like disappointing him. It wasn't his failure or mine, but sometimes those negative pregnancy tests felt way more personal than either of us wanted to admit.

What if it never happened for us? What if it was me? What if it was him? What if it was both of us?

There were too many what ifs.

While Hale and I had a daughter, neither of us had anything to do with Elara's conception. Yes, Elara was a Davenport, but she was not Hale's. He adopted her the day she was born, and I adopted her the day we got married. We loved her as our own, and if she was the only child we ever had, she would certainly be enough, but we still wanted to try for more.

I promised no more crying, but sometimes my body just did what it wanted. Tomorrow my cycle would start all over again. Another month gone by, another reason to try not to cry.

Doctors & Their Bedside Manner

"It's been over a year, Doc. Something's wrong."

My OBGYN stilled with only one foot in the door and my chart suspended in his hand. "Rayne. Hello."

I planted my hands in the lap of my paper gown and gave him a moment to enter the room and get situated.

He scrolled through my records as he sat on the wheely stool. "Date of your last menstrual cycle?"

"The twentieth to the twenty-eighth." I'd just recited all this information to the nurse and it annoyed me that I needed to go over this crap again. There had to be some malfunction with my ovaries or uterus. I was sure something was wrong and that was what we should be discussing.

"Any lifestyle changes?"

"Well, there's been a lot more tension in the bedroom."

"It's important that you stay relaxed during intercourse. Have you been taking the vitamins?"

"Yes."

He set the digital chart aside and stood to wash his hands. "Let's have a look."

God, I hated this part.

"Feet up."

I reclined on the paper-covered table, my ass hanging dangerously close to the edge of the table as he snapped on his gloves. Between the table, my gown, and the modesty blanket, there was so much damn paper I felt like a piece of origami. Every muscle twitch was amplified by the obnoxious crumpling.

"Scoot a little lower, please. A little more. Again."

For the love of God! The gown crinkled as I scooched as close to the table's edge as humanly possible. Another inch, and I'd be on the floor. And there went the blaring light.

I stared at the ceiling so not to blind myself as he scoped out Main Street. "Did you rob a stadium for that thing?"

A courtesy chuckle. "A little pressure."

He inserted the speculum, and I grunted. If men had to have their private parts pried open, I bet they wouldn't call it *a little* pressure. And they'd certainly design more ergonomically comfortable tools than the vagina jack is currently cranking open my cooch.

"Nice weather we've been having."

Why did gynecologists get chatty the moment they were staring up your hoo-hah? "Yup."

"Have you been timing your intercourse with your ovulation?"

"Yes, but that's not helping matters in the bedroom." Some nights, I got so neurotic I might as well have brought a stopwatch and worn a whistle around my neck. "The calendars are sort of a mood killer."

"Trying to conceive can be emotionally challenging, especially when faced with difficulties."

Difficulties? Did he find something alarming? Did he know something I didn't know?

He wheeled back and removed his glove with a snap. "It's important to have a strategy for coping with the stress. There are a lot of emotions associated with procreation. You can sit up."

I lowered my feet from the stirrups and scooted back, my gown crinkling with the subtlety of a frying pan falling down a flight of stairs. "You said difficulties. What did you mean by that?"

"Only that patience is a virtue and a difficult one at that."

"So there's nothing wrong? You didn't see any red flags."

"Everything looks healthy."

After a year of trying, one little peek at my mystic treasures didn't seem thorough enough. "Aren't there some tests we can run?"

"There are certain fertility tests to identify any potential issues, but we like to start with a wide net and narrow down the possibilities."

Yes, let's make sure the HMO get all the co-pays possible before we get to the actual bottom of my fertility obstacles. "So, what's the plan of action? Where do we start?" I needed answers.

"We can order some new bloodwork to check your hormone levels, and it might be a good time for some imaging."

"Imaging?"

"A pelvic ultrasound. A semen analysis for your partner is an option as well."

"Where does he get that done?" I highly doubted anything was wrong with Hale's swimmers, but it was worth a look. Whenever I pictured his sperm, they were swimming around in little Armani ties.

"They'll give you a referral at the front desk."

"Okay." My gut told me this was a me problem, not a Hale problem. "For the imaging too?"

"Yes." He made a note in his laptop. "It's important that you keep trying."

"We are. Every day."

"Well, that's good."

Was it? Sex was starting to feel like a football play.

Rayne's on defense. Hale's coming in on that final-yard line. The team's fired up, and there's the snap...

"What about IVF?"

"I'd say we're a ways off from that."

"Exactly how long is 'a ways'?" I needed solid numbers.

"Ovulation induction, insemination, or

in vitro fertilization are treatments typically considered after a thorough evaluation."

"Doc, we've been evaluating the…situation," I gestured toward my lady bits. "for over a year."

"Like I said, we need more tests. Moving forward with any ovulation treatment depends on each patient's unique circumstances." He stood and handed me a pamphlet. "There's some helpful information in here about counseling and support groups. It's important that you educate yourself before making any decisions."

Why did so many male doctors assume woman put no thought into decisions prior to entering their office. This was the only thing I thought about—every day—for more than a year.

"Thanks."

I glanced down at the cornflower blue brochure, and my heart stopped at the boldly printed word *INFERTILITY*.

The doctor continued to talk about information I needed to grab at the front desk but I was done listening. I stared at the brochure, wondering why it was in my hand if we still had 'a ways' to go and more to 'thoroughly evaluate.' Then the door closed and I wanted to cry.

It seemed like as safe a time as any. Hale wasn't here, and I was alone. Just me and my empty eggs.

I sniffled, and a tear fell from my eye, forming a blotch on the brochure where the happy couple held an infant. I had no idea how long I sat there, but it felt like years before I was dressed, packed up, and collecting my appointment card and scripts from the front desk.

On the drive home, I was numb. No recollection of traffic or even parking my car when I reached the office.

I filled my arms with the reports I needed to return to Remington and tried to compartmentalize my professional life from my personal drama.

"Hello, Rayne," Miles greeted in his chipper British accent as he entered the elevator. "I haven't seen you all morning."

"What?"

"I said, I haven't seen you. Is everything okay?" He pressed the button for the top floor.

"Oh, I had an appointment this morning."

"Well, lucky you. He's in quite a mood today. Stocks plummeted and he's been on a rampage. Something to do with a bill the senate just passed…"

Miles continued to update me in his eloquent, matter-of-fact way, but I couldn't hear a single word over the ringing in my ears.

What senate bill was he talking about? Was it another one that went after women's rights? What if we wound up needing IVF, but by the time we figured that out, some dickface part of the patriarchy took away that option?

In addition to everything else, I now felt a crushing sense of urgency. My mind started to panic, so I beelined toward Remington's office the moment the elevator doors opened.

"Uh, Rayne, he asked not to be disturbed," Miles warned, but I needed some sound advice.

Sophie, the newest receptionist whom I was pretty sure was sleeping with or trying to sleep with Remington, sputtered as I walked past. I didn't bother with appointments. I was Remington's right hand and daughter-in-law. We were family, so I marched right into his executive, corner office and shut the door.

"Ever hear of knocking, Meyers?"

I plopped into the club chair across from his enormous desk and slouched dramatically like a broken doll. "I'm barren."

His bushy white brows furrowed. "Start over."

I rummaged through my bag and withdrew the sad little brochure, tossing the crumpled paper onto his desk. "I went to the doctor this morning, and they want to run more tests."

"Run more tests, meaning they haven't concluded anything yet?"

"Well, no, there's nothing since my initial labs. But something's gotta be wrong, Remington. We've been at it for months!"

He set the brochure aside and glanced at his watch, debating the time. "Sometimes these things take time."

"It's been over a year. What if it just doesn't happen for us?"

"Nonsense. Hale's a Davenport. We have strong swimmers and a potent bloodline."

"But what about me?"

I was a Meyers. We didn't have a potent bloodline. Ours was instead a weak line of runaway men and commitment-phobic women. There were a lot of childless relatives in my gene pool, now that I thought about it. Even I was an only child.

My mom had to have a sex life after my father, right? He left when I was a little kid. Yet, I never had any siblings.

"I'm sure you're fine, Meyers. You're young and healthy. For once, don't overcomplicate something simple. Just keep at it in the bedroom, and eventually, you'll wind up in a nursery."

He moved to the wet bar in the corner of his office and cursed. Returning to the desk, he stabbed a finger into the telephone and buzzed the secretary.

"Sophie, where the hell are the glasses?"

"Your reading glasses, sir?"

He rolled his eyes. "No, my damn martini glasses."

The door to his office opened, and a flustered Sophie walked in carrying a tray full of stemware. "I put them in the mini-fridge to chill." Every curve of her twenty-something, perky body was displayed in the skin-tight burgundy dress she wore.

"Next time, leave them where they are."

"Yes, sir."

She bent to open the fridge and both I and Remington silently tipped our heads to admire her perfect heart-shaped ass. Jeez, did the girl live in a Pilates studio?

Bet her ovaries were fine...

She set two frosted glasses on the bar beside the shaker. "Would you like me to mix you a drink, sir?"

I rolled my eyes. Just what Remington needed, another pretty, young thing to fawn over his every desire. Was she even old enough to handle alcohol? Apparently it didn't matter that Remington was approaching his seventieth birthday.

"That's all for now."

She backed out of the room, her expression demure and her body language inviting.

As soon as the door closed I scoffed. "Please don't sleep with her."

"While you enjoy broadcasting your private business, Meyers, mine is not up for discussion. I'll keep whatever company I want."

"She's barely twenty, Remington."

"She's twenty-three."

"And how old is Miles?"

He frowned. "I haven't a clue."

"Exactly. Why do you even know her age?"

"She told me."

"Because you asked?"

"What's your point?"

"It must get tiring always having to pour their milk and cut their meat." I was surprised she didn't add on a few months and say she was twenty-three and a half.

He filled the shaker with ice. "You're being especially judgmental today."

"You're one to talk."

Why couldn't he be satisfied with his long-term girlfriend, Odette? I liked Odette. She was normal. Very different from his bat-shit crazy wife who he kept stashed far away in the south of France.

He poured vodka over the ice, capped the shaker, and rattled it loudly. Poking at me, he smirked. "She did tell me she's a Sagittarius."

"Oh, my God." Horoscopes were not the way into a man like Remington's heart. "And you kept a straight face?"

He glanced over his shoulder, filling the martini glass with the accuracy of James Bond. "I'm a gentleman, first, and a critic, second, Meyers."

"You're a horny old man who likes pretty toys."

"Nothing wrong with that." He crossed the room and handed me a martini.

"I can't."

He scowled. "Why the hell not?"

"The doctor said I'm not supposed to drink right now."

"That's not until you get pregnant, Meyers. Alcohol's historically proven to help make that happen. Drink it."

I took the cold glass from him, mostly because I didn't feel like arguing. My gaze drifted over its cloudy contents to the clock on the wall as I sipped. Ten a.m.

Remington returned to his desk with a matching martini. "I never tried to get any of my wives pregnant."

Remington got more than a few wives pregnant over the years. Although, technically, Jasmine—Hale's beautiful-cheating-manipulative-ex-girlfriend and Elara's biological mother—was now married to Remington as part of a legal hush settlement. But I was sure there were plenty of other accidental *whoopsies* over the years. There seemed an endless line of gold diggers who looked at Remington Davenport like a retirement plan. His age never seemed to matter to any of them.

But for me, he was just a friend, a boss, and a father figure. "We don't know if the issue's with me or Hale."

"That's your problem, Meyers. You worry

too much." He sipped and flinched. "What the hell kind of olives does she have stocked?" His finger punched into the receiver on his desk, and he barked, "Sophie, where did you get these olives?"

"At the Winn-Dixie, sir."

He shook his head. "I order my olives from Southern Europe. Get on the computer and get me some ..."

"Spanish Queens," I provided, knowing far more about this man than anyone should.

"Spanish Queens," he snapped, then disconnected the intercom. Fishing out his sad little olive, he examined it and tossed it back into his glass. "No one cares about the minor details anymore."

I set my martini down and went back to slouching. There were no answers for me here, but Remington had comfortable furniture, and at the moment, I felt safe and hidden in his oversized chair. His office was my favorite place to procrastinate.

"Schedule the tests, Meyers. Then, when you see nothing's wrong, you can unload that worry and get back to old-fashioned fucking."

I winced. "Remington."

"Are we pretending a stork's going to bring the baby? Grow up. Babies come from fucking. Just keep having sex, and you'll get it right one of these times."

Why did men simplify everything down to sex? "Well, you've been no help at all."

"Last time I helped, I got in trouble. Something tells me your other half would prefer you not share these details with me."

He was right. Hale was very private, especially where his intrusive father was concerned. "On that note..." I stood and waved a hand at the documents I brought in with me. "Your reports are finished and I emailed over the stats on the Highlander deal. I'm still waiting on the analytics for the new account, but everything else is done."

"Don't let that Davis fella push you around, Meyers. He told us we'd have the analytics by Tuesday, and it's now Wednesday. We're taking our business elsewhere if he doesn't have something in your inbox. Show him you have sharp teeth behind that smile. It'll feel good to take your frustrations out by firing someone."

I hated letting people go, so it was more likely to add to my stress than anything else. I had checked my emails while waiting at the doctor's office that morning, and I already knew Davis hadn't emailed the analytics report yet.

"Let's just give him until—"

"Meyers." Remington met my stare with stern authority. "We don't make exceptions. If people want to do business with us, they meet our deadlines. If the analytics aren't there when you get back to your desk, fire him and hire someone more dependable."

"Fine." He knew I hated confrontation. "But aren't you at least curious about his—"

"No. I take no interest in incompetent people. Now, get to work."

I pressed my lips into a flat line and stood, slugging back the rest of my chilled martini. "As always, this has been a real treat. Thanks for your help."

"I gave you sound advice."

"Thanks for that," I mumbled as I left his office. Because without Remington's revolutionary advice, I might have never concluded that sex could lead to pregnancy. Things would be much easier now that I figured that out.

When I got to my desk I spent twenty minutes avoiding my inbox and tidying up my work from yesterday. As expected, there was no email from Davis.

"Shit."

I opened the file with the scripted letter I used to fire the last seven candidates for the job. With a quick copy and paste, we were good to go.

"Dear Mr. Davis," I read, making minor adjustments to personalize the text. "Unfortunately, despite our shared efforts and expectations, the deadline was not met. I understand that unforeseen circumstances can sometimes affect our ability to meet obligations, and I appreciate the effort you put forth in attempting to complete the task. However, meeting deadlines is a crucial part of success. Yada, yada, yada, and send."

I stood to stretch my legs and groaned at the uneasy feeling that always came with firing an employee.

My phone pinged, and I opened a text from Hale. He was in California at the moment, which was why he hadn't gone to the doctor's with me.

GOOD MORNING, BABY. HOW WAS THE appointment?

. . .

I QUICKLY TYPED OUT A REPLY.

APPOINTMENT WAS FINE. THEY WANT to update some labs and run some tests. When are you getting home?

HE'D BEEN GONE FOR THREE DAYS, AND three days without Hale was usually my limit.

I SHOULD BE WALKING THROUGH THE door around ten tonight. Wait up for me?

ALWAYS.

I ATTACHED A LITTLE HEART EMOJI and a kiss and slipped my phone back on my desk. A pile of work waited for me, and it was going to be a late night. Cuing up the latest resume submissions, I started searching for Davis's replacement.

I worked well beyond five that day but figured it didn't necessarily count as over-working myself because Hale wasn't around to give me grief about working beyond my pay grade. When I heard him pull up, I shut my laptop and pretended I'd been watching a movie.

I didn't know why I hid my overtime from him. Or maybe I did. It was just something I made a habit of doing to avoid more confrontations between him and Remington.

I must have been more exhausted than I thought because the next thing I knew, the sound of Hale entering the bedroom woke me up. For real. From sleep. Maybe I was developing narcolepsy. I made a mental note to add that to tomorrow's Google list.

The soft creak of the door pulled me from sleep. Peeking through my lashes, my body soft and tucked deep within the covers, I watched Hale's shadowed silhouette quietly creep into the dark room. Rather than say something to let him know I was awake, I took a moment to simply watch him.

He set his suitcase by the closet and loosened his tie. The lethargy of his motions told me it had been a long day for him. Once he stripped away his clothes, he climbed into bed. His hand slid slowly up my body, tracing the curve of my thigh to the jut of my hip.

"You asleep, baby?"

I moaned softly and rolled to my back, blinking up at him through the dim glow cast by the television. My hand cupped his jaw where stubble had grown. "I missed you."

Rather than kiss me, he pressed his forehead to mine and shut his eyes, giving our emotional connection a chance to entwine once more. "It's good to be home."

After Care Beats Foreplay Every Time

I lifted my arms over my head as he removed my shirt, kissing his way down my throat to my breasts. Warm hands framed my ribs. He awakened my body with delicate nips and licks. As he moved over me, my knees bracketed his hips and his hard erection weighed heavily on my stomach. I reached between us to stroke him slowly.

The moment my hand tightened around his flesh, he groaned against the curve of my throat. "Yes." His shoulders trembled as his breath quickened. "There's nothing better than feeling your hands on me."

Nudging his shoulder, I eased him onto his back and straddled his hips. "It's my turn to take care of you."

His chest expanded on a deep inhalation as my hands combed slowly over his muscular shoulders. He was so beautiful that at times I still struggled to understand how he was mine.

Curling my hands around his thick length, I stroked him slowly and guided him inside of my body. Slowly, I lowered over him and we both moaned. That first tight stretch after a few days apart always felt incredible.

His hands cupped my hips as he guided me into a slow canter. Our languid pace escalated the pleasure, allowing us the quiet space to feel every delicious tremor and tingle. The hunger he stirred inside of me built slowly, until it consumed me, controlling my need for more.

"Fuck, Rayne," he breathed, his fingers digging into my hips. "Your body fits mine perfectly."

Leaning forward, balancing my weight over his relaxed body, my hips rose and fell in a seductive rhythm. He pulled me closer, his hand dragging to the center of my back and pressing me low so he could trap my nipple between his lips.

A low moan escaped my throat in a needy plea as my body tightened around him. His fist moved to my hair, and suddenly, he took control. His torso rippled in a wave of chiseled muscle as he lifted his upper body off the bed, holding me by the hair as he sucked my nipples and pumped his hips hard.

Releasing my hair, he caught my hips and guided my rhythm. I gripped his broad shoulders and leaned back, trusting him not to drop me.

"Who's pussy is this?" The fingers of his free hand teased my clit.

"Yours."

"That's right." He flexed his hips. "*Mine.*"

He flipped me to my back, once again the aggressor. Pushing my thighs wide, he fucked me hard, ramming his cock deep to emphasize his possessive claim. My body was his.

He cupped my breast, demanding my full attention as his hand dragged higher, closing gently around my throat, and something shifted in the air. My heartbeat rolled into a thunderous roar, pounding wildly from my pulse beneath his thumb, just below my jaw, all the way to my swollen clit.

"Ah," I gasped as my sex contracted like a fist. Then I was coming.

Hale cursed, and pumped his hips harder,

forcing his release deep inside of me. It was unexpectedly fast but perfect just like it used to be, before the schedules, before the basal thermometers and fertility tests, before the disappointment of negative pregnancy tests, and before the inevitable sense of failure that haunted me.

My stomach had never felt so achingly hollow until this past year. Logically, I knew none of this was our fault, but it was sometimes impossible not to feel like a failure, even when we were both trying our hardest to succeed.

"Hey." His hand brushes my cheek. "Where'd you go?"

"I'm here," I lied. It was obvious my mind had gone somewhere else.

He kissed my forehead. "Whatever you're thinking about, put it away for now, Rayne. All the worry. All the stress. We can deal with it tomorrow. Let's just give ourselves this moment."

My mouth curved into a gentle smile. How did he do that? How did he know exactly what to say to calm me down the way no one else could?

When he pulled out, the ache that came in his absence nearly brought me to tears. I could go three days without him, but any more and I was always overly emotional when he returned.

"I think I reached my limit," I confessed, remembering the days when we only had a long-distance relationship and spent weeks apart. I could never go back to that.

I need Hale like a drug—not just for the intimacy but for my sanity. He was my anchor in the storm, my harbor light in a dark sea.

He nestled close and tucked a strand of hair behind my ear. "Talk to me, Rayne. What's going on?"

Maybe I was being dramatic. Maybe I wasn't. "I just missed you. Sometimes all these business trips get to be too much."

"I'm sorry, baby. Believe me, I'd much rather be home with you and Elara. You could come with me next time."

I'd tried that. Traveling with a toddler was a lot to manage, especially when I had to bring my work and Hale was tied up in meetings most of the trip. Time passed faster when we stayed home, but I still missed him like crazy.

"I'm just being needy."

"That's okay. I like feeling needed."

My body shivered, and goosebumps rose on my skin. Hale dragged the covers over my chest. I should have been lying upside down, letting gravity do its work, but it felt too nice to simply lie in his arms.

We lost a bit of the aftercare when our objectives changed. "I miss this."

A satisfied chuckle rumbled from his chest as he pulled me closer, cradling me like a baby. "It's been a while since you've let me hold you like this." His fingers traced slowly up and down my arm.

Why did I deny us these tender moments when they felt so damn good? "I'm sorry I get so crazy about all this baby stuff, Hale."

"You're fine, Rayne. I get it."

Did he? Did he feel the sense of failure the way I did? Did he know how hard it was to take an inventory of my body and feel nothing but emptiness? Basic indigestion could create false hope, and damn, that hope hurt when it turned out to be nothing more than a flutter of gas. Maybe I wasn't ready to have a baby if this was how my mind worked.

"Rayne."

I met his stare. "Yeah."

He tugged me close and looked me square

in the eye. "There is nothing wrong with you or your body."

God, I was so transparent. "I know. It's just hard. The other day, the doctor used the phrase *geriatric pregnancy*. I'm thirty-two!"

Hale laughed. "Baby, you're far from a geriatric. I mean, for Christ's sake, you still watch cartoons."

"Only because Elara likes it when I watch them with her."

"Elara's a little young for The Simpsons, Rayne."

"I watch The Simpsons for current events, Hale. Everyone knows that show is a modern-day Nostradamus."

"Simpsons aside, you're still too young to be a geriatric anything."

"I know! I mean, technically, a woman has to be thirty-five to fit that category. You just know someone with a penis coined that term."

He chuckled. "Sometimes I think you imagine the patriarchy as a room in a club where a bunch of men sit around smoking cigars and passing misogynistic laws."

I cocked my head. "That's actually pretty accurate to what I imagine. It's like the dogs playing poker painting but with stuffy old men that look like Mr. Potter from *It's a Wonderful Life.*"

He kissed my forehead. "You're young." He kissed my nose. "And beautiful." Then he threw off the covers and kissed my stomach. "And healthy." Dropping lower, he nuzzled my hip with his nose and placed his palm over my belly. "But you're not very patient, Mrs. Davenport."

I rolled my eyes. "Tell me something I don't know."

He formed a heart with his hands, framing my belly button. "I will. I'll tell you something even The Simpsons haven't predicted yet. It's going to happen for us, baby. We just have to give it time. Trust me on this." He kissed my stomach and pulled the covers over us.

"You're right. We just need a little more time and sex."

"Much more sex." He tugged me to his side and turned off the television. "After some sleep of course."

Because it's icky...

I never got the whole biological clock nonsense until I realized it wasn't nonsense, my uterus was literally a ticking time bomb, and I was deep in some Edgar Allan Poe shit. That metaphorical *tick, tick, ticking* was driving me fucking crazy!

"Why don't you come up to the city for a bit," Phina, Hale's sister, suggested.

I called her for emotional support after taking yet another negative pregnancy test. "I don't know. I'd have to make arrangements with Andrew for Elara because Hale has to fly out to Bangkok tomorrow.

"We could have lunch at La Crocodile and drinks afterward at Per Se," she tempted in a cajoling heiress tone she probably mastered at age six. "Come on, Rayne. It'll be a perfect day and probably just what you need right now."

I sighed. Phina did know how to make a girl feel special. "When?"

"Let me look!" Pages fluttered as she flipped open her day planner. "Oh, darn. I'm booked solid this week, but next week I'm open. How about Friday the eleventh?"

My gaze moved to the calendar. Elara had a pediatrician visit earlier that week, but nothing else scheduled. However, the eleventh was blocked off for other reasons.

Seeking out the non-fertile day, I suggested, "How about that following Tuesday?"

"You want to come on a Tuesday?" she asked in surprise.

"Mid-week is easier to plan with Andrew, especially if Hale's away. I don't think Per Se would be as relaxing with a toddler running around."

"True. Okay. Tuesday the fifteenth works."

I jotted it down. "Thanks, Phina. I'm looking forward to it."

"Me too. I'm even going to book us a

little treat at the spa, so make sure your flight gets in early."

Ah, the spa. That touchy-feely kind of pampering Seraphina loved to partake in. I personally couldn't stand being touched by anyone other than Hale and found massages to be less indulgent and more along the lines of awkward torture. But I didn't want to rain on her parade.

"Great. I'll text you my flight details as soon as I have them."

Traveling meant doubling up on my workload with school and Remington plus spending extra quality time with Elara and Hale before I left, which was fine because all of those distractions took my mind off other things.

I plowed into my syllabus, moving full speed ahead until about two o'clock when a splitting headache developed behind my right eye. That was when Remington called, asking if I was in the office or working from home.

"I'm home. Did you need something?"

"I, uh..." His voice drifted.

"Remington?"

"I forget what the hell I called you for."

"Oh." I frowned. Remington wasn't usually the forgetful sort. "What were you doing before you called?"

"I was..." he muttered something, and I gave him a moment to collect his thoughts.

I disliked seeing signs of aging in Remington, so I attributed his forgetfulness to simple busyness. The man had a ton of crap on his plate.

He growled in frustration. "Forget it. I'll call you when I remember."

The line went dead, and I sighed. I was used to his abrupt and rude phone etiquette, especially when he was preoccupied, so I didn't think much of it.

I read a few more chapters from my supply chain management text and that put me right to sleep. A few hours later, I awoke hunched over my notes with back-breaking cramps just as Andrew walked in the door with Elara.

"Mommy!" she called, charging for me and hurling herself onto my lap.

"*Umph!* Hey, Peanut. How was your adventure?" Elara wasn't in preschool yet, but Andrew kept her pretty busy. She had a full social schedule of playdates, museum tours, nanny circles, and fun kiddie adventures.

She held up her pudgy fist, showing off

the smeared stamp on the back of her hand and frowned. "Uh-oh."

I laughed. She was her father's daughter. Knowing little blemishes like this stressed her out, I tried to celebrate it as a good thing. "How pretty! Did you go to the petting zoo?"

Moaning, she climbed off my lap and went to the kitchen, not distracted in the least from the horrific smudge on her hand. "Up!" she demanded, pointing to her stool by the sink.

"She's been begging to wash it off all day," Andrew commented, moving to help the little princess. "What do we say when we need help, Elara?"

"*Pease*," she pleaded, leaving out the L.

I wasn't sure if her OCD was an environmental trait she picked up from her neatnik father or something genetic. Maybe I should mention it to the pediatrician next week. And it wouldn't hurt for Hale to curb his need for perfection around the little one.

Ha! Like that would ever happen.

I got up from rayne sofa and folded the lap blanket, setting my forgotten textbook and notes on the coffee table. "Andrew, next week I'm going to New York. Are you okay with that?"

"Hale's here, right?"

"Yes. He'll be back by then." I typically tried to travel only when Hale was away, but this trip felt...necessary. I wasn't sure why.

"Then that should be fine. I'll put the dates in my calendar now."

"Thanks, Andrew."

He shut off the faucet and helped Elara dry her hands. "All better."

I reached into the cup of pens by the phone and clicked a purple one open. "Oooh, look what I found." Elara immediately looked at what I had. I drew a small heart on the back of my hand. "Pretty."

She frowned and gasped. "Uh-oh, Mommy." She tugged me toward the sink.

"No, I don't want to wash it off. I like it."

She whined as if this somehow broke the laws of nature, her tiny body helplessly tugging me toward the sink.

"Andrew, don't you think it's pretty?"

He lifted his head from the calendar he'd been marking and fawned over my heart. "Very pretty! Can I have one?"

I drew a star on his hand, and Elara screamed. We both looked at her in surprise and laughed.

"Elara, we don't scream like that."

She marched over to Andrew and pointed at his hand. "No!"

He cradled the scribbled star protectively to his chest. "I like my star."

Her eyes filled with tears, and she pouted in frustration, stomping her little foot angrily.

"Do you want one, Peanut?"

"No." She pulled her pudgy fists protectively close and backed up.

"Okay. You don't have to have one. But you can't get mad at other people for wanting one." My little anti-control lesson cut off as a sharp cramp plunged from my back, through my stomach, and into my legs.

I must have gasped because Andrew's face instantly contorted with concern. "Are you okay?"

"Mmm. Yeah." I grimaced, holding my side. "Just a little stomach issue." Pain radiated through my back and Elara's prior distress shifted to concern as she watched me double over and grip the counter.

"Can I get you something?" Andrew offered, but there wasn't anything he could do. Cramps were cramps.

"Do you mind if I..." I gestured toward the steps, needing a few moments to myself.

"Go. I've got her. We were about to take a swim."

I nodded my thanks and slowly lurched up the stairs. I needed my bed.

Later that night, after the red devil made its debut, I fed Elara dinner and put her to bed. Hale was working late and didn't get in until around eight.

"You look cozy," he said, joining me on the sofa.

"I'm not. I got my period."

He brushed a loving hand over my head and peeked under the blanket, finding the usual suspects—a heating pad, a bag of truffles, and a box of tissues. He glanced at the screen where Dolly Parton's face was frozen. "*Steel Magnolias*?"

"I needed a good cry."

He sighed. "Did you eat?"

I'd eaten everything in sight, but he didn't need to know that. "There's a steak on the counter for you. It's from Spencer's." Hale didn't marry me for my culinary skill so he wasn't surprised to come home to takeout.

I hit play as he warmed up his dinner and set the table. The lengths he went to for propriety made me laugh. I gave him credit, though. Hale could hire a house full of servants to wait on him hand and foot, but he preferred his privacy and liked to take care of himself.

"Will you sit with me?"

I paused the movie, wrapped myself up in the blanket, and took the seat across from him, settling in like a disheveled burrito. He held his fork in his left hand, tines down, and gracefully cut into his filet. Peeking under the table, I smirked at the napkin appropriately draped over his lap.

"Good?" I asked as he took the first bite.

"Delicious. Do you want some?"

I ate earlier, but I was always a little extra ravenous this time of the month, so I leaned forward and opened my mouth like a good little carnivore.

"Mmm." It was even good reheated. Maybe I had an iron deficiency. "How was your day?"

"Same old." He sliced off another bite and fed it to me. "Yours?"

"I caught up on school stuff." I dipped my finger into his mashed potatoes and sucked it clean.

"I can get you a fork."

That reminded me... "I, uh, wanted to talk to you about something."

He glanced at me, swallowing his food before responding. "Sounds serious."

"Not really." I didn't want to make too big of a deal out of it. "Elara had a bit of a meltdown today over a stamp on her hand."

He frowned. "Who put a stamp on her hand?"

I should have known he'd see her side first. "The petting zoo."

"What year are they living in? Haven't they heard of bracelets?"

"Hale, you're missing the point. She flipped out because there was a mark on her skin."

"A mark made of ink that could trigger an allergic reaction. Not to mention the transfer of pathogens from repeated use."

I rolled my eyes. "Forget I said anything."

He caught my hand and stilled when he noticed the faded heart. "Is that what this is about?"

"My cootie mark, yes. I was trying to make a point, but I can see I failed."

He traced his thumb over the faded heart. "You shouldn't draw on yourself."

"Why? Has ink poisoning and pen pathogens become a leading cause of death?" I teased.

"Because it's not right to mark a work of art."

I shoved him affectionately. "You're sweet." I blushed, then I licked my finger and smudged my saliva over the mark. "It comes right off."

"Oh, God." He looked away in disgust.

I laughed. "Suddenly, my saliva's gross to you?"

He reeled in the germaphobia and hid his aversion to my natural disorderly conduct. "What's the point here, Rayne? Are you afraid Elara's like me?"

There was no doubt she was her father's daughter. Sometimes, I forgot she wasn't his biological child. While they still shared a genealogical link through Remington, chances were this was more environmental than anything else. "I just think it would do her good to get a little dirty now and then."

"Why?"

"Because dirt's healthy, Hale. There are all kinds of studies about the benefits of soil and good bacteria."

"Good bacteria?"

"I'm sure there's a more scientific explanation than I can offer, but my point is, she needs to be okay with a little disorder in life."

"She knows how to make a mess."

"Hale," I pleaded. "Do I need to spell it out?"

He knew what I was getting at. He was a perfectionist with deep-seated OCD tendencies. Hale liked cleanliness because, in his mind, it assured he was in control. But Elara was reliant on more than just Hale, and sometimes her high standards for perfect order took a toll on those who took care of her—namely me. I wasn't a slob, but compared to Hale I was far from tidy.

"No, I get it. I'll try to be a little more lax around her regarding subtle messes."

I chuckled. As he made that promise, he imperceptibly angled his glass so that it was the exact distance from his plate that it was when he started eating.

"Thank you."

"How about you? Do you need anything other than some soap to wash that slobber and pen off your hand?"

I smiled, thinking him the sweetest man tight-ass in the whole wide world. "I could use a cuddle buddy."

He glanced back at the television. "Do we have to watch *Steel Magnolias*?"

"Yes."

He sighed. "Okay. Let me shower and change, then I'll be your cuddle buddy."

I stood in my burrito blanket and kissed his head. "You're the best."

"Wash your hands," he called as I headed back to the sofa.

I Am A Mother-Fucking Goddess!

I met Phina in the city on Tuesday morning and we started the day with brunch. I hadn't drank in a while, so it was nice to have a mimosa or six. The champagne was hitting just right when Martel Sharoski, my personal New York driver and ex-mercenary, drove us to the spa.

I frowned when we pulled up to a discreet doorway with a leaf illuminated above the awning. "This isn't the spa we usually visit."

"I changed the plan," Phina said with a feathery wink of false lashes.

"Huh?" Knowing Hale's sister, this could be anything. I wasn't in the mood for injections or IVs or any sort of chemical peel. "What is this place, Seraphina?"

"It's a Reiki healing lab. Come on."

Marty opened the door, and I sent him a desperate look to save me as Phina pulled me inside. The scent of incense assaulted my senses, but my nerves quickly calmed at the soft, tranquil plunking of chimes. Okay, this place seemed pretty chill.

A woman appeared with her hands folded in front of her waist and an easy smile on her natural face. "Welcome to Serenity. Can I help you?"

My gaze traveled down her silk genie pants to her bare feet. Her hair was long and wavy, hanging down to her bare belly where a piercing looped through a thin belted chain.

"We have an appointment for the Reiki healing."

I looked curiously at the various displays of crystals and pretty glass things. My hands stayed balled at my side because I feared accidentally breaking something fragile.

"Wonderful. You must be Seraphina and Rayne. I'm Skye. Follow me, and I'll get you settled in the Intentions Cave."

We were going to a cave? I sent Phina a panicked look, but she appeared unconcerned.

We followed Skye down various flights of

stairs that seemed to date back to the last century or older. The musty air smelled of earth and dampness the deeper underground we traveled, and I thought I heard faint trickling along the walls, which were stone and lined with melted candles. The far above sounds of the city muffled, and I grew more concerned the lower we traveled.

The temperature dropped as Skye led us into a small stone room that seemed carved out of some mystical cave. "Make yourselves comfortable." She lit a candle and held a small bundle of dried herbs in the flame. It smelled a little like reefer.

"What is that?"

"Just some sage to cleanse the space." She waved the singed bundle to the corners and wafted the aromatic smoke across the walls with a fan made of feathers. I discreetly coughed.

When she finished, she set the bundle in an opalescent shell where it continued to smoke. She lifted a small copper singing bowl and tapped the side with a wooden mallet. As she dragged the mallet around the rim of the bowl, it rang like a bell.

"This space is clean. Set your intentions and take a moment to meditate. Manifest your goals. Iris and Willow will be with you shortly."

Who the hell were Iris and Willow? As soon as we were alone, I sent Phina a wide-eyed look and waved away the sage smoke. "Seriously?"

She laughed. "Don't make fun. Let's try it. We might discover something great. Gwyneth Paltrow does it."

"Oh, well then, by all means."

"Shut your eyes and concentrate." She bumped my shoulder with hers. "We're supposed to be manifesting."

"I don't even know what that means."

Seraphina took a deep breath, hummed serenely, and lifted her chin. "It means we set a goal and will it into existence."

This little rock room would have a bouncer and a line out the door if it were that easy. I mimicked her posture and shut my eyes.

I'd never meditated before, so I wasn't sure if I was doing it right.

Did I remember to pack my slippers? I wonder if Andrew found my note about Elara's ear drops. I should text him about that. Are we allowed to use phones here? There's probably no signal. Someone could murder us down here, and no one would know. It's giving... 'put the lotion in the basket'.

Shit. I'm not doing this right.

I shook my head to scatter my thoughts.

My mind is clear. My mind is clear.

There's a little purple lamp. That's cozy. How about a recliner?

I got lost in the imaginary decorating of my mind when the door suddenly opened, scaring the crap out of me.

"Seraphina?"

My imaginary room burst into flames, incinerating to ash. Damn it.

"That's me." Phina stood, appearing fully manifested and at peace with her experience thus far.

"Hi, I'm Iris. We're going to have a wonderful experience today. Are you ready?"

"Yes." Phina smiled, fully embracing this kooky place.

Iris bowed her head toward me. "Willow will be down for you in a few minutes. You can enjoy the sanctuary a while longer."

"Great."

Phina and Iris disappeared, and the energy of the stone room shifted from that of a prison cell to a mausoleum. I must be missing something.

And why was I thinking about spiders. How did one clean a cave?

There are probably those long centipede things down here...

"Oh, God." Where the fuck was this Willow chick?

I pulled out my phone, but there was no signal this deep in the earth. "Shit." I used my flashlight to search crevices for bugs but found none.

My foot tapped anxiously and the strange acoustics muffled the sound, making everything feel closer. I didn't like it. Nor did I feel serene or connected to the universe in this weird majestic place. I just felt trapped.

But I wanted to feel the serenity. I wanted the Paltrow special. I needed the full manifestation experience to improve my life so I could find complete contentment with the state of things.

I took a deep breath of the musty, cool air and focused again.

Set an intention... I want to be present. I am present. I am in a cave deep in the earth. How far is the subway—

Nope.

I'm in a majestic sanctuary on a spiritual

journey. I own my destiny. I am one with Mother Earth.

That sounded good. The moment I thought about the earth, the trees, and the mountains, I felt connected to something, sort of anchored.

I am manifesting babies. Wait, is that too greedy?

I am manifesting fertility. I'm a fertile woman ready for implantation. My uterus is a beautiful garden wherefore life can grow.

Now I was getting the hang of this.

I will have Hale's baby. We will conceive a child together. My body is young and healthy.

I kept repeating positive affirmations in my head until I forgot where I was. When the door opened, it scared the crap out of me and I jumped.

"Rayne?"

"Yup." My heart raced as I recalled I was still stuck in this Ghostbusters dungeon.

"I'm Willow. Are you ready to begin your Reiki healing journey?"

I nodded and stood, grabbing my bag and following her down a narrow hall. We entered a dimly lit room with a massage table. Candles illuminated the shadows, and crystals covered every square inch of the shelves.

"Why don't you tell me a little about what brings you here today."

"Um, my sister-in-law brought me here."

"Okay," Willow smiled. "That was thoughtful of her. Have you ever done Reiki therapy before?"

"No. I'm a virgin."

"Well first, let me say thank you for trusting me. I've been practicing for nineteen years, and I hope you'll find the experience mind-opening. Do you have any goals for today?"

"Not really." As a skeptic, I wanted to see what she inferred from as little information as possible.

"Okay. Then why don't you settle in on the table so we can get started? Lie on your back and find a comfortable position. I'm going to get warmed up."

I stared at the table and then back at Willow. "Is this a, uh, naked thing?"

"No." She chuckled softly in a non-judgmental sort of way. "You can keep your clothes on. Or don't if that makes you feel more in tune with your surroundings. Reiki works best however you're most comfortable."

Definitely clothes on.

I climbed onto the table and laid back. Several dream catchers and crystals hung from the ceiling, flickering as they gently turned and reflected the flickering candlelight.

This room was much more relaxing than the underground cave. Native American flute music played from hidden speakers, instantly putting me at ease. The soft scent of lemongrass and lavender wafted in the air, and my body relaxed on the heated, cushioned surface.

"Let me know if the table gets too warm for you."

A toasty blanket draped over me, and I shivered. "Ooh." Now she was speaking my language.

"Let's take a moment to ground and center before we begin. Relax your jaw and close your eyes if you feel comfortable doing so."

I felt very comfortable doing so, so I did.

Gentle fingers lightly pressed to my forehead. "Take a few slow, deep breaths, inhaling through your nose and exhaling fully through your mouth."

I could sense her moving around me, but I didn't have a clue what she was doing. Was that her hand on my forehead or had she set something there. Mindful not to make it fall, I tried to stay as still as a statue.

"With each breath, feel yourself becoming more relaxed and present in this moment."

A soft bell rang, then another. The scent of various oils swirled in the air around my face, and I grew more relaxed. The slightest movement sent a breeze over my skin. I sank deeper into the heated table, safely cocooned under the cozy blanket.

This was a million times more my style than a naked massage, so I sighed happily. Was it rude to nap here? Probably.

"Now, I want you to bring your awareness to your body, Rayne. You and your body are one. Feel the weight of your limbs and the power hibernating in your core."

Did core mean vagina? Or was she talking about my stomach? Should I ask? I didn't want to disrupt the process so I just concentrated on both.

"Sink into yourself. Feel your body rooted to the earth and grounded like the strong trunk of a tree."

Strangely, my body did feel heavier. Was this one of those weighted thunder blankets, or was she doing that with only her words?

"Imagine your roots growing deep into the earth below you. Feel those roots anchoring you securely to the earth's energy, providing you with stability and support."

Oh, this was nice. Sort of like Mother Earth was protectively holding me in her bosom. I was safe and warm and so very relaxed.

"As you breathe deeply, visualize a beam of light extending from your crown toward the sky. Feel yourself connecting to the universe, drawing on its incredible light and energy and wisdom."

I was suddenly very wise and lighter than a feather. Maybe this Willow chick was a witch. The good kind, of course, like Glinda.

"Now, imagine the earth's energy rising up through your roots, filling your body with strength and vitality. Her incredible energy empowers you. You possess the natural magic to self-heal. Do you feel how safe and supported you are right now, Rayne?"

"Mm-hm," I moaned, too comfortable to fully answer.

"You are connected to the wonderful healing energy of the universe all around you."

Damn right, I was. I was a motherfucking ethereal goddess.

My breath hitched as her hands pressed lightly onto my shoulders, sliding upward into my hair. She encircled my head, framing the sides of my face and gently massaging my temples, forehead, and scalp.

"You are connected to the divine energy that surrounds you, Rayne. Surrender to the infinite wisdom and guidance of the higher realms so that your spirit can awaken. Open your mind and heart so that you can receive the gifts the universe has in store for you."

I am open.

Open like a quickie-mart.

Twenty-four-seven, wide open for business.

Universe, come on in...

Something cool rested on my forehead, and I stilled, this time certain it was not her hand. Was she putting crystals on me? It had to be.

"Your inner eye is open to intuition and insight. The physical world does not limit you. Trust your higher self to guide you on your true path."

I no longer envisioned a dark room with a Barcalounger and lamp. Now, my mind was an enchanted forest with an illuminated path. Birds sang quietly while bees buzzed. Elara's laugh drifted from beyond the trees as my inner self moved in toward the sound as if walking through a dream.

Willow placed another crystal on me, this time setting it lightly over the shallow indent of my throat. "You speak your truth with clarity and confidence, Rayne, so that you may express your authentic self honestly. Here, you're free of judgment and have nothing to fear. Tell the universe what you want in your heart of hearts, so that your voice can call it into existence."

Was I really doing this? I'd laid down a non-believer, but something was shifting inside of me. Maybe it was the calming oils or the crystals. I wasn't sure. But suddenly I was all in.

"A baby," I murmured, my voice small and weighed down by emotions.

"The universe accepts your desires and plans to serve you with everything you need."

Her hands moved to hover over my chest without actually touching me. It was strange that I could feel exactly where she was even though no part of her body touched mine.

"Feel your heart open to love and compassion, not just for others, but for yourself as well."

It was then that my energy shifted, and

my throat constricted. My eyes burned, and my brow furrowed. Self-compassion was not a strong suit of mine.

"I feel your struggle, Rayne. The *Anahata*, or heart chakra, is your connection to others. I sense that you love very deeply, but sometimes, in the past, this has wounded you. You must let go of past pain and grievances so that forgiveness and healing energy can flow freely into you."

Things were suddenly getting a little too heavy. I thought of my father, and Elle, and ex-coworkers who drove me crazy. This was starting to feel like therapy more than a spa visit. My relaxing experience intensified, and I desperately wanted to get back to that peaceful feeling I had moments ago.

When I peeked through my lashes, I was surprised to find my eyes wet with tears. Willow placed more crystals on my upper body, her hands moving around me as if pulling away cobwebs and cleaning the energy surrounding my heart.

"I see a bright green light over you. It's siphoning the negative energy away. Breathe deep and release that negative debris, Rayne."

I took a deep breath, fighting the constricting tightness of my lungs as the heaviness in my chest increased. Blowing out a breath wasn't easy. At first, the air shook, and my lips trembled, but then I felt the unwanted weight pulling away, and a sense of openness gradually returned.

"Very good, Rayne."

She continued to work on my heart chakra. The longer she spent there, the lighter I felt. When she moved to my stomach and concentrated on my solar plexus, she reminded me of my power within. I'd always thought that was IBS, but what did I know?

When she moved lower, she claimed to ignite my spirit, reminding me to have fun and let pleasure guide me. She suspected I had a good sex life, which was true, but she sensed the tension in this area and said it was forming a blockage.

I worried that the blockage might be my crusty, old, geriatric lady parts, but she said it was a mental block that could be easily moved with consistent practice and open-mindedness. I liked her outlook a hell of a lot better than mine.

When the session was over, I felt extremely flowy, as if all that stagnant energy inside of me had become unstuck. The possibility of finally letting go of some of those past pains no longer seemed so impossible.

"Hydration will help flush out the remaining toxins, so drink plenty of water over the next few days. You can maintain your connection to the earth by eating a nourishing diet, rich in plants. Journal, meditate, and spend a little time in nature whenever you feel overwhelmed."

This woman was a wizard of calm, and I'd do anything she suggested if it meant keeping this peaceful buzz. My ADHD had never been so quiet. I wanted to ask how long this sensation would last, but I figured each client was different.

When I met Seraphina on the main floor, she did not appear as serene as I felt.

"Ready?" she asked, stuffing her wallet into her designer purse.

"I have to pay."

"I handled it."

"Oh. Thanks."

I looked back at Willow, unsure if it was customary to hug a Reiki healer after a session. I decided that might cross some personal boundaries, so I just said, "Thank you so much for everything, Willow."

"You're welcome, Rayne. I'm sure I'll see you again."

The moment we were outside on the pavement, Phina mumbled, "Doubtful."

I frowned at her unusual negative attitude. "Didn't you like it?"

Marty opened the limo door, and she slid into the back of the car and scoffed. "If I'd known this was a hands-free massage, I never would have booked it."

"But didn't you think it was neat how you could feel the energy shifting?"

"What are you talking about? All I felt was awkwardness. She just stood over me pretending to wave energy around."

I hid a smirk. I was the one who usually felt awkward. Everyone loved a regular massage, but I hated the feeling of a stranger's hands roaming freely over my bare skin. *Ick!* But no contact Reiki? I was a big fan!

After lunch and more cocktails, I checked in to The Plaza penthouse and called Hale to tell him about my day. "It was amazing, Hale. I could feel space opening up inside of me."

"Sounds...neat."

Okay, the Davenports were just different. They didn't understand spirituality at this level. I'd obviously gone through some sort of awakening that was beyond his comprehension. Maybe he just needed to experience it for himself.

"Anyway, I ordered some stuff for the house. Just put any shipments aside until I get home if they get there before me."

"What kind of shipments?"

"Some…crystals and rocks and stuff." It wasn't like I was joining a cult. I just liked the way certain pretty things made me feel. There was no difference between this and liking jewelry, and I wasn't really into jewelry, so maybe this would be my fancy thing.

"I'll have Alfonse keep an eye out for any packages."

I frowned. "Why Alfonse? Where are you going?"

"I'm heading to the tarmac right now."

"What for?" His travel plans were news to me. I put him on speaker and opened the shared calendar app on the phone. He had nothing booked this week.

"I missed my wife."

I stilled. Warmth spread through all that newly emptied space Willow created in my chest. "You're coming to New York?"

"I should be there in four hours."

"Hale!" This was a fabulous surprise.

"What?"

"I wasn't expecting this."

"Don't you want me there?"

"Of course, I want you here! It's just... You could have come with me."

"I had meetings today, and I knew you wanted some girl time with Phina."

"Well, this changes everything! I'm going to nap, so I'll be awake when you get here."

"Good plan. I'll text you as soon as I land."

As soon as we hung up, I texted Seraphina.

YOUR BROTHER'S FLYING IN. CAN I send Mr. Parcel over to your boutique to pick up an order?

SHE PINGED RIGHT BACK.

OF COURSE! GO ONLINE AND SEE WHAT you want. I'll have Lilly put the order together for you.

. . .

A QUICK PERUSAL OF SERAPHINA'S website and my cart was bursting with porn-tastic lingerie. Hale was going to go nuts!

"Percy?" I rang the bell, and the butler appeared.

"Yes, Madam?"

"They're putting together an order for me at Seraphina's boutique. Could you see that it gets here in the next two hours?"

"Of course."

"Thanks!"

I quickly straightened up the penthouse and moved upstairs. While Percy was preoccupied with other things, I ran a bath. After a long, peaceful soak, I napped. When I awoke, the boutique bag was waiting on the dresser.

I checked my phone. Hale was about thirty minutes away. That gave me plenty of time to prepare.

I Prefer Him Primal

I sent Percy home before I changed into my new duds. I didn't typically wear lingerie, so I expected to blow Hale's mind.

As I inspected my reflection, I chewed my lower lip. It was hot, but it was also unlike anything I'd ever worn for him before. I nervously pulled at the short, plaid skirt and adjusted the tie of the shirt that barely covered my boobs.

Maybe fantasy play was too weird for us.

No. I looked cute and playful. The whole point was to escape reality, and this was definitely far away from normal for us.

I twisted my hair into two messy buns instead of my usual single one. Then I put on my blue light glasses and some fruit flavored gloss. Perfect.

If only I'd been this hot in high school.

The door opened and I rushed to the steps, making sure it was Hale.

"Rayne?"

"I'm up here," I called, rushing back into the master bedroom and dropping to my knees on the carpet. "Ouch." I stretched to the bed and stole a pillow, stuffing it under my knees as I faced the door.

My heart raced as his footsteps climbed the stairs. Too late to back out now. "Did you ea—" His words cut off. "What..." He laughed nervously. "What's this?"

I held out a sheet of paper I'd ripped off the notepad in the drawer. "I didn't do my assignment, sir."

He tossed his carry-on by the door and rubbed his jaw. "You bad girl."

His words sent a wave of excitement through me. I nodded repentantly. "Yes, I've been very, *very* bad."

"Jesus, Rayne." He chuckled and crossed the room, never taking his eyes off me. "Where did you get that outfit?"

"What do you mean? This is my usual school uniform."

He closed the distance. Towering over me in his tailored suit, he dragged a finger between my boobs where the blouse gaped open. "And you say you didn't do your homework?"

I shook my head, looking up at him with big eyes. "I'm sorry, sir."

He caught my chin in a gentle grip, dragging his thumb over my lips and smearing the sticky gloss to my cheek. "How sorry?"

"Very. I was hoping there might be some extra credit I could do for you."

"Hmm." He circled me slowly. "First, you'll need to be disciplined."

My head cocked. "Disciplined?" That was a little off-script, but I decided to go with it.

"You want to make this right, don't you?"

"Yes, sir."

The metal of his belt clinked as he loosened his clothes. "Then get your ass over here." He lowered onto the bench at the foot of the bed and patted his lap.

I moved to stand—

"Eh, eh, eh." He held out a finger. "Did I say you could stand?"

Hiding a smirk, I shifted to my hands and knees and crawled to him. "How do you want me, sir."

He stretched out his legs and patted his lap. "Face down, ass up."

I swallowed tightly, a little nervous and completely surprised by how quickly he jumped into his role. Was he really going to punish me? "Hale—"

"It's Mr. Davenport."

My heart rate spiked as I looked down at his lap, noting the bulge of his erection. "Yes, Mr. Davenport." I climbed over his lap and lowered my torso to his legs so my hands were planted on the floor, and my ass pointed in the air.

"That's better." His hand trailed slowly up my thigh, lifting the skirt and exposing the silk thong wedged between my ass cheeks. The press of his arousal prodding at my rib served as a constant reminder that he was turned on.

"What was the assignment, Rayne?"

"Um..." It was hard to think with the blood rushing to my head and his fingers tickling my ass.

He scraped his fingernails over the soft skin of my ass, and my spine lengthened. I was extremely ticklish on my butt, and he knew it. "I'm waiting."

I blurted the first thing that came to

mind. "The principles of operational man-agement!"

Shit. I inwardly winced. Those damn principles were impossible for me to memorize, even after Hale spent hours trying to help me study them last semester. I was pretty sure my professor was a sadist who hated me for my new last name. I barely ended up passing that class.

Hale's chuckle was low. He had me right where he wanted. "And what are those principles, Rayne?"

I could have picked anything. I could have said the Pledge of Allegiance or state capitols. Anything that would have been easy, but no. I chose the one thing my brain was determined to forget.

"Um—*Ah!*" The sound of his palm slapping my ass echoed through the cavernous suite and I blinked in shock.

He spanked me. He literally spanked me. It took a second to process.

"*Um* is not a principle."

Holy shit he was actually planning on disciplining me. Role-playing just got very real as my ass started to burn from the imprint of his palm.

"I'm waiting."

"S—strategic m—management," I stammered, racking my brain for the principle concepts.

"And what is strategic management, Rayne."

Hale could be a tenured teacher at any university for all he knew about business. I, on the other hand, was a low B student on my best day and a C student on most days.

"Or—organizational strategies!" I rushed out.

"More detail please." His nails scraped over my tender ass.

Shit. I was so fucked. "Organizational strategies and formulation within competitive environments."

"You're missing something."

I panicked and blurted, "While understanding industrial dynamics and the effects of globalization." Holy shit! I couldn't believe I remembered that.

"Very good." He rewarded me by gently massaging my ass cheek and soothing away the burn. "What's the next principle."

Well, fuck.

It had something to do with style and technique, but I couldn't remember the name. "*Ah!*"

"That's for making me wait. You clearly haven't studied."

Clearly. "I'm sorry, sir, I must have been too busy fucking my husband."

He stilled. "Is this a joke to you?"

I smothered a laugh. "No, sir. I'm taking this very seriously, as is my ass."

He swatted me again, this time a little harder, and my body rocked forward. "Watch your language."

"Sorry, sir." My fingers splayed over the marble floor as the blood rushed to my head, making it difficult to think.

His touch gentled as he traced the seam of my ass, pressing his fingers against the wet silk of my panties. I moaned, surprised by how turned on this was making me.

"Repeat after me, leadership and organizational behavior require a high emotional intelligence and an appreciation for team dynamics."

I seriously should have had him take that final for me. "Leadership behavior requires a high emotional intelligence and team dynamics—*Ah!*"

"You missed some words."

"My ass is on fire—*Ah!* Damn it, Hale!"

"I warned you not to cut corners. And

once again, it's Mr. Davenport. Now, do I need to teach you what happens to naughty girls with filthy mouths?"

That sounded fun. More fun than spanking. "Maybe."

His nails scraped down my heated flesh, and my ass cheeks reflexively clenched. "I think you're too eager." He wrenched my panties aside and dragged his fingertips through my wet folds. "Look at what a dirty girl you are." His fingers sank inside of me. "I think you like being disciplined."

Well, I certainly didn't like The Principles of Operational Management. Obviously some part of me enjoyed what he was doing, but I wasn't really sure why. "I like what you're doing now, Mr. Davenport."

He stilled. "Do you?"

"Yes."

"And now?" He pressed deeper, and I moaned.

"Yes, sir."

My head shot up when he spread my cheeks wide and pressed his thumb against my little rosebud, his fingers still buried inside of me. "And now?"

My breath quickened. My arms were getting tired from holding my weight and things were intensifying quickly.

"Tell me whose ass this is, Rayne."

"It's yours—sir."

"Good girl. Back down you go." He pressed a hand between my shoulders directing me back into position.

I forced my body to relax and let my head hang low, only I lurched forward when he applied pressure and breached my tight hole.

"So tight. So obedient." He stroked my back affectionately. "Look how good you behave for me." His grip tightened on my ass cheek as he slowly stroked his fingers in and out. "Such a beautiful view from my angle."

My eyes flashed open at the recognizable shutter sound of his phone taking a picture. "Hale!"

"Quiet please." He pumped his fingers faster. The press of his erection became more pronounced, and my legs trembled as I tried to stifle my moans. "I bet you want to say something indecent, don't you Rayne?"

My body rocked with the pressure of his thrusting hand. The wet sound of his finger sliding in and out of my body played like a filthy symphony and I whimpered, trying to keep quiet. Typically, Hale loved it when I made noise. In a way, he'd conditioned me to be loud during sex because it added to his pleasure, but now he was turning things around and I was going to burst if I didn't scream soon.

"Your pussy's so wet, and your ass is so tight. I can't wait to stuff my cock inside of you. Which hole will it be, Rayne? Here or your ass? Or maybe that dirty mouth of yours?"

I couldn't keep quiet. "Fuck!"

A slap landed on my ass and I lunged forward, the searing sting only adding to my pleasure.

"Hale!" I winced. "I mean Mr. Davenport!"

"Mr. Davenport, what?"

His fingers pounded harder. I was going to come, but there was no way I could stay silent through the orgasm he was building. "I'm sorry, Mr. Davenport!"

"Sorry for what?"

"Not doing the assignment."

He twisted his fingers, adding pressure exactly where I needed it most. "The assignment's changed. Now I want you to beg for my cock."

"Please give me your cock, sir."

"Louder."

"Please, sir, fuck me with your big cock!"

He withdrew his fingers just as I started to come and spanked my ass hard, his other palm rubbing wildly over my clit as my screams of pleasure echoed off the opulent furnishings. My release gushed over his fingers and down my thighs, but he left me little time to relish in the aftermath.

"On your knees. It's time for your second lesson."

He had a pillow waiting the moment I lowered to my knees. The knot of my shirt had loosened, and when I tried to tighten it, he swatted my hands away.

"Leave it." He paused. "On second thought." Reaching between my breasts, he yanked the knotted fabric and ripped it open, exposing my bare breasts. "That's better."

My nipples pebbled tight as he rose to his full height.

"Take out my cock like a good girl."

My hands shook as I loosened his belt. When I leaned back to rest my weight on my heels, I bolted forward. The burn on my ass cheeks singed with surprising heat.

Noting my realization, he chuckled. "Open your mouth."

My lips parted but he didn't slide his engorged length down my throat. Instead, he caressed my cheek with a gentle touch and whispered, "Do you still want my cock?"

That delicious pivot between gentle and aggressive undid me every time. I nodded, desperate to please him.

"I'm not going to be gentle."

"Yes, sir. I understand."

"I want you to swallow all of it, Rayne, just like I taught you that first time we did this. Do you remember?"

My body quivered at the memory of that first time. How could I forget? But when I didn't immediately answer he frowned.

"Rayne?"

"It just seems like a waste of perfectly good—"

His fist locked around my buns, forcing my attention to his face. "That's not the assignment. I want you to swallow every last drop, Rayne. Do you understand?"

"Yes, sir."

"Good girl. Do it right, and I'll make sure your tight little pussy's dripping with cum by morning. Fair enough?"

More than satisfied with his plan, I nodded. "Yes, sir."

"Open."

The moment my lips parted he slid to the back of my throat. I relaxed my jaw and gave him control. As promised, he wasn't gentle, but I'd have it no other way. I loved when Hale lost himself like this. Loved the fact that I could do this to him.

When my eyes watered, he dashed away my tears and told me I was a good girl. Sometimes, he held himself as deep as he could fit, cupping the back of my head and watching me closely as I stared up at him.

"God damn, you're good to me." If I choked, he groaned and pulled back, only to wrap his hand around my throat and do it again. "Feel how deep I am. I love when you take all of me."

Hale was a big man, but I'd become accustomed to his length and thickness. By the time he finished, I expected my mouth to be slightly swollen and my throat a little sore. But I didn't mind.

As my lips stretched around his hard shaft, I moaned. He didn't just fuck my throat, he praised me and told me how much he loved the way I spoiled him. His words were a drug and I gobbled them up as much as I greedily swallowed down his cock.

"Fuck." He thrust harder, holding my hair in both hands as his hips bucked wildly. "That's it, baby." His dick pulsed at the back of my throat. "Open your mouth. Show me that tongue."

I knelt before him, mouth open wide, tits and tongue on full display. He jerked his stiff cock, as hot jets of cum spurted across my lips and chin. His shoulders twitched as a shiver noticeably raced up his spine and he caught his balance on the bed post.

"Jesus, Rayne." He caught his breath, glancing at me with a satisfied grin. "Stay just like that." He reached for his phone on the bed and my eyes widened as he snapped several pictures of me, bare chested with my tongue out, and his cum dripping down my face.

He tossed the phone aside and dragged his finger along my lips, feeding them into my mouth. "Now, swallow it."

I sucked his fingers clean.

"Such a good girl. I think you earned those extra credit points you needed."

"You have to delete that picture, Hale."

"Not a chance."

"Hale."

"It's still Mr. Davenport." He held out a hand and helped me off the floor.

"Mr. Davenport, I think your wife will murder you if you don't delete those pictures."

He walked me to the bed and turned me to face the mattress. Mr. Davenport seemed to be on a bit of a power trip. Totally my fault. "We can discuss it later." He nudged my feet apart and pressed me forward, lowering my upper body to the satin coverlet. "Hands behind your back."

Rolling my eyes, I did as he said. I'd delete the pictures after he fell asleep.

"Is your ass sore?" His fingers scraped over what I was sure was a red hand print.

"Yes." I yelped when he slapped my butt again.

"Yes, what?"

"Yes, sir."

The shutter sound of his phone sounded, and I looked back in outrage.

"Hale!"

He pinned me down with one firm hand at my back. "Look how sexy you are. Tell me you wouldn't want a picture."

Well, he had a point. The photo he took was fucking hot.

He swiped his thumb. "This one's my favorite—so wet and swollen and pink."

Damn, my ass looked fine from that angle.

He tossed the phone onto the bed. "I'm going to fuck you so hard tonight you'll still feel me inside of you tomorrow. That's what bad girls get when they don't do their homework."

Were we still doing that? "I'm sorry, sir."

"You will be." He stripped off his clothes and his thighs brushed mine. Yanking my hips back so my body folded over the edge of the four-poster bed, he positioned himself at my entrance and then nudged inside.

My breath hitched as he stretched me. Hale was always a tight fit, but my body adjusted once he was seated to the hilt.

"Feel how wet you are for me. You love sucking my cock, don't you, baby?"

I moaned, my mind entering a soft subspace of pleasure where it became difficult to think or talk. "Yes, baby."

He thrust forward, and the bed creaked. Sometimes he'd move fast and other times he'd slide out slowly, stroking along my channel to drag out the pleasure. When he pressed all the way in, he'd sometimes hold himself there, his hand planted on my back to make it perfectly clear who was in control. But he never hurt me or pushed my body too far. No matter how wild he got, he always made sure I was comfortable and okay with what he was doing.

He leaned down and bit my shoulder then he whispered, "Do you remember my promise? I'm going to fuck your tight little pussy until cum's dripping down your thighs. Is that what you want?"

"Yes, sir." That was all the permission he needed.

Hale went wild, plowing into me like a primal animal. He used my body like it belonged to him, which, in a way, it did. I was his greatest treasure and he handled me with such care, knowing exactly where my limits were and how far he could push me along that hazy edge of pleasure and pain.

He fucked me so many times I lost count. And when he was finally finished, he'd kept his word. My body trembled under a mixture of his release and mine as cum dripped from my weak thighs.

I was spent. Every muscle in my body had been worked until I could hardly move.

"Don't fall asleep yet, baby."

I barely roused when he lifted me to his bare chest and carried me from the bedroom. The soft scent of lavender filled the steamy air as we entered the bathroom. I must have dozed long enough for him to fill the bathtub.

"I've got you." Holding me close, he lowered us into the warm water, and I sighed at the soothing heat. "Just relax and let me take care of you."

With my head resting on his shoulder, I drifted in and out of sleep as he gently washed my body. Once I was clean, he wrapped me in a thick robe and carried me back to bed.

His lips pressed to my forehead. "You get an A-plus, baby. Now, get some sleep."

I moaned and smiled, too exhausted to form words or open my eyes.

Hale chuckled and kissed my forehead one last time. "I love you, Rayne. So much."

God, I loved him too. More than words could say.

"I have a surprise for you."

I looked up from my toes and a glob of polish landed on my phone where I was watching TikToks. "Shit. Hand me a tissue."

Hale pulled two tissues form the box. "Why don't you have them do that for you downstairs at the salon."

"Because I like the challenge, and it feels nostalgic to do poor people things for myself from time to time."

"I'd hardly call painting your nails poor people things."

"Well, I was just a broke bitch before I met you so I have years of experience when it comes to doing things like this for myself."

"For having years of experience, you're not very good at it. There's more polish on your skin than the actual nail."

Realizing how much this was probably making him twitch, I laughed and accidentally dabbed the red polish on my foot. "Oopsy. Will you look at that?"

"Rayne."

I looked up at him with feigned innocence. "What? I slipped."

"Give me that." He took the polish and lifted my foot to rest on his lap. "You've mangled them."

When he sniffed the nail polish, I laughed. "You know I struggle with the girlie things, Hale."

He dunked the brush and wiped away the messy spots on my skin. "I think it's more about concentration than being girlie." He focused on painting clean, straight strokes with my nailbed.

I wiggled my toes.

"Hey. Stop that."

"What was your surprise?"

He never broke concentration. "I made us an appointment."

"For?"

"There's a world-renowned reproductive

specialist here in the city. We have a consultation with one of the doctors this afternoon."

"Oh." Usually, Hale had great surprises. This one felt more like an oil change.

"You sound disappointed."

"I'm just surprised."

"Well, I said it was a surprise."

"Yeah, but..." We were having such a nice getaway, I dreaded spoiling it with bad news. "Is that why you came here?"

He stopped painting my toenails. "Rayne, I thought you'd be excited about this. She's one of the best fertility specialists in the country. It's not an easy appointment to get on short notice, but if you don't want to go, we can cancel it."

If that was true, we couldn't cancel now. Then we might get blackballed and never get an appointment again. "Is it a doctor's office just for women?"

"No, they see men, too."

"So, we're both going?"

"Of course. I wasn't going to send you there alone. We're planning for *our* family."

"So...if they want to run some tests on you...?"

"I'll do whatever they need me to do."

I smiled, pleased with his effort. Even

though his test probably came down to filling a cup. Why was it women got *a little pressure* and men got an orgasm when it came to fertility tests?

He squeezed my ankles. "Hey. Relax. We're just going to hear them out and get some information. There's nothing to be afraid of."

"What time's the appointment?"

He looked at his watch. "We have to be there in an hour."

"Hale!" I shot off the couch. "I'll never be ready!"

"Watch the carpet. Your nails are wet."

"Exactly! I can't shower now."

"So don't."

"Hello? Are you new? Lady doctors check *everything!* I still reek of *boduissy!*"

"What the hell is boduissy?"

"*Boduissy!* Booty, dick, and pussy!"

Laughter belted out of him. "So go shower."

I growled and waddled toward the bathroom. "So much for my pedicure."

An hour later, we were sitting in a sterile, Ikea-style waiting room. The place smelled of opposition, mixed levels of hope, and privilege. I wouldn't exactly call it welcoming or homey. There was a super-enlarged baby poster on the wall. What did it say about me if I found that kind of closeup creepy?

Elara could totally be a model. She was way cuter than any of the kids plastered on the walls here.

"Mr. and Mrs. Davenport?"

Hale stood and took my hand, raising a brow when he felt how clammy my fingers were. I don't know why I was so nervous.

What was wrong with my doctor at home? Sure, he was about a decade past retirement, and his bedside manner had room for improvement, but these New York doctors intimidated me.

"Dr. Seacrest is waiting for you," the nurse said, directing us toward a scale. "I just need both your weights and a quick urine sample from Mrs. Davenport."

That was easy enough with my nervous bladder. I accepted the cup while Hale got on the scale. His weight never fluctuated more than half a pound. Mine, on the other hand, yo-yoed all over the place on a weekly basis.

The one time I needed to pee in a straight stream urine came spraying out of me like a sprinkler. After washing my hands and tightening the lid over a few salvageable drops of urine, I returned to the hall. The nurse took the cup and instructed me to step on the scale.

I glared over my shoulder at Hale. "Turn around."

He pivoted, and I read the scale. Yikes. That was quite a few pounds higher than I was used to weighing. "Are you sure this is right?"

Hale laughed, and I glanced down to find his foot on the corner of the scale.

I smacked his shoulder. "Jerk!"

When he lifted his foot, the scale settled back to my usual weight -- plus ten. Which was normal. I guess.

"Perfect. Come with me." The nurse led us into an office rather than a patient room, and a beautiful woman with dark, curly hair rose from behind a white veneer desk.

"Mr. and Mrs. Davenport, welcome to Blossom Fertility." She shook both of our hands, and we sat.

To stop from fidgeting, I buried my hands in my lap. This place looked more like a med spa than a doctor's office.

"I've gone over your medical history and the good news is, so far, everything looks great."

"It does?" How did she get our medical history?

Dr. Seacrest nodded. "Your recent tests show no red flags, and we're at a good place to dig a little deeper. I want to conduct a personal interview with the two of you so that we can fill in some missing information your other doctors might not have considered collecting. Do you mind if we get started?"

Hale nodded his consent, and she opened a slim laptop, her focus moving to the screen.

"How frequently do you have intercourse?"

"Daily."

I gaped at him. "We do it pretty frequently when Hale's around, but he travels a lot."

"Would you agree that you have daily intercourse on the days he's home?"

I don't know why I was suddenly embarrassed, but we sounded like whores. "Yes?" I leaned forward and explained, "We're newlyweds."

Were we still newlyweds? It had been over a year since the wedding. Did other couples have sex as often as we did?

"And how often do you travel, Hale?"

"Weekly. I'm usually away on business for half the week."

"And…" She clicked her mouse. "You have a daughter?"

"Yes."

I cleared my throat, but Hale only looked at me.

"Rayne?" The doctor questioned my expression.

I looked at Hale, giving him one last chance to fill her in. Was he seriously not going to explain Elara? Fine. "Full disclosure, I adopted Elara about a year and a half ago and…" I looked at Hale, waiting for him to jump in. Last chance. Going once. Going twice. Sold to the big coward in denial. "Hale's not her biological father either. He adopted her when she was born."

I glanced at Hale, as he stared intensely at a small mark on the wall behind the doctor.

"Okay. That's important information." She typed a few notes into her computer. "Do you use any lubricants or other products that could affect sperm mobility?"

"Um…" I looked at Hale again. This was his idea, yet he left me to answer all the tough questions. I kicked his foot and he snapped out of whatever haze he'd been in.

"We use lube on occasion."

"For vaginal intercourse?"

"Anal."

World, swallow me now.

"When you typically have vaginal inter-course, what positions do you use?"

"All of them."

My cheeks burned. Why not just show her the slideshow of pictures from last night? That reminded me I needed to delete them from his phone.

"Good, variety helps."

Thank God she wasn't the sort of doctor to judge people.

After a few more questions, the doctor closed her laptop and smiled. "Since Rayne's recently had comprehensive bloodwork, I won't order more labs for her. But I would like to arrange an ultrasound. And, Hale, I'd like to get a sample from you. From there, we should be able to get a clear picture of where we stand."

"Sounds good."

I stood. "Do we make the appointment with you or at the desk where we checked in?"

"Oh, no. We're a fully equipped clinic. You can head right to imagery from here."

"But...I haven't been to makeup. I'm not ready for a close up."

She laughed. "There's nothing to worry about, Rayne. The ultrasound is completely painless, and you should be finished in under twenty minutes. Hale, you can return to reception, and they'll show you where to go from there."

She was separating us? I looked up at Hale with wide eyes and he immediately read my panic. "I'll go with Rayne."

The doctor paused. "That's not really necessary—"

"I know. But it's what I'm doing." He took my hand and kissed my fingers. "Come on, baby. We're in this together."

Having Hale close by calmed my nerves, but the experience was still awkward as hell. They put me in a paper gown and told me to wait in a dark room with a large screen. The paper blanket covering my lap crinkled even when I laid still.

"I hate these paper outfits."

"Are you sure you have it on correctly? I thought the ties usually go in the back."

"They're not examining my asshole, Hale." I sighed, trying to ignore the obnoxious crinkling that accompanied my every breath. "These beds are comfortable. Do you think they're made by the same people who make regular mattresses?"

Hale wiggled the stirrups, inspecting the engineering. "Why don't you put your feet up?" He glanced back at the monitor of the ultrasound machine, but the screen was dark.

Not thinking anything of it, I did as he suggested. That was more comfortable.

"It's a little cold in here." When he reached under my paper blanket, I slammed a hand between my legs. "Hale!"

"What? You're my wife. It's not like I haven't seen it a million times before."

"First of all, it's not an *it*, it's a *her*. Second of all, don't be inappropriate."

He sat back, crossing his arms over his chest, and stared at the stirrups. "We could have one of those delivered to the house."

Before I could yell at him for being a pervert, the door opened, and a cheery redhead waltzed in. "Hello!"

Well, wasn't she chipper?

"Sorry to keep you waiting. We'll have you out of here in no time. And, good, you're already in position."

I adjusted the modesty blanket and opened my gown, exposing my belly.

The tech turned on the monitor and faced me with an enormous wand. "Oh, the doctor ordered a transvaginal ultrasound so you can keep your gown closed."

I blushed and covered my stomach just as she rolled a condom down the long penis-shaped stick. That's when I understood that enormous dildo was a camera. My eyes widened.

"That's how you collect the images?" Hale grinned and I rolled my eyes.

"Why don't you just ask for some popcorn, Hale. It's not a movie premiere."

The tech chuckled as she squirted a blob of lubricant on the end of the giant wand and handed it to me. I looked at her questioningly. "Um?"

"You're going to insert the transducer into the vagina, and I'll guide it from there."

If Hale's grin got any bigger I was going to smack him in the head with the big dildo. "I just, uh, put it inside?"

"Yup."

Face burning, I bent forward and slipped the rod inside. It didn't matter that there was lube and a condom, this was the most unsexual situation I'd ever been in.

A black-and-white image moved on the screen. "Great. I'll take it from here."

She reached between my legs and gripped the end of the probe. Was this what the crop circle aliens did when they abducted people?

"Go ahead and lie back and relax, Rayne. No reason for you to be uncomfortable."

If only she knew me.

Her gaze was glued to the screen.

Hale wagged his brows, and I shot him fireballs from my eyes.

"Try to relax. You're tensing."

Jesus, she could feel that?

"How exactly does this work? Is it sonar?" It was reassuring to see that my husband still had some maturity left. He frowned at the blurry images on the screen.

Was that what my internal organs looked like?

"Yes. The transducer emits high-frequency sound waves that bounce off internal struc-tures and create images of the pelvic organs." She moved the wand, and my eyes went wide. She was really freaking up there. "There's your wife's cervix. And this area here is the rectum."

"I thought I recognized that."

I was going to kill him.

The tech laughed. "And that right there is the bladder."

It was official. Hale had finally seen every last inch of me. While he made jokes and she took pictures, I did what I did best and worried. "Does everything look okay?"

"Oh, I just take the images. The doctor will go over the results with you."

That sounded ominous. Why did we have to call them results? Maybe they were just selfies? Whatever happened to good old slides?

Hale took my hand. "You okay, baby?"

Oh, look who finally showed up for emotional support. About freaking time. "I'm fine. Just lying around with a big old wand up my cooter."

He squeezed my hand lovingly. "Just a typical Wednesday afternoon."

What was with him today? My eyes narrowed. "You're cruisin' for a bruisin', Mister."

He chuckled and blew me a kiss.

The tech took several pictures of my insides, and then the wand was gone, and I was instructed to get dressed.

As we walked to Hale's side of the building, I joked, "I hope they didn't find any pictures of old school rings up there."

Hale growled. "Not funny, Rayne."

"Oh, you're the only one who can make jokes today?"

"Those are the rules."

I rolled my eyes.

To Hale's disappointment, I was not allowed in the sample room with him. "Is there a nurse who can offer a little prostate stimulation if he needs it? Sometimes that helps."

"Rayne," Hale snapped, and I snickered. *Payback was a bitch.*

"I don't need that," he assured the nurse.

"Uh, we don't offer that," she said, missing the joke. She slid Hale a cup, and I plopped into a waiting room chair, wincing.

Of course, Hale noticed, and his expression instantly turned to concern. "You okay, baby?"

I rubbed my bottom. "Yeah. My butt's still sore from last night."

He grinned. "I bet it is." He tossed the cup up in the air and caught it in one hand. "I'll be back in ten minutes."

"Oh, honey, you never take that long," I teased loudly. His eyes narrowed as he disappeared into the private room. He was going to spank me again.

After our appointment at the fertility

clinic, we were told to grab dinner at a local restaurant and return to the clinic when we finished to review the results of our tests.

"So, how was it?" I asked Hale once we placed our order.

"Which part? The part when my wife took a ten-inch dildo or the part when I got to jerk off to porn?"

"They gave you porn?" I scoffed. "See! This is exactly why I hate the patriarchy!"

"You think those imaginary old men around the poker table ordered that porn for me?"

"They *are* the patriarchy."

"Of course they are."

"And that dildo-cam could have been a few inches shorter. I blame them for that, too."

"Right."

When our drinks arrived, we did a quick cheers. "To fertility," I said, taking a big gulp of my margarita. "God, I miss tequila."

"Then why did you order a virgin margarita?"

"I'm trying something new. Plants and stuff. It's supposed to keep me more grounded and connected to nature."

"And the plant that grows the margarita is...?"

"A lime. Duh."

"Of course."

My spiritually awakened appetite took a nose dive when Hale ordered a steak. "Make that two," I said, changing my order at the last second.

"Do you want that *with* the salad or without?"

"You can cancel the salad."

The waiter nodded and walked away. Hale arched a brow.

"Don't judge me. Cows eat grass. I'm getting nutrients from somewhere."

He held up his hands. "I never told you to eat plants and give up alcohol or meat. I like you happy and a little drunk."

I pursed my lips. "That's because I'm a cheap date."

"Oh, I don't know about that." He lifted my left hand and traced his thumb over my wedding ring. "You've cost me more than any other woman."

"Just wait. Your daughter's been in princess training since birth."

"She's your daughter, too."

"I know." And I did know. I loved that

little peanut with every ounce of my heart. Sometimes, I worried it would be impossible tolove a second child as much.Elara already owned so much of my heart. "You're lucky I'm so down to earth, otherwise you'd really have your hands full."

He kissed my hand. "I am lucky."

I sipped my margarita, which was really just a slurpy with an umbrella in it. "Do you think the universe gives us exactly what we need?"

"I think the powerful people have power because they know how to take control."

That theory didn't help us out when it came to family planning. "You can't command everything, Hale."

"If I covet something, I'll stop at nothing to get it." He touched my wedding ring again. "Case in point, I have you."

"You're such a sexy, savage capitalist. Tell me more, Big Daddy. "

He sipped his old fashioned. "Men who have everything they want don't need to brag."

"You don't have *everything* you want."

His fingers laced with mine. "It'll happen, Rayne."

I wish I had his confidence.

After dinner, we returned to the clinic. I was once again nervous for reasons I didn't understand. We waited for Dr. Seacrest in a small conference room where I critically judged the minimalist decor.

"Do you think the different holding areas are for different purposes?"

Hale looked up from his phone. "What do you mean?"

"Like, does us waiting in here imply something about our results?"

"No, I think our chart tells them about our results."

He was always so logical. "Do you think you gave them a good sample?" I made a fist and flexed my muscle. "Strong?"

"Did you just ask if my semen was strong?"

I shrugged. "Well, they should be, right? That's a long ass journey for those little guys. Plus, it's a race. I like to picture them storming my ovaries as *Flight of the Valkyries* plays."

He silently chuckled then said, "Yes, they were strong."

"Good." I chewed my lip nervously. "I hope my ovaries were photogenic."

The door finally opened. "Davenports, how was dinner?"

We pushed through the tedious small talk, but I was anxious to get to the results. "Did you find anything concerning?" Hale took my hand, silently urging me to calm down.

"Actually, I did."

I clenched. This was it. This was the moment she told me I was as barren as the old west during a high noon shoot out.

"You can relax, Rayne. I have good news. I'm almost certain I've figured out the issue."

"So, there is an issue?" Hale asked, shifting in his seat to sit a little straighter.

Oh, God. It was me. I was a faulty model. Or was it him? Maybe his swimmers were just a bunch of doggy paddling lost boys.

"A minor one," the doctor clarified.

"Mine or his?" I blurted, unable to bear the suspense. "Just give it to me straight, Doc. It's me, isn't it? My plumbing's all clogged, isn't it? I knew it. The Reiki lady said I was stuck. I eat a lot of dairy."

"Rayne, baby, let her talk." Hale squeezed my clammy hand in both of his.

But my hands weren't sweating. That was Hale's sweat. Oh, God, if Hale was nervous, we were screwed. He was supposed to be the calm one!

"It comes down to timing," Dr. Seacrest explained. "All of your test results were healthy. Sperm mobility is good and I saw no uterine abnormalities. You have a thick, well-developed endometrium, Rayne, which is optimal for conception."

"So...we're just not doing it *enough*?"

"Well, from your interview, you seem to be enjoying frequent intercourse. Females with shorter menstrual cycles can sometimes ovulate earlier than expected. There's a chance you've just been missing the window. Lifestyle factors, such as stress, can also lead to delays in ovulation and impact fertility. Can you think of an obvious source of stress in your life?"

"No, not that I can..." My words drifted off as soon as I met Hale's stare. Okay, maybe there was one source, but that seemed like a stretch. Or was it?

We both sighed and said, "Remington."

"What's Remington?"

Hale grimaced. "He's my father and Rayne's boss."

"Do you consider your job stressful, Rayne?"

"My job? No." My phone buzzed. Speak of the devil. I sent the call to voicemail. "My boss, however, can be a bit of a handful."

"And your boss is also your father-in-law?"

"Yes, but I have a very different relationship with him than Hale. We're more like friends." If one friend always bossed the other around and made them pick up their dry cleaning and headhunt minions.

"He's a malignant narcissist who expects the world to revolve around his needs," Hale explained. "If he can't profit off of someone, he views them as a waste of time."

"I see."

"That's a little harsh," I mumbled.

"Harsh, but true. He's a source of stress in both our lives," he told the doctor and I gaped at the little tattletale.

"I wouldn't say that—"

"How many times has he texted you since we've been here? Ignore the fact that you're using your personal time, he knows you're away with your husband, and that you have a doctor's appointment today."

I casually slid my phone into my bag. Stunned Hale would throw me under the bus like that. Yes, Remington had called several times, but that was only because I was a crucial part of his daily operations.

"I'm an indispensable part of the company," I explained, refusing to look at Hale who knew that was a lie.

"He was probably looking for paperwork on collectible cars, or something equally unimportant. He has no respect for your personal time."

"It's not like I can't ignore him." I bunched my shoulders, feelings slightly under attack. "He knows I'm busy, that's why I haven't answered him. I'll call him back when I feel like it." My purse vibrated in my lap, and I winced.

Hale gazed at the bag. "That's him right now, isn't it?"

"So? You don't see me rushing to answer." Just then, the Imperial March blared from my work phone. If Remington was using the emergency line reserved only for emergencies, it must mean that whatever he needed couldn't wait. Hale held my stare, daring me not to pick up. I almost didn't, but the longer it rang, the more I worried something was wrong. "I'm sorry, I have to get this."

I discreetly lifted the phone from my

purse, and the *Imperial March* silenced. "Remington? I'm at a doctor's appointment. Did you need something?"

"Meyers, what did you do with the paperwork from the marina? I want you to see about moving my yachts closer to the cabana lounge."

I closed my eyes as Hale glared at the phone. The room was small and silent, so there was no chance they couldn't hear how ridiculous and not-urgent Remington's question was.

"This is exactly what I'm talking about," Hale told Dr. Seacrest. "She needs to establish boundaries." He cupped his mouth and spoke loudly toward the phone, "This. Is. Her. Personal. Time."

"Remington, I'll have to call you back." I hung up the phone and it instantly started ringing again. I silenced it, stuffing it all the way at the bottom of my bag as my blood pressure rose.

"That was an emergency?"

"You know how he is, Hale." I didn't want to argue about this here, so I faced the doctor. "Obviously, there are some changes I can make. But it's also stressful that Hale refuses to get along with his father when he's such a prominent part of our lives."

There. I said it.

Was I going to look at Hale now that I told the truth? Abso-fucking-lutely not. So I stared wide-eyed at the doctor like a total psychopath.

"Well, it seems like you've identified some areas you can work on. A few boundaries and perhaps some minor lifestyle changes, and things should improve."

Was she dismissing us? That was it?

Her advice was fuck more and stress less? Who wouldn't benefit from that?

What a waste of a tank of gas. I mean, it was great we both got a clean bill of health, but we weren't necessarily given a solution. I thought this lady was supposed to be the best of the best? We were at least happy before we came here. Now, we were both pissed off and not speaking. Great. This was exactly why I preferred to be non-confrontational in all things.

A Truth for a Truth

As soon as I walked into the penthouse, I tossed my purse onto the table and barked at Hale, "I'm taking a bath."

Five minutes later, I was stewing in a steaming tub of irritation and denial. Not only was I pissed off about him throwing me under the bus, I forgot my damn book downstairs, and I was at a good part. Normally, I would just call Hale and ask him to bring it to me—which he would—but there was no way I was asking anything of him now.

"Rayne." Hale barged in to the bathroom.

"Ever hear of knocking?" I slunk below the bubbles, rolling my eyes.

"Let's get one thing straight, a door will never keep me from you."

"Oh, really? Will this work? Go. Away."

"My flight leaves in two hours. We should talk."

"I think we said enough."

He dragged the vanity chair closer to the tub and sat down, staring at me for a long moment. "You can't deny that he puts too much stress on you."

"I'm his personal assistant, Hale. It's a twenty-four-seven responsibility. And what does it matter, if I don't mind doing it?"

"I mind."

The room temperature dropped several degrees as the air between us chilled. I'd always suspected he minded, but he never admitted it. In fact, he denied it.

"Well, that's new."

"No, it's not. I've tried to be supportive, but he's only become more intrusive. Now, it's literally impacting our family life."

"Oh, bullshit."

"Rayne, the doctor said—"

"There is no test that spit out an actual result that said our inability to conceive is Remington's fault, Hale." I flung my hand out of the water and started ticking off facts.

"One, she's not even my official doctor. She's a specialist we had *one* consultation with. She doesn't know anything about us. Two, your job is way more intrusive than mine. You leave every week, and I'm left alone for days. I have to care for Elara, do my job, and go to class. Did you ever think that maybe I need Remington as much as he needs me? Marta feeds us and takes care of our daughter when Andrew or I can't. When I'm overwhelmed, I can go there to catch my breath. Your dad might stress you out, but he helps calm me down. I like knowing I'm a part of his world when mine feels empty. You're away a lot, Hale. And sometimes..."

I didn't understand why I was suddenly crying. When I wiped my eyes I got bubbles on my face and sputtered, trying to keep them from going in my mouth.

"It's really hard knowing I have a partner but also feeling like I'm a single parent half the time. Plus, school's super stressful, and everyone's younger than me in my classes, so it's not like I have friends I can study with. If I was going to cut back on stress, I'd start there. But none of that matters because it takes two to tango, bucko, and this is not just my fault. You want to point fingers and place blame, let's put it all on the table. The situation between you and your dad has been the biggest freaking elephant in the room since we've met, and we've been stepping around it for years. *That's* intrusive!"

"Bucko?"

"I'm too tired to pick my words carefully."

He glanced away and sighed, not the least bit frazzled by my emotional explosion. "My job has always required a lot of traveling."

"Well, my job has always required a lot of Remington."

"I don't want to fight with you, Rayne."

"Then why did you say all that to some stranger in a lab coat? She said our timing was off, and you dumped all this personal crap on the table. You could have at least spoken to me about your feelings in private."

"I'm sorry. You're right. That wasn't the best place to bring this up. But it usually bothers me most when you're running out the door to help him, so there never seems to be an appropriate time to discuss it."

"Oh, my God." I sank lower in the tub, strongly considering going underwater and holding my breath until he left the room.

"What?"

"Hale, I love you, but I am not going to be a part of your rivalry with him. He might be my boss, but he's also my father-in-law. He's the only father figure I've got, and I love him. You can't ask me to stop worrying about his health or stop scheduling his appointments and checking that his medications are correctly sorted just because I'm off the clock. That's what a good daughter does. And, as his son, you should be grateful I care so much."

"I am grateful."

"Then why is it so hard for you to accept? Can't you just admit that you love him, too?"

His jaw twitched. "Sometimes, I overlook how much you do when I'm not around. I know I rely on you a lot with Elara. I'm sorry if I've taken you for granted."

Of course, he'd breeze right over the Remington stuff. "She's my daughter, Hale. I do it because I love her, not as a favor to you. Now, can we go back to everything else I said and have a real discussion?"

He bolted out of his chair and paced the bathroom like a caged lion. His fingers forked through his hair, leaving it abnormally tousled and standing on end.

"I can't stand it when you're upset with me. Tell me how to fix this."

Fix it? He was the one who started it.

Maybe this wasn't even about Remington, but Hale was so used to blaming him for the problems in his life that he naturally went there.

"Hale, do you even know what I go through every month?"

"What do you mean?"

"I mean, this part of *trying* is more than just *having sex* for me. Every few weeks, I pee on that little stick, and my heart gets broken —over and over and over again." Saying the words aloud brought the pain of the last fifteen months to the surface.

No matter how many times I told myself it was no one's fault, I still piled most of the blame on my shoulders.

"I sit on the toilet and I cry. Every month." Tears welled in my eyes now as I considered how many times I prayed and made promises, only to be disappointed again and again.

"Rayne." He dropped to his knees and rubbed my shoulder. "Baby, please don't cry."

I sniffed and wiped away my tears. "The worst part is knowing that I have to disappoint you."

"Baby, you could never disappoint me."

"Just once, I wish that test would be positive. Just so I could see you beam with pride."

"You don't have to be pregnant to make me proud, Rayne."

"I know." I wiped my eyes, ready to get out of the bath and go to bed. "And I'm not telling you this to make you feel bad. But if you want to know where my stress comes from, it's that. You're so perfect and used to getting everything you want. It's incredibly stressful to be the one letting you down."

"Come here." He pulled me into a hug, careless of the way I dripped all over his clothes.

"I'm sorry," he rasped, pressing a kiss to my lips. "I was a complete prick today. The thought of you crying over any of this..." His jaw ticked and his eyes glazed. "I never want to hurt you."

I nodded, accepting his apology. "I know that. This is just...life. Nature's complicated."

"But this is about us. I should be there with you when you take the tests so you never have to go through any of this alone. I *want* to be there. I'm so sorry I haven't been."

"It's fine—"

"No. It's not fine. When I say we're in this together, I mean it. I promise to do better. And you're right. I need to work out my shit with my father."

I drew back in surprise and studied his eyes. "Really?"

"Really."

I owed him an apology, too, but I was so blown over by his admission and promise to try where Remington was concerned that I could hardly think of what else I needed to say. This was tremendous progress.

I turned his wrist and checked the time on his watch. He had roughly one hour before he really needed to get moving.

"Hand me a towel," I whispered.

He opened a towel and helped me out of the tub. After he gathered me in the plush fabric and dried me like a child, he lifted me into his arms and carried me directly to bed.

I shivered and pulled him down with me. "I love you, Hale." I pressed my lips to his.

"I love you, too, baby," he whispered against my mouth as I loosened his tie.

His hands traveled over my damp skin as he kissed a trail down my stomach. My fingers raked through his hair, pressing him lower until his mouth was between my thighs. The warm lick of his tongue had me arching into him and closing my eyes.

Hale could be demanding in bed, but he was never selfish. He always saw to my pleasure first.

My heels dug into his back as I writhed and moaned. The slow climb of my climax was a languid build that spilled over me in soft delight.

When my shivers calmed, I pulled off his shirt and pulled him in for another kiss. My hands fumbled at his belt as I urgently tried to get his pants off. "Take these off."

As soon as he stripped off his clothes, he was filling me—slow, deep, and divinely passionate. My nails scraped down his shoulders as he kissed my neck. When he found that sensitive spot by my ear, my toes curled, and my legs trembled.

"Don't go," I breathed, pleading for him to stay.

"I wish I didn't have to."

My heart hurt every time we said goodbye. The ache never got easier to bear.

"Then give me something to remember you by. I want to feel you still inside of me even when you're thousands of miles away."

His hips slammed forward, and he buried himself deep. Locked in passion, we battled our denial, knowing full well that we only had a few minutes before he'd inevitably have to say goodbye.

I wondered how I got so lucky to find a man I loved so completely, a man who accepted me at my best and my worst. But no one prepared me for the agony that accompanies such unconditional love. If I ever lost Hale, the loss would kill me. He was more than my husband. He was my heart, my soul, the breath in my lungs, and the song in my voice.

"You're my world, Hale."

His brow pressed to mine as if my confession struck like an arrow to the chest. "You're my entire universe, Rayne." His breath shuddered as his release filled me.

I clung to his shoulders, desperate to hold him a little more. "Don't let go yet. Just stay inside of me for a while longer."

His arms slid beneath my back, our bodies still connected as one, as he pulled me onto him. I rested my head on his shoulder, savoring the safety I felt in his arms as I listened to his steady, familiar heartbeat.

Breathing in his scent, I committed this moment to memory, storing it beside a million other priceless moments we shared. It would be three long days before I could have him like this again. Bearable, but difficult.

"I'll miss you," I said, my only way of letting him know I would never willingly let him go, but I was ready to face reality all the same.

"I'll miss you too, baby. More than you'll ever know."

I Am A Unicorn, Therefore I Sparkle

"More crystals?" Hale looked up from his laptop as I casually decorated every child-safe, unadorned surface of the house.

"You *hush*. I like them. They keep me centered and calm."

"That used to be my job," he mumbled, his gaze drifting back to the iPad.

"This one's a moonstone. Willow says it can help balance my hormones."

"Who needs Western medicine when we have rocks?"

"Western medicine can't energize the divine feminine, Hale. And it's not a rock, it's a crystal."

"And crystals are...?"

"Shut up. It's supposed to strengthen my cycles and help with conception."

"Sound advice from a woman you met in a cave below the New York subway."

"Um, your sarcasm is not appreciated. And that cave-dwelling woman gives me the confidence that we will get pregnant."

"The Reiki lady, not the renowned fertility specialists who collected actual scientific data."

"That's correct."

"Just checking."

I returned to organizing my crystals into cute little displays and ignored my husband's skepticism. Hale liked facts and order. If he couldn't make math out of something, it didn't exist. The man didn't have a spiritual bone in his body. I, on the other hand, was accessing my inner goddess and traveling down a fertile path to enlightenment.

Willow had taken on a prominent role in my life since my visit to New York. When she told me she worked with virtual clients all over the world, I hired her as a spiritual coach, sort of like a therapist.

Sure, she lacked some credentials, but she grounded me in a way few could.

She and I had a weekly recurring meeting,

during which I expressed my worries, and she advised me. I didn't see any difference between this and any other sort of coach, church leader, or advisor.

Did Hale think I was in a cult? Probably.

Was I?

Well, I wasn't shaving my head or running around in robes yet, so I considered it more of a high-interest hobby. And even if it was a pricey placebo, Willow's advice was helping me.

My IBS—a condition I'd struggled with since puberty—was less frequent. My breakouts had cleared up. And I seemed to have a natural glow that wasn't there before.

My job was still stressful. Hale was traveling as much as ever, and Elara was burning through my energy faster than a kettle that never stopped steaming. But my stomach issues were calm, and my mood was Zenner than ever. I wasn't living off plants or doing that whole no-alcohol thing, of course. I mean, come on. I was never going to be *that* Zen. Chocolate and booze had been my crutch for far too long, and I owed them my loyalty, even in a time of pure enlightenment.

"If Willow sells you any more rocks, she

might be able to relocate to a nicer place above ground."

"Joke all you want, Mr. Davenport. But as the newest Davenport, I'm expected to have a few weird, rich-girl interests. It's in the gold digger handbook. This can be my first frivolous, eclectic hobby as your wife."

It still felt strange calling myself rich. Every time I signed into my bank account, I felt like I was shoplifting. The monthly statement was obscene, and my brain still thought like a girl who sometimes bounced checks and regularly paid overdraft fees. It would be impossible to overdraw my accounts now.

"We're not rich, Rayne."

"Uh, I beg to differ."

"Rich is unstable. We're wealthy."

"And wealthy is somehow more stable?"

"Wealth is generational, so yes, it's much more stable."

"Could you be more pretentious?"

He met my stare. "Your rock is crooked."

"It's a crystal!"

"And a crystal is..."

"A pretty rock. Why are you picking on me?"

"Because you're cute when you're flustered."

I wondered how cute he'd think I was once I saged the house. "Just think of them like jewels. You love buying me diamonds. Now, you can buy me crystals." I abandoned the shelf I'd been decorating and brought him a palm stone. "Hold one." I placed it in his hand. "They all have different meanings. This is rose quartz. It represents unconditional love and emits a healing vibration. It's a symbol of love and joy."

He turned it in the light. "Pretty."

I smiled and took it back from him. "I think so."

I never did well with houseplants. And Hale's home was already decorated when we got together, so this was technically the first time I tried changing the aesthetic.

"Do you mind having them around?"

"Why would I mind? This is our home. Decorate it however you want."

I rushed back to the sofa and kissed him.

He caught my hips. "What was that for?"

"Just for...being you."

"Well, if you wanted to really thank me..." He glanced at his watch. "Elara and Andrew won't be back for another thirty minutes."

I slithered off of his lap, landing on the

floor between his knees. "Is this what you had in mind?"

"That's exactly what I manifested."

I laughed and unzipped his pants.

Despite all of Hale's teasing, he really did listen to me and love me enough to support anything I was into. A few days later a package arrived. I waited until Hale got home since it was addressed to him, but when he saw it, he smiled and handed it to me.

"It's for you."

"For me?" I loved prizes.

"Open it." He handed me a knife and I sliced the carboard open.

"It's another box." I pulled the luxe white box from the paper and set it on the table. "It's heavy." The suction of the lid made it difficult to lift off. When I finally got it open, a piece of foam covered whatever was inside, so I suspected it was fragile. I tossed the foam board aside and gasped when I saw pale pink rose quartz in a cushioned bed of satin. "You got me a crystal?"

I carefully pulled the tower from the box and gasped. Hale laughed. "Do you like it?"

I tucked it in my lap, blushed, and whispered. "Hale, this is a penis."

"Actually, the proper term is *wand.*"

I ran my fingers over the smooth flared head. The pink quartz was heavy and cold in my hand, but it was definitely a dick. "Well, we can't display this on a windowsill."

"It's not for display. It's for you."

I looked up in shock. "What do you mean?"

He took the crystal *wand* and dragged it between my legs. "You know what I mean."

I gaped at him. "It goes inside?" I whispered.

He nodded. "Not the sort of vibration you're used to, but according to what you told me..."

"Oh, my God. You're going to Reiki my vagina?"

"What do you say we give it a spin?"

It turned out, that not all sex toys were created equal. Most of the toys Hale added to our collection were soft or chargeable. This was nothing like the others and when he used it on me, it was unlike any other time.

Hale teased the cool crystal over my skin slowly. He took his time and was excruciatingly gentle. He didn't fuck me with the *wand,* he made love to me with it. It was sensual and scintillating. He worshipped my body, anointing every inch of flesh with the crystal, until I was begging for the real thing. And when he pressed inside of me, there was something powerful about his intentions.

"Can you feel me, Rayne?" He pulled me onto his lap, his arms winding around me as he closed his mouth over mine and flexed his hips. "Can you feel me inside of you, deep in your core? Feel me in your heart. I'm there, Rayne. Always with you."

My lips dragged over his jaw as he pressed deeper. "I feel you."

"Can you picture what it will feel like when our child's in there?"

"Yes."

"A piece of me, growing inside of you."

Every slow stroke enunciated his whispered words. My entire being became part of him in that moment as he held me in his arms and made love to me.

"That's what I want, Hale."

"You know I'll give you anything you want, baby. I'll always take care of you."

My head tilted back as my pleasure peaked. His grip tightened as his swollen cock pulsed inside of me, and we shivered. I had never felt so connected, so unified with another person as I did in that moment as our bodies fused as one.

Even if that wasn't *the moment* of conception, it was a fundamental moment for us, one where we recognized each other's commitment and poured all of our love into one shared purpose. That night, Hale healed something in me. He reminded me that while our lives would be fuller with a second baby, our love was far from empty. And that was a truth I needed to remember.

The following week I was at Remington's organizing the outdated file system he used in his house. "Remington, why do you still have the rebate paperwork for a vacuum you no longer own?"

"Meyers, don't ask stupid questions. Do I look like the person you should be asking about vacuums?"

He was right. I pulled out the overstuffed file bursting with outdated manuals and rebates and went to find Marta.

She was making something that smelled divine in the kitchen. "Hey Marta, do you have a second?"

"What is it, Niña?"

I dropped the heavy file on the counter. "Could you look through this and tell me what appliances he no longer has? I'm trying to make some room in the filing cabinets. The man is still holding on to his tax returns from 1970."

"Of course. You sit. I'll make you lunch."

Oddly, I wasn't that hungry, but I never turned down Marta's cooking. "What's on the stove?"

"Today, I make a white bean chicken chili." She set a steaming bowl before me with a spoon and a linen napkin.

"Smells good." I lifted the spoon to my mouth and blew on the creamy chili to cool it off.

"It is good for you, Niña. You need all the protein and nutrients you can get in your condition."

I stilled, a mouth full of beans and delicious chicken on my tongue. "Huh?"

She looked at me with a knowing grin and whispered, "*Estas embarazada.*"

"No compre-hendo. English, please."

She glanced at the door and then stepped closer, planting her hand flat on my belly. "You have a baby in you, Niña."

I lowered my spoon. "Nuh-uh."

"Whatever you say." She tapped my hand with little conviction. "Eat up before your food gets cold."

I numbly finished my lunch, and she said

nothing more about it as she sorted through the file. When I left the kitchen, I went right to Remington's office. "I, uh, have to go deal with something."

He didn't look up from his desk. "Are you coming back?"

"Maybe."

"Who's going to clean up these files, Meyers?"

"I have a system. Just leave them. I need to... It's an emergency."

At that, he glanced up from his work. "Is everything all right?"

"Mm-hm."

Everything was fine. It wasn't like Marta was some sort of prophet. She was a housekeeper who liked to cook spicy food. However, she did tell me that the first time she met me, she knew I was going to be essential to the Davenports. Apparently, her intuition influenced Remington's decision to hire me, which, now that I thought about it, was really odd. She also once told me that she had a bad feeling the day Remington fell from his heart attack like she knew something was going to go wrong that day.

A flutter of excitement rippled through my belly. "Is Marta psychic?"

He rumpled his bushy white brows. "What? You do realize we have actual work to do, Meyers. Go deal with your *thing* and get back here to clean up this mess. I want to review these reports tonight. Marta's making chili, so bring Elara back with you and we can do the reports after dinner."

"Uh-huh." I grabbed my purse, not hearing a single word he said.

Twenty minutes later I was washing my hands and staring down at a pregnancy test. I promised Hale I'd wait for him the next time I took one, but he was in Colorado visiting wind farms for the next three days.

Only in the land of wishful procreation did three minutes take this long. Seconds passed like fortnights as I impatiently tapped my foot and stared at the unchanging stick.

"Ugh!" The wait was killing me, so I called Tyler.

He answered right away. "Calamity, what's shaking?"

"You busy?"

"Just developing some photos I took last weekend."

Tyler had recently discovered a love for photography after speaking to Rarity Lockhart, the photographer at our wedding.

She gave him a bunch of old equipment, and he'd started taking night classes. He even booked a few local gigs around town, which was exciting.

"Pictures of what?"

"Just a few architecture shots and some landscapes. I'm experimenting with shadows and light."

"Cool."

"What's up with you?"

"I'm currently sitting on the toilet waiting for a pregnancy test to process."

"Shit. Really?"

"Yup."

"Is that... I mean, are you and Hale trying?"

"We've been, but it's not as easy as it seems. My expectations are low."

"Oh. Well, how long does it take?"

"We've been trying for over a year."

"No, how long does it take for the test results, Rayne?"

"Oh. Three minutes." I stared down at the tiny window where one blue line appeared.

"This is a big deal. I feel so special being a part of it."

"Shh." I couldn't think or blink and

Tyler's words were making it harder to see. I just needed him on the line for emotional support.

"You called me."

"I think I see something."

"What do you see?"

Was that another faint line? It was so light. Sometimes that happened, but it never got any darker. I swallowed tightly, an uncomfortable tension headache developing behind my eye.

"Ray?"

"Oh, my God."

"What is it? Should we Facetime? I can't see your face."

"Tyler... I'm pregnant."

Turns Out, I Can Grow Things

I kept the news to myself for three whole days. Marta, Tyler, Willow, and my doctor, who confirmed the results, were the only people who knew I had a bun in the oven. Keeping such a big secret was *killing* me, but I wanted to tell Hale in person. Thank God he was on his way home.

I dropped Elara off at Remington's for an impromptu sleepover. It always gave me a little thrill when I hijacked his plans for some surprise grandpa time. He bitched and moaned, but then he melted because, let's face it, Elara was irresistible.

As soon as I got home, I got to cooking—not something I usually did--but this was a special occasion. Hale was scheduled to arrive in less than an hour and it had been a while since I used my culinary skills, so I needed every second.

The baby spinach salad was prepped, the baby carrots were glazed and ready to go in the skillet, and the baby back ribs were already roasting in the oven. It didn't take a genius to sense the theme. But in case Hale missed it, I also made a playlist—all songs with baby in the title.

As the Supremes crooned *Baby Love*, I carefully wrapped the baby hotdogs in their little blankets because nothing screamed pregnancy like little wieners swaddled in pastry. For dessert, I picked up two baby cakes from Chef Dubois—one with pink frosting and one with blue.

The table was set, and things looked good, but something smelled off. I rushed to the kitchen and sniffed the air, trying to locate the culprit. The ribs were cooking nicely, and carrots were bubbling on the stove. Everything was calm. So why did I smell smoke?

I scanned the kitchen, not seeing anything out of the ordinary. Then, I tracked the smell to the dining room but found nothing amiss. The table looked fine, and all the taper candles were straight—"*Oh shit!*"

I ran into the living room and found the source of smoke. A pillar candle I had set on the side table flickered with a five-inch flame, singing the corner of some work of art that probably cost more than my car.

"Fuck, fuck, fuck!" I blew out the candle and pulled the heavy frame off the wall. Flames climbed up the canvas, melting the gilded frame.

I held the painting between my out-stretched arms, angling it away from my face, and spun in a circle, not sure what to do. "Oh, no!"

The center of the portrait bubbled with a heat blister and opened as the flame melted through the underside. The smoke detector started to blare.

"What do I do?" I panicked and rushed through the smoky living room toward the back door. Wrenching open the glass, careful not to catch myself on fire in the process, I screamed. The highly flammable oil paint blazed like a torch the second the wind came into play, and I screamed.

"Son of a bitch!" I hurled the painting into the pool the second I smelled burnt hair and the flames went out with a hiss.

Panting for breath, I stared at the floating

work of art as it singed on the surface. "Well, that's ruined."

I dusted off my hands and went back inside to beat the smoke detector off the ceiling with a broomstick. Coughing, I shut off the air conditioning and opened the windows to air out the house. Then, I made sure there were no more fire hazards.

The front door opened just as Mariah Carey kicked off *Always Be My Baby.* "Rayne?"

A little frazzled, I rushed to greet Hale. "Hey. Welcome home." I untied my apron and tossed it behind me into the kitchen.

Hale glanced around the house at the candles and sniffed the air. "Is something burning?"

"I made dinner." Rising on my tippy-toes, I pressed a kiss to his lips and took his bags, setting them by the door. "Come have a seat."

"What's the occasion?" He asked as I towed him toward the table. "Why are all the doors open?"

"I was in the mood for some fresh air. Do you want some wine?"

"Sure." He stopped and did a double take of this set table. "Are we having company?"

"Nope. Just us. Elara's at your dad's for the night."

He frowned. "Anniversary's in April. We started dating in June. Your birthday's in May. Why do I feel like I'm forgetting something?"

I cut him off as he made his way to the wine fridge. "I'll get it. What kind do you want?"

Pleased, but suspicious, he said. "That depends. What's on the menu?"

"Um, ribs." I wanted to get him situated and seated before I started with all the baby-themed stuff.

"Ribs?"

"Is that okay?" Hale didn't typically enjoy messy food.

"It's fine. I, uh, guess I'll have...a beer?"

"Oh, I have beer!" I raced to the fridge and removed one of the cute pony bottles I grabbed at the store.

His hand engulfed the small bottle, and he chuckled. "Where's the rest of it?"

"What? It's cute." I steered him toward the dining room table and pushed him into the seat at the head of the table. "You stay here. I'll be right back with our first course."

He caught my hand as I tried to leave. "Wait. How about a kiss?"

I paused and bent to press my lips to his. He deepened the kiss, sliding his hands up my back and into my hair. "I missed you."

I smiled against his mouth. "I always miss you."

"Wait," he said as I tried to pull away again. "Where are you going?"

"I have stuff on the stove." I laughed nervously. "We wouldn't want anything to catch fire."

"Fine." He let me go.

I quickly tossed the salad, stirred the carrots, and checked on the ribs. I returned to the dining room with nicely dressed salads topped with candied pecans, goat cheese, and sliced apples.

"This looks delicious, baby. What kind of lettuce is this?"

"It's baby spinach."

"I'm impressed."

"Me too." I dug in, suddenly ravenous. The apples smelled so fresh and the sweet vinaigrette was delicious. "Oh, my God, I'm an outstanding chef." I shoveled in another bite. "These pecans are orgasmic!"

He chuckled, taking his first bite with

much more decorum than I could muster. This eating for two thing was real.

"Mmm. Delicious," he praised. "So, what did you do while I was gone?"

I heaped another bite onto my fork. "Elara had her checkup. She's cutting her second molars, and the doctor said it's time to start hardcore potty training."

"Really? I guess we need to read up on that."

"I went to the store and got some potties to put in the bathrooms. I also made a reward chart for her."

He smiled. "You're cute when you do teacher stuff."

I shrugged. "It's the only thing I'm officially trained in."

He neatly sliced his salad into manageable bites while I wolfed mine down as if someone might steal it from me. "Do you ever wish you stuck with it?"

"Teaching? Oh, no. I'm not a fan of kids."

"Just ours?"

"Well, yeah. Elara's special. I think she was always meant to be mine."

He smiled and met my stare. "That's how I feel."

I leaned over and kissed him. "Willow would say the universe chose us for her."

He pressed his lips tight, choosing to take another bite rather than comment.

When we finished the salad I brought out the pigs in a blanket. "Munch on these while I get the baby-back ribs and baby carrots."

Hale lifted a wiener and examined it with a frown. "What are they?"

"They're pigs in a blanket."

"Pigs in a what?"

"It's regular people appetizers. Try one. They're good."

He took a tentative bite and raised a brow. "Not bad."

I transferred the baby back ribs to a platter, slathered them with barbecue sauce, and set them down on the table with a huff. "Those things are heavy."

Hale's eyes widened. "Is all this for us?"

"I went grocery shopping when I was hungry. You know how that goes. I also have baby carrots. I'll be right back."

He cocked his head but made no comment as I rushed to retrieve the carrots.

"Oh, napkins!"

When the table was finally set with the main course, and we were ready to eat, Hale hesitated. I plated his food, giving him a good sample of everything.

"Dig in," I said when he looked anxiously at his food. "You can cut the meat off the bone if you want."

Had the man honestly never eaten a rib before?

I lifted a rib and took a bite, moaning at the savory flavor. Hale rolled up his sleeves and moved his tie out of the way, draping it over his shoulder. He had yet to touch his main course.

"So, you just decided to make ribs?"

"*Baby*-back ribs," I said, gnawing the meat off the bone. "And *baby* carrots."

"I didn't know you liked ribs that much."

I shrugged. "Who doesn't like a rib?" Maybe Hale didn't. "Are you going to eat?"

He lifted a rib, careful not to touch the sloppy bone with more than two fingers. When he took a bite, he strategically used his teeth in a way that ensured no sauce touched his skin. I, on the other hand, had already dirtied several napkins.

"Good God, Hale, you'll be here for years at that pace. Don't you like pork?" Sauce smeared over my lips and cheeks, but it would take the jaws of life to pry this sucker from my hands. Goddamn, I made a good rib! *Who knew?*

"They're very tasty. They're just...messy."

"So, get messy. *Life* is messy."

He took another calculated bite. The tension in his body was clear on his face as he battled severe tactile revulsion. After every neat, little bite, he compulsively cleaned up his hands and lips. From what, I have no clue. There wasn't a speck of sauce on him.

Okay, maybe the ribs were a bad choice for Neatnik Hale. I started to doubt my plan. The stress of eating messy food was sort of overshadowing the ambiance.

"What exactly are we listening to?"

I paused and cleared my throat, thinking I also could have considered my song choices more carefully. "This is, uh, *Baby Got Back* by Sir Mix-A-Lot."

"Okay, Rayne." He dropped the rib and wiped off his hands. "What's going on? Did I miss something? The candles, the 90's rap, the weird food..."

"It's not weird food."

"It's weird that you're cooking. Since when do you do that?"

"I was in the mood for baby-back ribs and baby carrots and baby spinach."

"You have to admit, that's a weird combination of cravings—"

I watched the moment his words registered. His head lifted as the blood bleached from his face.

"Wait." He looked up at the speaker in the wall. "Baby Got... Oh, my God..." He jumped to his feet. "Are you pregnant?"

I laughed, and he gave me no time to answer. Scooping me out of my chair, he kissed my messy mouth. I still had a sloppy rib in my hand, which got sauce all over his collar and ear. "Sorry."

"Fuck the rib. Are you really pregnant? We're going to have a baby?"

I nodded, and he howled with the joy of a thousand touchdowns. His hands flew into his hair as he grinned widely. He was speechless and beyond happy, which made me the happiest woman alive.

"This is amazing! When did you find out? How?"

"Well, you see, Hale, when a boy puts his penis in the girl's vagina—"

"I mean, how could this be? You took a test—"

"The test was wrong."

"You took another one?"

"I had to. Marta totally freaked me out."

"Marta?"

I told him the whole story about the chili and what his father's housekeeper said. "She's always had eerie intuition. Does anyone else know?"

"Just you, Tyler, Willow, and Marta. Oh, and the doctor. I wanted to make sure it was official before I told you."

"Wait, how long have you known?"

"A little over sixty hours. But you can't get mad at me for keeping it a secret from you. I wanted to tell you in person."

"I can't believe you could keep it to yourself for that long."

"It nearly killed me. We have to tell everyone else soon because I hate keeping secrets. I bought Elara the cutest big sister shirt to wear at your dad's tomorrow."

His hand went to his chest. His hair was a mess, and he had crap all over his face. It was rare to see Hale so shaken, but I loved it. He looked like a true father.

"I can't believe this." He covered his mouth then wiped his eyes. "We're having a baby!" When our gazes locked, he crossed the room and hugged me tight, his face wedging into the curve of my neck as he sniffled. "I love you so much."

"I love you, too."

He drew back and wiped his eyes. "We should celebrate. Champagne?"

I smiled at the irony of his question.

"Oh, wait." He laughed. "You can't drink. Right. I forgot."

"You can, though. Don't let me stop you."

"No, it's fine. I just feel like we should do something special." His gaze dropped to my stomach, and then he pressed his palm over my belly. "I can't believe this. My baby's in there."

"Well, I think I play a small part in the procreation, so technically it's *our* baby."

He smiled at me with such awe. "Our baby. How amazing is that?"

Turned out, we didn't need champagne or a fancy meal to celebrate. We only needed each other. Hale carried me upstairs, where we made love late into the night.

As he kissed my stomach, he whispered secret promises to the little bean growing inside. Considering my track record, I always assumed I'd be terrified once I reached this point,

but I was so overwhelmed with relief and gratitude that I was oddly calm. It was as if I was
truly ready for this next chapter of our lives.

Afterward, I lay in a mess of blankets and
pillows, more satisfied than I had felt in
months.

The bathroom light flicked on as Hale
cleaned up. On his way back to the bed, he
paused by the balcony door. "Rayne, why is
my Renly portrait in the pool?"

I bit my lip. "Is that something you really
want to know?"

"I guess not." He chuckled, leaving the
window and climbing back into bed.

As he fussed over my body, taking more
care than usual, my stomach soured with
guilt. "Was it expensive?"

"I got it for a steal at an auction."

Uh-oh. A steal for me was a two-for-one
at Costco. Hale's definition was probably
much different. "How much of a steal?" I
braced.

"Fifty."

"*Thousand?*" I was going to be sick.

"Yeah."

There was no way I could replace a work
of art like that. And if that was what he con-

sidered a bargain, that probably meant it was worth twice that. "I'm sorry, Hale."

"Nothing could upset me right now, Rayne. Don't sweat it." He kissed my head. "I'll just have to find something I like better to replace it. Maybe a nude of my beautiful wife. I have a few on my phone I'm fond of."

"There will be no nudes of my body hanging in the common areas of this house. And you promised to delete those!"

"I don't remember that."

"Hale," I said sternly. My maternal voice was already developing.

"Shh. Baby, I'm trying to sleep."

My lips pursed. I was never getting those damn pictures off his phone. "What's our baby going to think when he learns his father's a big old pervert."

"He?" Hale chuckled. "What if it's another girl?"

I smiled. "I'd be happy either way." My hand cradled my flat stomach as a sense of warmth spread through my chest. "Our baby."

Hale's hand covered mine. "Our baby."

Mind the Zygote Please

We caught the pregnancy early, so at this stage we were basically dealing with a zygote. But that tiny, little fertilized egg quickly became our whole world.

This was different from the first time Hale was expecting. When Elara's birth mother revealed she was pregnant, she wasn't exactly on good terms with him. That led to the blowout between Hale and Remington, and then Remington had a heart attack and broke his foot. A few weeks later, I was hired and put smack dab in the middle of their dysfunction. The rest was history.

But this time, Hale was determined things would go differently.

I awoke to an enormous breakfast in bed.

"Oh, my gosh." I scooted back to the pillows, making room for the loaded tray. "We had eggs?"

"I went to the farmer's market. They're organic."

"When?" It was barely light outside.

"I've been up for hours. Too excited to sleep. Besides, your body needs nutritious food. I also picked up some vitamins and fruit and a variety of dairy products—"

"And flowers!" I leaned forward and sniffed the lilies in the vase. I searched the tray for coffee but didn't see it. "Is there coffee?"

"It's probably a good time to start limiting your caffeine."

"What? Who says?"

"Doctors. Even half a cup of coffee a day could impact the baby's weight."

"Maybe a small baby isn't such a bad thing. Keep in mind, junior's entering this world through a very small hole."

"Rayne, everything you put in your body over the next fifteen months matters."

"Fifteen? Am I gestating for an elephant?"

"Well, I figured you'd breastfeed for the first few months. That means no raw fish or fish high in mercury of any kind, no deli meats, alcohol, caffeine, or unpasteurized cheese."

"I can't have cheese? What the hell am I going to eat? And what about sandwiches?"

"No *unpasteurized* cheese."

"That's probably the good kind." I crossed my arms and pouted.

"I promise to keep you well-fed and fully satisfied. We can get a chef if you want."

A chef sounded nice. Someone I could order around to meet my every craving... *Did I just graduate to a new level of bougie?* "What about a maid? I should probably take it easy now that my body's a sacred vessel creating life."

"Whatever you want, baby. Say the word and I'll deliver."

"Huh. This is working out better than I expected."

"I want to make this the healthiest, most stress-free nine months of your life."

Well, that sounded lovely. "I should marry you."

He leaned over the tray and kissed me. "Eat. Then let's inform Elara that she's going to be a big sister."

I smiled and took a bite of the buttered toast. "Oh, I bought a doll for her. I read that it's supposed to help young kids learn how to treat the new baby. She can practice her big sister skills with it."

"That's perfect. I was thinking we should give her a present so she doesn't feel over-looked in any way."

"Done! You gotta admit, we make a good team."

When we got to Remington's, Marta greeted us in the foyer and pinched Hale's cheek. "You're glowing like a proud poppa."

"Daddy!" Elara raced into the foyer and sprung into Hale's arms.

Since Daddy disappeared for several days each week, he tended to be a hotter com-modity than Mommy, who was always around and, therefore, old news.

I pulled the big sister T-shirt out of my bag. "Come here, peanut. I have something for you." I slipped the T-shirt over her night-gown and grinned. "Let's go find Grandpa."

Holding Elara's hands, we walked into the den where Remington was already midway through his morning. "About time you showed up."

"Pop-pop," Elara crashed into Rem-ington and climbed up his legs to get to his lap. He helped her up, and she pulled on her shirt. "Uh-oh."

He glanced down at the pink T and read the words BIG SISTER. "Uh-oh, indeed." He looked at us for clarification. "I imagine this was the *thing* you had to deal with the other day."

I nodded and smiled. "We're due in March. He or she will be an Aries. I know that stuff's important to you."

"Well." He sat Elara down and came to shake Hale's hand. "Congratulations to both of you."

"Thank you." I hated how formal Hale acted around his father. All morning he'd been elated. Now he acted like this was nothing more than a wise business merger.

Remington looked at me, smiled, and held out his arms. "You're carrying some precious cargo, Meyers."

I lunged at him, hugging him tightly to make up for the cold handshake he'd just shared with his son. "I'm going to demand the best maternity package you can afford."

"Now, wait a minute. How did I know this was going to somehow cost me money?"

"Mr. Davenport." Miles entered the room

with an arm full of paperwork and stilled. "Sorry. Am I interrupting?"

Hale looked at me, and I smiled. No point in keeping it a secret. "Not at all. We were just telling Remington that I'm pregnant."

His eyes bulged. "Pregnant? Well, congratulations!" He shook Hale's hand. "Great news."

Next, we told Alphonse and the other members of the household staff. Elara took a bit more explaining. We gave her the baby doll, but she threw it on the floor and went to find Meep Meep her sheep.

When we got home, we had a video call with Seraphina and Barrett, where we let them read Elara's shirt. Then we did the same thing with our moms. By the end of the day, I was exhausted, but it was well worth it. I had everything I wanted and needed. I couldn't ask for more.

Closed for Business

There I was, just peacefully enjoying my banana and yogurt when it hit. Like a kamikaze meteor hurtling toward Earth, my stomach detonated. There was no cramping. No warning burble. Just complete and sudden anarchy.

"Oh God!" I bolted from my seat and rushed in the direction of the toilet.

"Rayne?"

There was no time to explain. I needed a vessel and the bathroom was too far! There was a demon inside of me, and it needed exercising!

I made it as far as the hall when Vesuvius erupted out of me. As my eyes bulged, I covered my mouth as my shoulders locked, but there was no stopping it, so I rushed to the umbrella stand and exercised that fucking demon all over Hale's Swarovski umbrella.

A warm hand pressed against my back as I shivered and hugged the narrow umbrella stand. "Are you okay?"

I was in shock, shaking and fighting back tears. "I'm sorry."

"It's fine. It happens. Can you stand?"

"I need a minute." I'd puked before. I was a college student at one time. But I'd never experienced anything quite as sudden and violent as what just happened.

"Let me get you some water." He disappeared and returned a moment later with an uncapped bottle.

I took the bottle with a shaky hand as he casually carried the bin of umbrellas outside. At least they were waterproof.

"Was that morning sickness?"

"That was…" I swallowed a small sip of water and wiped my mouth, fearful it might trigger another episode. That was unlike anything I ever felt before. And not in a good way. I was speechless. "I feel really weak."

"Take my hands and I'll help you up. Not too fast." Hale wrapped me in his arms and ushered me to the sofa. Elara carried on from her high chair, trapped and irritated that we forgot about her.

"Just sit for a minute. Try to drink some water. I'll find you a cracker to settle your stomach."

The sweat on my skin chilled and I shivered, pulling the lap blanket up to my chest as I tipped onto the pillow and groaned. He helped Elara down from her tray and I heard him tell her, "Mommy needs a hug", with a warning to be gentle. "Her belly hurts."

She toddled over to the sofa, dragging Meep Meep in her wake, and stared at me curiously with a cocked head of curls, still wild from sleep. "Momma sick?" She climbed onto the sofa and nestled into the nest of my knees. "Baby?" She pointed to my stomach.

I smiled weakly. "That's right. Baby." Or a demon. The verdict was still out.

She frowned. "Mommy ouch?"

I didn't want to confuse her, so I just said, "Mommy sleepy."

She gave me Meep Meep, which was extremely high currency in the world of Elara. I cuddled him close to my cheek, breathing in the familiar scent of baby shampoo tinged with traces of milk.

"Thank you, Peanut."

She scooted off the couch and kissed my forehead, returning a minute later with her baby doll. She showed it to me and then threw it on the floor. We had some work to do there.

Sounds of Hale hosing out the umbrella stand carried from the front door. We should probably keep more vessels around the house if this morning sickness crap was going to be an ongoing thing. Or maybe I should travel with those plastic doggy bags, just in case.

My stomach still felt unstable and sour, so I decided not to think about it until I was out of the eye of the storm.

Unfortunately, the morning sickness continued over the next few weeks. It usually struck before work and then again around two p.m.—not technically morning, but Mother Nature didn't care much for man's time constraints, so she basically did as she pleased, and apparently, it pleased her to torture me.

"Rayne?" Remington knocked on the bathroom door.

"I'll be out in a minute." The use of my first name showed his concern. I'd been hugging the toilet since lunch and it was now—

oh, God—I'd been in the bathroom for over an hour.

"Would it help if Marta made you something?"

No doubt Marta hovered outside of the door with him. "Niña," she said with great concern. "I can make you a nice broth with a little toast."

The thought of any food turned my stomach. Even water was becoming hard to keep down during these challenging moments. "I'm okay. I just need a minute please." I hated the idea of them standing close enough to hear me retch, and every word made me fear that it would happen again.

"Well, call if you need anything."

"Mm-hmm," I mumbled, holding back another explosion.

When I finally staggered out of the bathroom you would have thought I spent the night pledging for Greek life. Remington, Marta, and Miles stared at me with unblinking concern.

Remington rushed forward to take my arm. "Do you want Alphonse to drive you home?"

Even a five-minute car ride seemed dicey

at the moment. "I just need to sit down for a few minutes."

Stock market numbers played across the bottom of the television. His laptop and paperwork cluttered the coffee table, and his iPad hung from the stand to the left of the couch. Miles picked up the phone he'd abandoned to let the person on the other line know that Remington had stepped away and would return shortly.

"Just sit for a while. Find your sea legs."

I groaned, not wanting to think about the sea. I pulled a blanket out of the ottoman compartment and curled into a ball. "I'm sorry."

"Don't apologize. It's easier to blame Hale. He did this to you." I smiled because beneath his feigned anger was real concern. "Do you need anything?"

I was typically the one waiting on Remington, so this felt especially awkward. "Eating and drinking only make it worse. I just have to wait it out."

"How about some medicine?"

I shook my head. "There's not much I can take while pregnant."

He frowned. Powerful men like Remington and Hale had difficulty accepting situations that rendered them powerless. "Well, lie down and rest. Miles will get you some water just in case."

I pulled the blanket up to my chin and shut my eyes. "Thank you."

I must have dozed because the next thing I felt was a gentle hand touching my hair, and Remington wasn't touchy-feely with me.

"How long's she been sleeping?" Hale's voice roused my mind, but when I opened my eyes, I was confused to see my daughter on Remington's lap.

The sun was setting and the sky over the pool was a vibrant pink. "What time is it?"

"Momma," Elara slid off Remington and rushed over to me. She kissed my eye. "Look! Dall, dall, dall!" She held up a marble decorative ball that usually sat in a bowl in Remington's foyer.

"Should she have that?" It could quickly become a weapon for shot put.

Hale took the ball away from her and handed it to Marta. Elara screamed and I winced.

"Come, *Princesa*, I have a treat for you in the kitchen." Just like her mother, Elara toddled dutifully after Marta, wholly seduced by the idea of food.

Speaking of which, I was starving. I pushed myself into a seated position and folded the blanket. Remington closed his laptop and gathered up his work. He was flying out to see Odette tonight and wouldn't be back for a few days. He made no comment about me missing an entire day of work.

"I can't believe I slept that long."

"You probably needed it." Hale sat beside me and ran a gentle hand down my back. "Are you hungry?"

My belly felt hollow and achy. "I'm starved."

"Do you want me to have Marta whip up something light like soup?"

"No. I want a pizza with black olives and meat. Slightly burned."

He drew back. "You sure about that?"

"Yeah. Make it sausage. And see if they can put some of those banana peppers on it. The spicy kind."

"Right." He pulled out his phone and called in an order.

Remington made a quick goodbye before heading to the airport with Alphonse. The house was always different whenever Remington was away. Miles hung around and joined us in the kitchen, as did Raoul, Marta's husband. As much as I was a part of the Davenport family, I was also a part of the service family, and I loved how easily Hale infiltrated that tight-knit group because he knew my work family was important to me.

I ate my pizza while everyone else enjoyed takeout sandwiches and appetizers. We laughed and told stories. Marta picked on Hale in that sweet, adoring way a grandmother would. Hale's real grandmother, who was on his mother's side, was in a home in New Jersey. She didn't remember Hale anymore, so it was nice that he had this connection with Marta, who had been an employee of the Davenports for more than three decades.

When we got home, Elara was passed out. I wasn't tired due to my long afternoon nap, so I showered and found Hale reading over work stuff in bed—something we generally forbade.

"Um, are you working? It's ten o'clock."

"I just wanted to look over this contract—"

"Hale."

He met my stare, reading the warning in my eyes, and shut off his iPad.

"Thank you." I climbed into bed.

It had been weeks since we had sex, and I was beyond ready to put aside my procreating miracle status to return to moonlighting as Hale's naughty little wife. I took my time moisturizing my growing body, taking special care to hit all the areas where stretchmarks were known to scar. Then I gave Hale *the look*.

"Goodnight, baby." He kissed my forehead and shut out the nightstand lamp.

I frowned, unsure what just happened.

Did I smell? Was I not putting out the right pheromones? Maybe I was reading the room wrong. This pregnancy had me all jacked up.

Easing under the covers, I recalculated. Husband—check. Baby asleep—check. Showered and smelling fresh as a daisy—check. What the hell did I forget?

Rolling to my side, I faced him and dragged a seductive finger down his shoulder. "Hi there."

He opened his eyes, smiled, and kissed my nose. "Sweet dreams." Then he shut his eyes again

I frowned. "Hale."

His eyes opened. "Yeah?"

"Why aren't we having sex? You haven't touched me in weeks."

He drew back, a little taken off guard by my bluntness. "That's not true."

"Uh, yeah, it is."

"I touch you all the time."

"Well, you haven't been inside of me in weeks. I'm developing a complex." Seriously, how was he managing it? "Since we started dating, you've always needed frequent sex. What's going on with you?" It was his fault I was horny. Before Hale, I was content to never have sex—ever again. He conditioned me to be this way. "I have needs, too, you know."

Oh, God. Why were my eyes tearing up?

I quickly turned away, but it was too late.

No, no, no. This wasn't a crying moment. This was a strong, confident woman moment. I was doing the big girl thing and expressing my needs.

"Baby, I'm sorry." I flinched when he touched me, but only because any show of gentle concern when I was leaking led to more leaking. "I guess I was just trying to give you space while your body adapted to all this—"

"Gah! Don't try to be all understanding, Hale! And can you not touch me right now?"

I angled away from his comforting caress before I started sobbing uncontrollably.

"I'm confused. Do you or don't you want to be touched?"

"Of course, I want to be touched. Just not...that way." Did he ever hear of just fucking?

He sat up and turned on the lamp. "Rayne, I need you to be a little more clear. What do you want?"

"I told you to have sex with me, not get all comforting and sweet. Can't you see I'm an emotional mess right now?" My voice pitched as more tears spilled. "God, this pregnancy has my hormones all over the place!" I snatched a tissue from the box and blotted my eyes. "And now I'm sad!"

"Baby, take a breath."

"I can't. My nose has been stuffy for weeks!" I blew into the tissue, but nothing came out. I just sounded like a dying elephant. "I'm the most unsexy woman in the world right now. No wonder why you don't want to have sex with me!"

He drew back in horror. "That's not true!"

"Of course it is. I'm always puking or crying or in the bathroom. My body's getting all weird and I have no control over my emotions. This baby has completely hijacked my body and it's taking over my life."

"Rayne, honey, I happen to think you're more beautiful than ever. You're glowing. And I know you haven't felt great with all the morning sickness, but you're growing a human being inside of you. That's amazing. Think about it. You're completely stunning."

I paused and glanced up at him, wiping snot on the back of my hand. "I am?"

He shook his head and smiled. "You're adorable."

I drew in a shaky breath and swallowed. "You really think so?"

"I know so." He tucked my hair behind my ear. "If you're ready to have sex, I'm more than willing. I just didn't want to put pressure on you while you were so exhausted and adjusting to so many changes."

I whimpered and lost my battle against the next sob.

"Hey," he said, clearly unsure why I was still so upset. "Baby, talk to me."

"I can't." I started to cry again. "Because when I say stuff you say stuff, but your stuff's all sweet and nice, and I'm just this leaking puddle of hormones dripping all over the bed. Who wants to have sex with that?"

He chuckled. "Would you rather I was mean to you?"

"No." I was a blubbering basket case. "I just want you to have sex with me. Just sex."

"Just sex?"

"Yes. I need it." While foreplay was great, at the moment, I just wanted to be ravished. Some no-kiss fucking was precisely what the doctor ordered, but I could never ask for that. I wasn't like Hale. He could say whatever filthy thing crossed his mind. Me, on the other hand... Not so much.

"Okay..." He hesitantly leaned closer and laughed when I drew back. "Can I kiss you?"

"Why?" I dragged my hand under my nose, eyeing him suspiciously. "I'm all drippy and gross. Can't you just...do it?"

"Rayne, this isn't how I like to operate."

"Hale," I whined. "You're making this harder than it needs to be."

Frustrated, he threw up his hands. "I'm making it harder? You're asking me to have sex, but you won't let me touch you."

"Do I have to spell it out? Fine! I just want your dick inside of me." The faucet was now set to firehose. "Why can't you just love me?"

"Okay, okay. Take a breath, baby." He held his hand up, but made no contact. Instead, he sort of gave me an air-pet for comfort. "Whatever you want."

"Thank you." A jagged breath ripped past my lips. I had never been this level of unattractive, so I reminded myself that marriage was in sickness and health.

Hale pushed off his pants. "Should I just..."

"Yes! Just do it."

"Yelling isn't helping, Rayne."

He spoke calmly, but you would have thought he raised his voice for how quickly I cowered and pouted.

He mumbled something under his breath and rolled on top of me. "Is this okay?"

I awkwardly stared at him. Since when did Hale ask if something was okay? Typically, he just took what he wanted and made me have orgasms. Where was that guy now?

When he reached between us, stroking himself, it occurred to me that he wasn't even turned on, so I started to cry again. His horrified glare snapped to my face. "What's wrong now? I haven't even done anything."

"You're not aroused," I cried.

"You have to give me a minute, Rayne."

"Forget it. If you wanted me, you'd be hard." I pushed him off and clambered out of bed, rushing into the bathroom so I could sob in peace.

Hale cursed just as I shut the door, shutting him out. "Rayne?" He scratched at the door. "Rayne, I'm coming in."

Sitting on the closed toilet, I wadded up some toilet paper to mop my face.

His figure appeared in the mirror as he stepped behind me. "Enough of this." He turned me to face him, catching my face between his hands and planting his lips on mine.

At first, I tried to pull back, but he wouldn't let me go.

"No." His lips firmed against mine as his hand knotted in my hair. "The fact that you think I could ever not want you pisses me off."

His fist gave a gentle tug, punishing me for doubting him. His other hand drifted beneath my T-shirt and possessively took hold of my boob. I gasped at how sensitive they'd become.

"Take this off." He pulled me to my feet

and stripped me out of my shirt, leaving me bare and shivering. Turning my body to face the mirror, he planted my hands on the marble counter. "Look how fucking sexy you are."

His hands roved over my curves, cupping my breasts and teasing down the center of my stomach until his fingers disappeared between my thighs. His cock swelled and lengthened, sliding heavily against my ass.

He sank a finger inside of me, jerking me back to feel the fullness of his hard cock. "Do you see how much I want you?" His other hand dragged upward to cuff my neck. He held me by the jaw and tilted my head to kiss my neck in that place I loved. "Eyes open, Rayne. I want you to watch me fuck you."

I nodded as he kicked my feet apart and pressed my chest to the cold vanity. "Eyes on me, baby." The swollen head of his cock nudged into my body, and I gasped. He groaned and thrust, burying himself to the hilt.

Relief swept through me. This was exactly what I needed. No emotion. No talking. Just fucking. I shut my eyes.

"Open your eyes and watch, Rayne. I

want you to remember this the next time you think about doubting my attraction."

He drew back, practically leaving my body, then slammed forward. I reflexively moaned and stared at our reflection, my arms braced on the vanity and my breasts swaying with each hard thrust. He gathered my hair in his hand and kissed my shoulder. Then he bit me.

"Ah!"

"That's what you get for accusing me of not wanting you. Does this feel like I don't want you, Rayne?" He surged forward and I lifted up on my toes.

"No."

"Does my dick feel soft now?"

"No." It was so hard I found it difficult to keep my eyes open. "God, Hale, I love you."

"I fucking love you too." He cupped my sex, his hard length gliding in and out of my body as he strummed my clit. "Do you need to come, baby?"

"Yes." It was so nice to finally feel something good where my body was concerned. Maybe that's what this need was all about. I needed a reminder that I was still capable of pleasure. "Please, Hale."

His hips pounded into me as his fingers

worked their magic. I was panting and trembling as he possessively held me in that way they made me feel wanted and cherished and even a little bit sexy if I were being honest. My boobs looked fantastic!

When my orgasm tore through me, I reflexively shut my eyes. Hale slapped my clit and I gasped. "Ah!" My legs shook as another release started. "Hale, it's too much."

"Keep watching."

My nose was stuffed, I was thirsty, and my legs were getting kind of tired, but it felt incredible, so I did my best. "Let me just..." I lowered to my elbows, but the vanity was damn hard. "Wait. Maybe if we..."

His dick slid out just as he was about to finish. "Rayne, what are you trying to do?"

"I don't know. I... I want a bed." Maybe I was getting too old for kinky bathroom sex.

He huffed and scooped me into his arms, carrying me back to the bedroom and dumping me on the mattress. The second I landed, he grabbed me by the ankles and dragged me to the edge.

This was much better—*Hello!*—back inside of me he went.

I had my fix of orgasms, so at this point, I just let him finish. I realized then that Hale had been incredibly thoughtful by not bothering me for sex over the past few weeks because this shit was exhausting.

"Rayne!" My eyes snapped open. "Are you falling asleep?"

"No," I lied. "Sorry. Carry on."

He groaned and pulled out.

"Where are you going? Are you upset?"

"No. Go to sleep."

What man calmly accepted blue balls after delivering two mind-numbing orgasms? Hale, that's who! If I hadn't been so wiped out from the sex I'd probably cry again, because I did not deserve his level of understanding.

"I'm sorry," I mumbled, rolling to my side and shutting my eyes. He kissed my head and tucked me under the covers.

"You're fine. Get some sleep." A minute later the shower turned on and I imagined him finishing himself.

Poor guy.

Priceless Art

T he nausea slowed down around my fourteenth week, and my appetite returned. Good thing, too, because my doctor remarked about my weight. I was pregnant and growing a human, but down two pounds. I never could have predicted that in a hundred years.

She also emphasized how important it was that I ate enough protein and fiber and all of my fruits and vegetables. Oddly, the bakery sold none of those things.

"*Madam* Davenport!" Chef Dubois greeted me affectionately, pulling me into a carbohydrate-scented hug.

It was customary for people to hug their bakers, right?

He glanced down at me as he held my shoulders. "It's been weeks since I've seen you. I was getting worried."

"I know. I'm sorry. I've been busy."

"You look pale. I have just the thing to restore your pluck. Take a look."

I wandered over to the display and admired the variety of confections. The air in this place smelled like heaven on earth. "Ooh, you have éclairs!"

He moved behind the counter, opening a large box. "How many?"

"Two, please. No, four. I might want some tomorrow." I gasped. "And what's that?"

"That's tarte tatin, an upside-down caramelized apple tart with a buttery pastry dough, baked then flipped over so the caramelized topping drizzles all the way through."

Was it possible to get aroused by pastries? "Yeah, I'll take three of them."

When Chef Dubois rang up my order, four boxes were filled with sugary treasures. "I think you missed me, Madam Davenport," he teased.

"Well, I always miss you."

"I can tell." He slid the boxes forward. "You're my best customer."

"Well, I'm not alone. I'm actually ordering for two, now."

He glanced up from the antique register, his dark eyes widening under his bushy, white brows. "*Enceinte?* A baby?"

I smiled and nodded. Chef Dubois rushed out from behind the counter and hugged me.

"Congratulation! *Merveilleuse!*"

We danced about the bakery in an affectionate hug I was certain other customers didn't come close to experiencing with their baker. Yeah, I was definitely his favorite.

Chef Dubois helped me carry my boxes to the car and insisted I not wait so long between visits. He also told me to call him with any craving, and he would make it happen. It was like having secret access to James Bond, but better. On the drive home, I was strongly considering him for the godfather of my unborn child.

By my sixteenth week, I noticed some physical changes in my waistline—partially due to nature and partially due to my close ties to the baker. Jeans were a thing of the past. That was decided long before pregnancy because zippers and buttons were just a lot of drama. Leggings and underwear had always been my go-to, but even they felt tight now.

I bought some high-waisted granny panties and sized up so there was room to grow. My wardrobe was narrowing to loose-fitting sundresses and my coziest cardigans. With my puffy ankles, it wasn't very sexy, but it was comfy. And comfy was my jam.

Thanksgiving was around the corner and we were celebrating at the New England Riverton Estate. Marta was cooking at Remington's house and Odette was staying with him. We would crash at Hale's section of the estate with our mothers. Seraphina was staying at her portion and Barret was staying at his—with a girl.

"Who is she?" I asked Hale as he drove us to the ultrasound appointment.

"All I know is that he met her in New York, and her name is McKinsley."

"Wait, what? *McKinsley?* What the fuck kind of name is that? Is there a little C in there?"

"I didn't ask for her documentation, Rayne."

"Is she a model?"

"I don't know."

"Is she pretty?"

"I'd suspect yes."

"Is she fun? She's probably boring. She better not be one of those girls who eats half a crouton for dinner."

"I've never met her."

"Why don't you get more information when you talk to your brother?"

"Because he's my brother, not a covert op in espionage." He pulled into a parking lot. "We're here."

I wiped the sweat off my palms, not understanding why I was nervous. It was just an ultrasound, and we'd had them before. Maybe I was excited.

Nope, it was nerves. I could tell because as soon as I got out of the car and looked up at the office building, I had the urge to poop. Or puke. Or maybe I was just hungry. "I should have eaten that soft pretzel."

Hale took my arm and led me inside. Once we signed in, he and I waited on a set of blue chairs.

"You okay?" He took my sweaty hand and patted it in that soothing way that usually calmed me down.

"What if I can't see it? There was an episode of Friends when Rachel couldn't see the baby. What if I'm like that?" I was the mommy. I should be able to differentiate my unborn child from other ultrasonic goo. There was no doubt in my mind that Hale would recognize the baby right away, but what if I wasn't so lucky. Should I lie if I can't find it? What if I never found it until it came shooting out of me like a log on a flume? I needed to stop dramatizing the birth in my head. Everything was going to be fine. We were rich. Rich people had nice calm births with doulas and meditational playlists. What the hell was my Spotify password.

My foot kicked incessantly. "What about the sex?"

"Our sex? I guess I could take the rest of the afternoon off—"

I shoved him. "No, Hale. The baby's sex. Do we want to know the gender or not?"

"I would think yes."

"Really?" I wasn't so sure. I liked the idea of being prepared, but wasn't the surprise part of the fun. "No. I think definitely no."

"You don't want to know if we're having a girl or a boy?"

Human error was a real risk in these situations. I was afraid they'd assign the gender wrong, and we'd spend a fortune on stereotypical baby merch only to have to return everything after the refund period expired.

"I think I want to do things the old-fashioned way." I wanted to be an intuitive who had a natural connection to her child. Whenever I thought about the little bean, I felt a yellowy-orange glow.

Oh, I could go for some cheese fries. I dug through my purse for some snacks but just found a bag of dust that used to be a granola bar. I stashed it back in my bag for emergencies.

"Mrs. Davenport?"

"That's me." I stood, doing that dramatic pregnancy rise that mothers do while supporting my back and poking out my stomach. I wasn't showing much, but my back ached and for some reason, walking like an old man helped minimize the pain.

Hale and I followed the nurse to the ultrasound room. "You can have a seat on the table, and Dr. Levy will be right with you."

"Oh, uh, do I need to change?"

"Not for today's appointment."

She left us in the dim room, and Hale helped me onto the exam table. "I'm nervous."

"Why?"

I shrugged. "I don't know. I just want everything to go well."

He kissed my temple and gave my shoulder a supportive squeeze. "It will."

"Do you think we can get cheese fries when we're done here?"

"Sure. But I thought you wanted a soft pretzel."

"Can't we get both?"

He smiled. "Sure."

The door opened, and Dr. Levy entered. She was my favorite doctor so far. She was in her mid-forties and always smelled like fabric softener. She also had a tattoo of a moon on her wrist, which gave the impression that she was down to earth.

"Rayne, how are you feeling?"

"I'm good. A little nervous."

"Oh, there's no need to be nervous. Today's easy. You must be Dad."

"Hale. Nice to meet you." He shook the doctor's hand.

"Make yourself comfortable, Rayne."

I leaned back and blew out a breath. Hale took my hand and sat on the other side of the exam table, facing the machine so he could also see the screen.

"We'll start with a little warm gel on your

stomach. Can you lift your dress and lower your undergarments so nothing's covering the belly?"

I did as she instructed. Dr. Levy tucked some paper towels into the folded waistline of my undies and drizzled gel on my stomach.

Warmed my ass. That shit was ice-cold.

"Doing okay?"

"Mm-hm." I disguised my ongoing nervousness and nodded as she pressed the little scantron joystick thing over the blob of gel, smearing it around my slightly swollen stomach. My full bladder immediately registered the pressure, and I had to pee.

There was a soft swishing sound and then the steady beat of something more defined. "There's your baby's heartbeat."

I breathed in, my eyes focused on the black and grey screen as the sound intensified. Hale's hand squeezed tighter. "Look at that."

Panicked, I watched them both stare and smile. "Where?"

"Right here." The doctor clicked the mouse, and a small cross-hair cursor measured the screen. "Here's the baby's head. And you can see its profile there."

My heart stuttered. I hadn't expected the picture to be so defined and precise. There was a real person inside of me with an actual face. I could see its little nose and what looked like a mouth.

"He or she has a strong, steady heartbeat."

Beaming like a proud momma, my vision blurred, and I wiped my eyes, not wanting to miss a single detail.

"There's its arm, and you can see the fingers are starting to form. Oops." The image shifted.

My smile fell. "What happened?"

"They just moved a little. It's completely normal and healthy for them to be active at this stage. Have you felt any kicks yet?"

I shook my head. "Nothing yet."

"Well, you can expect them soon."

"Can you tell if it's a girl or boy?" Hale asked.

"It's still a little too early to determine. Did you want to know the gender?"

"We're not sure."

"Well, there's time to make up your mind."

It was over all too soon. She cleaned off my stomach and froze the screen on Little Bean's precious head. Or was that his butt? No, it was definitely his head. Or hers.

When we left, she gave us several printed pictures from the ultrasound and told us we could review the rest on the patient portal when we got home. I couldn't wait that long, so I signed into the portal on my phone as soon as we were in the car. I could stare at those pictures forever.

I breathed a sigh of relief. My baby was developing properly, and everything was great. I was a happy camper.

Hale and I stopped at a little pizzeria on the way home to get cheddar cheese fries, but as we were leaving with our order, he veered into a small boutique in the shopping strip.

"Hale, my fries. They'll get cold."

"I'll only be a minute. I need to grab something." He walked over to the display of picture frames and selected a ten-by-ten-inch square silver frame with white velvet matting. As he took his time paying, I snuck a few fries.

"Ready?"

"Mm-hm," I said around a mouthful of cheese and potato.

When we got home, he went to the dining room with his bag from the boutique. He stared at the vacant place his fifty-thousand-dollar work of ruined art used to hang and lifted the ten-by-ten frame.

My lips parted when I saw what he'd done. There, in the center of that little silver frame, was our baby.

"Priceless," he said, hanging it on the small hook in the wall.

I smiled and agreed, "Priceless."

Gold diggers, gowns, and saggy balls, oh my!

"I have to pee."

"We're about ten miles from our exit," the driver commented not fully understanding the severity of the situation.

"Um..." I looked at Hale and whispered, "I have to pee."

He frowned. "Can't you hold it?"

Did no one understand how these things worked? "There's a human on my bladder, and I haven't peed since we were on the jet. No, I can't hold it."

He glanced at the barren highway rushing by. "Rayne, there's nothing for at least six miles."

"I see trees and grass."

He looked appalled. "You want us to pull over?"

"That'd be great."

Hale cleared his throat. "Pull over up ahead, please."

"Sir, I'd much rather wait until we're on a safer road."

He looked at me, and I shook my head. I wasn't going to make it.

"I'm afraid it's an emergency."

As the driver eased onto the shoulder, I dug through my purse for some tissues. At least New England was woodsy.

Elara roused from her nap as soon as the car stopped. Hale handed her Meep Meep, but she tossed the sheep on the floor to her left and moaned to get out of her car seat.

"Not yet," Hale said. "I have to help Mommy."

This wasn't a group activity, so I scooted past him and darted for the trees. "I've got it from here."

"I'll block you."

I had to pee so bad I didn't care who saw, but Hale was the proper type. As soon as I was away from the car and out of the driver's view, I hiked up my dress and squatted.

"Whoa." Hale rushed to stand before me, opening his suit jacket so the driver didn't get a show.

"It's freaking freezing here!" My teeth chattered.

"Watch my shoes."

"Then back up. I can't stop once I've started." My knees ached from sitting for too long and I wabbled. "Shit."

Hale quickly grabbed my elbow for balance but it was too late. "Sorry!"

"Momma?"

"I'm going potty, Peanut! I'll be right there."

"I wanna potty!"

Hale looked down at his leather Berluti shoes and grimaced.

I quickly wiped and righted my clothes. "We should let her go."

"She can wait to use the bathroom at the house."

"Hale, the books say we shouldn't ignore her requests for a toilet."

"A tree is not a toilet, Rayne. This will just confuse her."

"If she was a boy you'd let her pee."

He ushered me back to the car, too smart

to get bated into a debate about gender biases. Once we were back on the road the driver avoided all eye contact. I stuffed my trash into a plastic bag and handed Hale a tissue for his shoe. He didn't complain about the marks on the leather, but I knew he wasn't happy.

"Guess you're not a golden shower sort of guy," I joked.

He scowled.

"Well, I feel better." That was really all that mattered.

When Hale's family showed up for a holiday, they really moved in. It was like watching an episode of *The Crown*.

Servants I didn't know the names of bustled about the estate, unloading ice-packed delicacies and filling liquor cabinets with favored labels. Remington arranged for a butler, a housekeeper, and a chauffeur in addition to his usual staff.

Hale and I preferred a more intimate setting, so we gave Andrew the week off. If we needed extra help, we could rely on our moms. They didn't get to see Elara as often as Remington, so they usually were a big help.

It was always interesting watching Hale's mom, Naomi, interact with Remington. She called him Remy, and the man turned into a teenager around her. It was adorable. I was curious to see how Odette took their subtle flirting.

Being pregnant and past the morning sickness stage, I had many requests for the Thanksgiving menu. Remington protested my requests, informing me that Hugo, the Belgian chef he'd hired, was the best of the best and not to be micromanaged.

"Dad, leave her be," Hale argued.

"It's handled Hale. Don't be difficult, Meyers."

"I'm not being difficult. I'm pregnant."

"Honestly, Remy, show a little compassion. She's giving us a grandchild," Naomi chimed in, earning some extra mother-in-law points. "If Rayne wants something different, she should have it."

I looked at Marta, who was standing by the door, wringing her hands. "Mr. Davenport, denying a pregnant woman a craving is bad luck. You will get a stye."

"Christ," Remington muttered. "Fine. God forbid we adhere to tradition and turn our nose at superstition."

I smiled victoriously. "Thank you, Remy."

He growled. Only Naomi was allowed to call him that.

My second trimester unleashed a whole new level of cravings. I wanted my food salty, sweet, and hot enough to cause a raging inferno in my mouth. Temperature had never been so important to me before, but now I needed my food piping hot and spicier than a habanero.

Marta's Mediterranean roots were precisely what the doctor ordered. The woman knew how to throw down some fiery food when it came to cooking, and I hovered around her like a mesmerized vulture waiting for any chance to taste what she concocted.

While the others anticipated traditional dishes like turkey and potatoes, I was seduced by Marta's descriptions of *callos a la madrileña, pimientos de padrón,* and *crema catalana,* a sweet custard dessert she made with citrus, cinnamon, and chili powder.

"Just make me a list of ingredients," I told her. "I'll see that everything gets here."

The estate was walkable, but the weather was a little too chilly for me, so I used one of Remington's many cars to navigate the grounds. When I returned to our house, Hale was out front chopping wood.

"Well, this is a new look." The man was a steaming, flannel-clad stick of eye candy. "How did you learn to handle an ax like that?"

"Frank, the groundskeeper, taught me when I was ten."

"My, oh my." I couldn't take my eyes off of him in those designer jeans. I didn't even know Hale owned denim. "Momma likey."

He chuckled. "If wood impresses you, I can show you some other varieties."

I glanced at the house, knowing full well my mother was inside. There were several little outbuildings around the historic property—lots of hiding spots. Feeling like a teenager about to slip a hand under a blanket during movie time, I glanced at the closest stone shed and twirled my hair around my finger. "What's in there?"

"That's the old smokehouse." Most outbuildings had shutters and glass windows so old they were marbleized by time, but this one didn't have windows. Hale set down the ax and brushed off his hands. "Come on. I'll show you."

I followed him into the old shed, and he closed the door. "Eh! Dark."

"Hold on." He lit a candle, and shadows

danced across the wood-planked walls. A wooden counter crossed the back wall. The entire space was no larger than ten feet in any direction. "Here." He removed his flannel and draped it on the counter, then lifted me to sit on the edge.

Pulling him into the space between my knees, I giggled. My hands crawled over his T-shirt. "This Paul Bunyan look suits you." Hale looked great in a suit, but it was pure novelty whenever he wore casual clothes. "You're really scratching an itch with my lumberjack fantasies."

"You've been fantasizing about lumberjacks?"

"Since my first Brawny commercial." I reached for his belt buckle.

"Is that so?" He tugged my knees closer and caught the back of my neck. "Give me that mouth."

His tongue stole past my lips as my cool fingers curled around his length. He thrust into my grip, his other hand working its way under my skirt. I moaned as he shoved my panties aside.

He tugged at my jacket, pulling it down my arms. "Lie back." He guided me down on the wooden bench, pushing my dress up then he stilled. "Holy shit."

I glanced down awkwardly. "What's wrong?"

He stared down at my stomach, unblinking. "You look so...different."

I bit my lip. It had been some time since he saw me like this, lying on my back, exposed. My stomach had definitely popped. "Sorry."

"God, don't apologize." He framed my belly and bent to kiss it. "Look at you."

"It so noticeable now, isn't it?"

"I wasn't expecting to find your stomach so...sexy."

"Really?" I didn't feel sexy, but I also didn't feel fat. If anything, I felt sort of magical, growing life and all.

"Fuck yeah. That's my kid in there."

"Shh. No cursing in front of the bean," I teased and we both laughed.

He shook his head in awe, then pushed my dress up higher to see my breasts, which had gotten substantially fuller. "Wow. I didn't expect you to look so different so fast."

"Good different?"

"Baby, you're always stunning." He caressed my breast, pulling down the lace of my bra to gently pinch the tip of my nipple.

A sharp gasp slipped past my lips.

"Did I hurt you?"

"No, I'm just really sensitive there."

"Really?" He bent to replace his fingers with his mouth and wet heat engulfed my nipple.

My body arched as he sucked, and his fingers returned to between my legs. Everything was feeling incredible. That familiar heaviness tightened in my core as my body pulsed under his touch. Building and stretching, like the waxing and waning of moon until I felt incredibly full and ready to burst. Then something mortifying happened.

"What the fuck?" Chin to my chest, I bolted into an upright position and looked down in horror. "What the fucking fuck is that?" I was leaking.

Hale stared at my body with wide eyes. "Is that supposed to happen?"

"I don't know!"

I covered my boobs and searched for a rag as Hale Googled from his phone.

The shed was severely understocked for leaky tits, so I used my dress to wipe up the trickle of liquid dripping from my nipples—

all sexy feelings gone. "I thought milk didn't come in until after the baby was born!"

"It's not milk. This says it's something called colostrum." He read from his phone as I tried to hide from any light. "It says oxytocin, the same hormone that triggers the letdown reflex during breastfeeding, can occur from orgasm." He read directly from the article, "Breast milk may leak or spray during sex."

"I'm sorry, did you say *spray*?"

He pocketed his phone. "That's what it says." He bent to my chest, and I grabbed him by the hair, jerking him back.

"Hale! What the hell are you doing?"

"What? You think I'm not going not to touch your boobs for the next four months because of a little milk?"

I stared, wide-eyed, as he pinned my hands at my hips and licked the liquid from my nipple.

He shrugged. "It's sweet."

"I cannot believe you just did that."

"Rayne, there's no part of you that could disgust me. Who cares? We drink breast milk from cows."

"Well, you're not drinking mine." I

pushed my dress back in place. "The baby needs it." I protectively covered my chest.

"You're being a prude. It's not like I was going to nurse from you. I tasted it. So what? Aren't you a little curious what it tastes like?"

"Not even a little bit."

"Fine." He chuckled in the same way he did the first time he tried to go down on me. Hale was always much more daring than me when it came to bed sport. "I'll just have to fill up on the rest of you." He yanked open my legs and went to town.

"Ah!" I dropped back and let it happen.

Three minutes later, I was howling and coming again, boobs dribbling like leaky old faucets. "This is terrible!"

"You're too in your head. Don't let it bother you."

This, coming from a guy who couldn't stand a smudge of anything on his body.

It didn't get any better when he was inside of me. They just kept leaking. I was mortified, but Hale—the pervert—loved it. The harder I came, the more they leaked. I should have known a man who loved to make me squirt would get a kick out of this. Give him enough time, and he'd have me operating like a full-fledged waterpark.

I left the smokehouse damp, shivering, and needing a shower. Hale arrogantly whistled his way back to the woodpile and swung the ax with more pluck and vigor then he had when I found him.

Slinking into the house like a mangey coyote, I tried to sneak upstairs unnoticed.

"Momma!" Elara called, racing over to show me her scribbled drawing of what looked like it might be a pumpkin. It was round and orange.

"Nice work, Peanut."

"You look flushed, Rayne," my mother said as she crocheted a blanket she'd been working on for the new baby. "I remember when I was pregnant with you. Your father and I couldn't keep our hands off each other."

"*Mom!* Ew!"

"What? That shed might not have windows, but I have ears."

My humiliation was complete. "I'm going to shower and erase my memories from the last hour." I skulked up the stairs.

The following day, everyone was settled in. Remington was sneaking work, which meant he was calling me every five minutes, which frustrated Hale to no end. I received more than enough impatient looks but he said nothing. My mother made things worse by always asking who was calling me. I ignored her, because everyone else knew it was Remington every time.

Naomi commented repeatedly about how needy Remy could be, which also didn't help matters. But to be fair, they didn't realize this was a hot-button issue between me and Hale.

As long as I played down the situation and didn't appear stressed by my bossy father-in-law's neediness, the situation was managed. But Hale still got frustrated.

"Just go over there," Hale eventually said. "But be back by five. We have that dinner tonight, and we're leaving at six."

Shock of shock, Hale was very persnickety about being on time. "It's fine. I can just—" My phone buzzed again.

"Just go, Rayne."

I hesitated, not wanting to make this a thing, but going over there would put an end to the incessant calls sooner so we could get on with our peaceful holiday. "Are you sure?"

When my phone buzzed yet again, he narrowed his eyes. "Yes."

With Miles out of the office visiting his own family and most of the staff gone at headquarters, there was only me, so it made sense that Remington would hit me up more than usual. As soon as I arrived at Remington's, Odette greeted me with a smile and a cocktail in her bejeweled hand.

"Rayne, I wasn't expecting you. I was just making a salad for lunch. Do you want to eat with us?"

"Sure." Odette was always sweet and stayed quietly in the background. When Remington paid attention to her, their chemistry was adorable.

As soon as Remington saw me, he looked befuddled. He was clearly surprised by my presence since he hadn't instructed me to come to him. Yet, there I was, ready to serve his needs for the sake of peace. He also overlooked that I was giving up a day with my family to help him—on a day that I had *clearly* scheduled for personal time.

"Meyers, we need to go through the proposal from Landry and compare it with the rundown we received from PCK. I want you to dig up everything you can find on both CEOs. *Everything.* Figure out their wives' names, who their mistresses are, how they voted in the last election, what allergies their children have, where they golf, and anything else of use. Leave no stone unturned."

This was the drill whenever Remington prepared a buyout. Most times, his victims didn't even foresee selling their companies. But Remington had a way of zeroing in on people's pressure points until they viewed him as an ally and confidant. In the end, he always looked like a savior and got exactly what he wanted.

"Sure."

I was elbow-deep in notes when Odette brought my salad to the dim study.

"You know," she said, setting my plate beside the open laptop. "It might not be my place to say this, but you could tell him no."

I laughed. "Have you tried that?"

"I do every day. At least twice. He's a demanding man, but it's good for him to feel challenged. The more he gets his way, the more demanding he becomes. It's healthy for him to face denial from time to time."

"Well, he only has me for another hour because I have my own demanding man waiting at home."

She patted my shoulder and left me to my work.

One of the men I researched was expected

to attend tonight's dinner party, so I supposed this was a time-sensitive issue. When I finally had all the information organized, I delivered it to the dining room where Remington had set up shop.

"Here. This is everything I could find."

He glanced up from his work and took the print out I prepared. His gaze moved over the information quickly. "What about the PCK fellow?"

"He'll have to wait. I need to get back to the house to get ready."

"I asked for reports on both."

"That's funny, Remington because I asked for a personal day." Our eyes met, and I dared him to say another word, especially when he had not even thanked me for giving him a few hours on my day off.

"Success doesn't take a holiday, Meyers."

"Well, I do. Hale's waiting for me."

He sighed and set the papers aside, realizing he wasn't going to win this one. "I hired a car for tonight."

I paused, hating the position I frequently found myself in whenever Remington tried to micromanage the minor details of our life. Sometimes, it was like navigating a minefield between the two of them.

Initially, I found Remington's gestures thoughtful. But over the years, I learned how much these little *helpful* moves irritated Hale. He saw his father's thoughtfulness as heavy-handedness. And Remington saw his son's reluctance to accept help as stubbornness. As far as I was concerned, they were both stubborn jackasses.

When I returned to the house, I fixed my hair. Hale was already dressed in his tux, and I was dreading my dress. Elegance was always a challenge for me, but being pregnant made it more so.

The pre-Thanksgiving dinner party was a tradition that the Davenports attended every year. No one really got excited about them, but skipping the affair was out of the question.

"Oh, I remember those old, dusty dinner parties," Naomi commented when she popped into our room to ask where Elara's extra bibs were. "The food's usually good."

I had somehow escaped this social obligation during my prior Thanksgivings with the Davenports, but I was running out of excuses and Hale was insistent that I attend with him this year.

"I look ridiculous in this dress." The Di

Lorenzo gown fell to the floor in soft chiffon ripples as I moved to the mirror. The low-cut neckline was black velvet and hung off one shoulder. I chewed my lip, considering what other options I had. "I should change."

"What? No." Naomi crossed the room and turned me slowly. "You look stunning."

I scrunched my nose. The skirt of the dress was intentionally sheer. The taupe layers were dotted with velvet, providing slight camouflage, but my bodysuit underneath was completely visible to anyone looking hard enough.

"I look like an eggplant." My boobs were bursting past the neckline, my belly was protruding, and I never knew what to do with my hair.

"You look lovely. Here, let me try something." Naomi set down the bibs and ushered me to the vanity chair. "You forget I owned a salon for half my life."

It wasn't that I forgot. It was that I never wanted to impose.

"And for the record, your *decolletage* looks sexy. It'll be a show stopper, for sure."

"Shows can stop for disasters, too, you know."

"Stop that." She unwound my hair and

heated a curling iron to add waves. Ten minutes later, she had me looking ready for a photoshoot. "You need something for your neck. Let me see your phone."

I handed it to her, unsure how my phone might help us.

She pressed a button and brought it to her ear. "Remy, do you still have your mother's jewels here?"

I frowned and waved for her to forget it, but she turned away.

"Yes, in the old chest. It's for Rayne. The black diamonds, I think. Perfect. Thank you." She ended the call. "He's having Alphonse run them over."

"Naomi, I can't wear Remington's mother's jewels."

"Of course you can. She left them to the kids. They're family heirlooms, and you're family."

Her presumptuousness was at complete odds with my typical fade into the background and impose on no one philosophy, but things were already in motion. "Okay, but just for tonight."

Getting down the steps in a floor-length gown with a protruding stomach that made it impossible to see my feet slowed me down.

Hale stood at the foot of the stairs, smiling appreciatively at me as he held out his hand. "You look incredible."

"So do you." The tuxedo was created for men like Hale.

Once I made it to the foyer, he lifted a coiled lock of hair from my shoulder. "Your hair's different."

"Do you like it? Your mom did it."

"You're gorgeous."

The door opened, and Alphonse stepped in, holding a slender jewelry box. "I have something for Rayne."

Hale looked at the box and frowned. Naomi intercepted, collecting the necklace before I could explain. "Perfect. Thank you, Alphonse."

"You're welcome. Mr. Davenport and Ms. Crawford are waiting in the limo out front."

"You can go ahead without us," Hale said. "Rayne and I will drive separately."

I knew that would happen, but I still smiled apologetically at Alphonse. "Thank you for bringing the necklace."

Hale came to see what his mother had. "Are those Grandmother's jewels?"

"Yes. Do you remember them?"

"Vaguely. Let me do this, Mom." He

swept my hair to one side, and I lifted it off my shoulders.

The cool weight of the black diamonds closed around my neck, draping heavily just over my collarbones. He latched the clasp, kissed my shoulder, and righted my hair. When he turned me to face him again, he looked down at my chest and smiled. "Perfect."

I don't think he realized that the dress was partially see-through, which was probably good since Hale could get a bit territorial around his peers. He wrapped me in a cashmere shawl and we were on our way.

The tradition of the formal pre-Thanksgiving dinner party dated back several decades. It was an opulent affair, with every detail meticulously planned to impress the guests, who ranged from various powerful positions.

When we arrived, a helicopter was landing in the back yard. "Oh, this is just like the cookouts we used to have in Oregon," I joked. "I hope someone brought potato salad."

Hale chuckled and rubbed his thumb along my fingers, something he did to calm me down when he sensed I was nervous. I usually wasn't at anything fancier than a Mc-Donald's drive-thru.

We were greeted by white-gloved servants who took our coats and led us to the main ballroom for cocktails. Hale used to order champagne as soon as we arrived at formal affairs, but that was currently off the menu for me, so he requested the waiter find sparkling water.

Women, ranging in age from twenty to eighty, were dressed in pristine floor-length gowns, and men wore tuxedos. A small orchestra played soft, tasteful classics in the corner of the main ballroom.

I relaxed the moment I spotted Remington and Odette. But as I took a step in their direction, Hale held me back.

"There's Phina."

I followed his gaze and spotted his sister holding the rapt attention of several well-dressed men. How that woman remained single was beyond me. Of course, Hale would prefer to mingle with his sister over his father, so we walked that way.

When we approached the cluster of men, they all chuckled at something Seraphina had said. She clutched a flute of champagne and cocked her head, appearing confused by their laughter.

"I wasn't saying it for a laugh. The soy crops are destroying the world's ecosystems."

Poor Phina. She had a philanthropic heart that went beyond the ordinary charitable acts wealthy people tended to do for show and tax breaks. The girl actually cared about something other than herself, and some people had a hard time comprehending that, including her brother.

Hale mirrored their amusement. "Pardon my sister, gentlemen. She brings a soapbox with her everywhere she goes."

I drew back at precisely the same time Phina frowned at Hale. She was very passionate about environmental issues and animal rights, and maybe this wasn't the best place to talk about the agricultural deforestation issue, but Hale shouldn't make fun of her.

"I would love to hear more about your thoughts," a man twice Phina's age remarked. "Care to find a quiet place to talk?"

I tried not to react to the impression that the old Dust Bowl relic wanted to do more than talk with Hale's little sister. I quickly tried to think of ways to bail Phina out, but before I thought up a rescue call, she laced her arm with the old geezer's and smiled sweetly into his cloudy eyes.

"Of course, Carlisle."

What the?

I glanced up at Hale, silently horrified, but he appeared completely unaffected by the bicentennial age gap.

The group of men dispersed and I clutched his arm. "Aren't you the least bit concerned that the captain of the Love Boat just kidnapped your sister?"

"Seraphina's a grown woman who can take care of herself."

"But..." I looked up at him in confusion. "She wasn't flirting with that old dude, right?"

"Rayne, my sister's dating life is not something I care to examine closely."

I scrunched my nose. Her *dating* life? Gross. That man was too old to be her dentist let alone her lover. I inwardly gagged as I thought about saggy balls and days of the week pill packs.

Phina was still in her twenties and beautiful. She could have her pick of any single guy in any room. Probably even some of the married ones. This had to be about charity.

Lights flashed across the large bay window as another helicopter landed in the lawn. Several women—mostly the younger ones—crossed the room and posed casually by the French doors. A moment later, Barrett walked in and I understood why they were acting like a bunch of horny jackals.

Hale escorted me across the room to the huddle of females surrounding his brother. A very tall, very beautiful woman with fiery red hair clung to his arm.

"Hale. Rayne," he politely disentangled himself from the hoard and brought his date forward. After shaking his brother's hand, he turned to kiss me on the cheek. "Holy shit, look at you!" His gaze dropped to my stomach. "You're so...*huge*."

"Watch it," Hale warned under his breath.

I rolled my eyes. "Thanks. Huge is exactly what a girl wants to hear when a man's looking at her body."

"Relax," he teased. "You're only huge in the stomach."

"Not making it better." I turned to his date. "You must be McKinsley. Hi. I'm Rayne, Hale's wife."

She glanced down at my stomach, and her

gaze skated away. "Barrett, what is that smell?"

O—kay. I put my hand away.

Berrett hardly acknowledged her question. "So, how are you feeling? Do you still have morning sickness?"

"Nothing like I did in the beginning." I watched his date place an order with the butler for something other than champagne. "Where'd you find this one, Barrett?"

"We met Saturday."

That seemed about right. Sex with a stranger...bring her to meet the entire family for Thanksgiving. Nothing weird there. "Right."

It occurred to me that Phina and Barrett's mothers weren't spending the holiday with us. "Where does your mom spend Thanksgiving, Barret?"

"I think she's in Rome at the moment."

I tried to lip read what his date was explaining to the wait staff. "McKinsley seems a little high maintenance." The girl hadn't stopped talking since they arrived. In all the time I'd been around the Davenports I'd never ordered people around the way she was. "Does she ever stop talking?"

"There are ways to quiet her down. She has a very talented mouth."

"Gross." I glanced up at Hale. "My feet are starting to hurt. When do we get to sit?"

"Let's say hello to the host. Then we can find our seats in the dining room."

The meal was an extravagant multi-course feast prepared by a team of talented chefs. The white-gloved staff delivered the luxurious dishes in an endless rotation that included lobster bisque, foie gras, and truffle risotto with wild salmon over a bed of tiny mushrooms.

Everything was presented with such flair. If the intention was to impress, they succeeded, but the company was too stuffy and pretentious to truly make the night enjoyable. However, the chocolate soufflés and crème brûlée at the end made it all worthwhile.

Each course had been expertly paired with a selected fine wine, which I couldn't taste. A local sommelier visited each table to describe the vintage. When I declined a taste, people looked at me questioningly. Did the rich not follow the no drinking while pregnant rules or did they just not realize my situation?

"Rayne's pregnant," Hale eventually announced.

The table responded with a tepid round of golf applause. It felt strangely like an old Victorian novel where pregnancy wasn't en vogue. But I had never been in style with these people anyway.

After dinner, rumors of my condition got out and men flocked to Hale to praise his virility. Hale possessively kept a hand on my back at all times. I felt a little like a cupcake in one of Chef Dubois' display cases as the men ogled my baby bump. Thankfully, no one tried to touch me.

Diamonds and crystal flutes sparkled under the chandeliers as the women in designer dresses moved about the ballroom, mingling with other females. It all seemed very segregated, with the men taking their after-dinner drinks in the atrium while the wives and girlfriends waited around, serving as much purpose as the floral centerpieces.

I was getting bored. "Why aren't people dancing?"

"It's not that sort of event," Hale explained as he sipped his brandy.

"Why not?"

Hale traced a finger down my spine. "Are you not enjoying yourself?"

I shivered under his touch. "It's a little

boring. No one's doing anything." Maybe this was what sobriety felt like. I'd never attended a function like this without a minimal buzz. It was like watching paint dry.

He glanced at the group of men playing instruments in the corner. The atmosphere screamed elegance and sophistication, but the vibe was more along the lines of a somber royal funeral. Despite the lavish welcome, exquisite decor, crystal stemware, polished silver, and meticulous attention to detail, these people didn't seem to like each other very much.

The women watched each other with judgmental stares, and the men competitively tried to outdo each other by casually mentioning yacht size and acreage. The old geezers circled young females like dirty vultures, and the mothers encouraged their barely legal daughters to fawn over men old enough to be their grandfathers.

It was like an auction for gold diggers and daddies. Speaking of which, my gaze scanned the crowd for Remington. I spotted Odette talking to a woman in her seventies, but no Remington.

"Where's your father?"

Hale briefly glanced about the ballroom. "I haven't seen him since dinner."

I searched the crowd for him, and spotted McKinsley. She seemed to be blending in fine with the socialites.

I decided it was an excellent time to use the restroom. "If a server comes around, can you order me a water? I'll be right back."

Hale stood and took my arm. "Do you want me to go with you?"

"No, I'll be fine."

I wandered toward the quieter wing of the house, certain there must be at least fifteen bathrooms in this place. The further I drifted from the ballroom, the more peaceful the house became. When I found an empty library with vaulted ceilings and ancient books lining the walls, I went inside.

A slender door in the corner led to a small powder room. I took my time freshening up, not expecting a line for the bathroom this far off the beaten path.

When I exited the bathroom, I stilled, startled that I wasn't alone. "Hi."

"Hello." The man had jet-black hair and eyes dark as coal. "I'm afraid I don't know you."

"I'm Rayne, Hale Davenport's wife."

"Ah. My apologies. The New York wedding."

"Yes. Were you there?" I winced. Was that a rude question? "I'm sorry, I don't know your name and...it was a big guestlist. Mostly Hale's friends. And now I'm rambling."

"I'm Xander. And I'm sorry to say I missed the wedding. Scheduling conflict."

"Xander. That's an interesting name."

"It's short for Alexander. Alexander Landry."

My breath hitched as I recognized his name. This was Remington's target.

His gaze dropped to my bodice. "I see Hale's been busy since the wedding."

My neck warmed, my blush crawling to my chest as he stared. "Speaking of Hale, I should probably get back to my husband."

"There's no rush. These dinner parties can be so tedious. Just once, I'd love to see a cat fight or something slightly amusing happen."

"Oh, I don't think anyone here would do that."

"You think those women out there are without venom? They all hate each other." He chuckled then rubbed his jaw. "But not you, right? You look... There's something different about you. Something... wholesome."

Being analyzed by a complete stranger was extremely off-putting—especially in a nearly see-through dress. Talk about direct. Remington would have his work cut out for him with this guy.

"Well, I don't know if I'd call myself wholesome, but I'm not vicious or venomous. I'm just Rayne."

"Just Rayne." He grinned. "What a curious name."

Okay, we talked for too long and now I was getting a weird vibe. It was time to wrap this up. "We're actually scheduled to meet next week."

He cocked his head. "Are we?"

"On the fifth. I work for Remington."

His brows lifted. "Maybe you should work for me. This is the first I'm hearing of this. I should fire the half-whit in charge of my schedule and hire you. Whatever Davenport's paying you, I'll double it."

I laughed nervously and edged toward the door. "Well, I'm not sure how my boss would like that." Another nervous smile. "He's also my father-in-law," I reminded, in case he was seriously suggesting I do something disloyal toward my Davenports. "Well, it was nice meeting you, Xander."

"Are you really in such a rush to get back to him? As Remington's right hand, shouldn't you take the opportunity to work the client?"

I did a double-take. Talk about being forward. "Excuse me?"

"He's had you research me, right? Find out where my stockholdings are, where I like to eat, who I like to fuck?"

My smile fell.

"Relax. It's an old game he's been playing at for years. You seem nice, so I'll save you some time. He's not getting my company."

This was getting uncomfortable. "I don't have the details of his plans."

"Let's not pollute this peaceful introduction with lies, Rayne." He rubbed his jaw and studied me. "You struck me as someone... honest. Am I wrong?"

The alternative was to call myself a liar. "Being honest doesn't mean I know my boss's intentions. He's a very complicated man with a very busy schedule."

"So am I." He grinned, flashing a line of pearly white teeth. "It's cute how you defend him. I'd bet there isn't another person at this party—including his children—who would think to protect a man like Remington Davenport. He must pay you damn well for that sort of loyalty."

"I'm just a loyal person. It has nothing to do with my paycheck."

A dimple formed in the dark stubble beside his mouth. "I'm beginning to see why Hale married you." His gaze moved over me. "I bet every man out there knows who you are."

"That's two bets in under a minute."

"What can I say? I can't resist a gamble. How am I doing so far?"

"Well, up until five minutes ago, you had no idea who I was. So I guess you're not always right." But he was doing better than I wanted to admit.

"Touché. But I know who you are now, and you're not easily forgotten."

I was too tired to unravel his innuendos. "If people know who I am, it's because I'm the only pregnant woman here."

"Exactly."

Okay, this was getting weird. Where was Hale when I needed him? "I have to get back. My husband's waiting for me."

"I bet he is." He cupped a hand at the side

of his mouth and whispered, "In case you lost count, that's three."

I laughed nervously. "It was, uh, nice meeting you."

"The pleasure was mine. Rayne."

As soon as I opened the door, I abruptly stopped. "Remington?"

He untangled himself from the arms of some young brunette. "Meyers? What are you doing down here? The party's that way."

I scoffed. Was he going to play this off like he wasn't just making out with some chick that had to be his daughter's age? And to think I was just defending him.

"What am I doing?" I looked at the girl, her lipstick smeared off her lips and her dress slightly disheveled. He was unbelievable. Odette was in the ballroom waiting for him. "I'm leaving."

I wanted to find Hale and go home. Leaving him and that slice of veal he was pawing in the hall, I went to find my husband.

Hale was getting his ear chewed off by Barrett's date. He appeared immediately relieved to see me. "Hey," I interrupted. "I'm ready to go home."

He frowned, surprised by my bluntness. "It's still early—"

"No, Hale. I'm ready now."

He excused himself from McKinsey and pulled me aside. "I arranged a surprise for you."

I had enough surprises for one night. Very aware of Odette's location in the ballroom, I averted my stare, afraid of what might happen if I looked her in the eye. "I want to leave."

Just then, the band changed from a traditional classical ballad to a more modern tune. Hale laced his fingers with mine and pulled me toward the center of the ballroom. "May I have this dance?"

My eyes widened. "What's happening?"

"You said you wanted to dance."

"No, I said no one was dancing. And they still aren't." The last thing I wanted was to become more of a spectacle.

He pulled me to his chest and planted a hand on my lower back. "Do you recognize the song?"

The familiar notes of Cyndi Lauper's *Time After Time* registered. It was the song we danced to at our wedding. Guests formed a circle around us and watched as Hale twirled me in a slow circle.

Remington appeared with a scowl, disrupting Hale's romantic moment. "Meyers, I need a word."

"Not now, Dad."

"Yes, now. It's important."

I glared at him, because even I had reached the end of my patience with him. "Not now, Remington."

Hale twirled us away from his father. "You're the prettiest woman in the room tonight, Rayne."

I was fuming. "That's great, Hale, but I just saw your dad making out with some chick in the hall."

"I beg your pardon?"

"He had his tongue down some woman's throat." I gagged. "What the hell is he thinking? Odette's right there." Why were bathroom visits always so complicated at these fancy functions? "Oh, and I met that Landry guy. He's creepy."

Hale's silver eyes darkened. "Why do you say that?"

"I don't know. Maybe because he followed me into the library and made me super uncomfortable."

His focus was no longer on me as he scanned the crowd. "What did he say to you?"

"It wasn't what he said. It was how he said it. Like being pregnant was some sort of testament to your virility."

"I'll kill him."

I grabbed him by the lapels. "Hey, can we not do the whole Neanderthal thing tonight? You've marked your territory and I could do without the whole let's pee a circle around Rayne spectacle." I pointed to my belly. "Everyone knows I'm yours."

"Exactly. So why would he say something to make you uncomfortable."

"Probably because he sensed your father closing in to buy out his company, and he knows I work for Remington. I think he was just trying to disarm the opposition."

"There he is."

"Hale—"

I was suddenly standing alone like a pregnant fool in the center of the ballroom. A plastic smile formed on my face as Hale made a B-line to Xander. Women whispered behind manicured nails.

Remington met my stare then his gaze moved to Hale and Xander Landry.

I was done.

Shoving through the crowd, I disappeared into the foyer and requested my shawl from the coat check. I gave the valet Alphonse's name and they called for the car.

The limo appeared a moment later, and Alphonse looked at me, confused and concerned. "Rayne?"

"Can you take me back to the estate?"

"Where is Mr. Davenport?"

"He's getting a ride home with the other Mr. Davenport." They could call an Uber for all I cared.

Alphonse opened the door and helped me into the vehicle. "Are you okay?"

I sighed. He was the only man to ask me that all night. "I am now. Thank you."

"I'll get you home." He shut the door and I sank into the seat, relieved to be alone.

The Turkey Shoot

"It's barbaric!" Seraphina cried, lifting her glass for yet another mimosa.

The men had disappeared early that morning for what was an age-old tradition in the Davenport family. They were off to hunt dinner.

No, not really. We had crab legs on ice, caviar, and a twenty-four-pound bird already marinating. This was just a dumb thing the boys did so they could dress like a Ralph Lauren spread and shoot guns.

"I doubt they'll kill anything. Hale doesn't know how to use a rifle."

Marta looked up from the bowl of custard she was whipping. Brunch had moved from the dining room to the kitchen because

I wanted to be where the food was. The housekeeper mumbled something in Spanish, and Seraphina laughed.

"Hasta la English, please." I scowled, despising when they spoke in Spanish. Sometimes, I suspected they specifically did that, so I wouldn't understand.

"Mr. Davenport is a very skilled hunter, *Niña*."

"He is?" This was news to me.

"Did you honestly think there was something Hale was not good at?" Phina asked.

"But Hale's not a killer. He doesn't hunt. He hates anything messy."

Phina rolled her eyes and emptied another bottle of bubbly into her diluted orange juice. "Hale hunts."

"No," I argued. "He sings lullabies and rescues ducklings."

"He's a killer, Rayne."

Odette sipped her tea and chuckled. "Are you a vegetarian, Rayne?"

"No, but that's not the point."

I still couldn't meet her gaze, so I gathered the crumbs on the counter into a pile. Maybe she and Remington had an open relationship.

"I find these things are less about the kill and more about the tradition," Naomi chimed in. "It's a part of the Davenport heritage for the men to go on these hunts. They like any excuse to showcase their privilege. They get off on the exclusivity of the event and other men beg for an invitation each year. Let them have it." This, coming from the woman who divorced from the man leading the slaughter.

"I think you're a little more indulgent than me. I don't believe in killing animals for sport."

"Someone killed that bacon you're eating."

I stilled then dropped the scrap of bacon right into Phina's champagne. "Thanks for ruining it."

"Look, it's the one time of year that Remy actually bonds with his sons," Naomi said. "Can we all just appreciate that?"

I couldn't imagine Hale and Remington spending this much time one on one together. They'd been gone since before the sun was up.

"What time are they coming back?" Phina asked, fishing the bacon out of her glass. "I might have Alphonse drive me into town before we get bombarded with testosterone. Want to come Rayne?"

"Wait, how many people are coming back?" I looked down at my faded T-shirt stretched over my stomach and my dingy sweatpants. I was in my house cardigan, the one with a hole in the elbow that I simply couldn't part with.

"All of the men. They should be back soon," Marta said, moving to set out refreshments.

"Hold on. Who's coming here?"

"It's mostly just the guys from last night." Phina, of course, was already dressed for the day in her ivory cowl neck sweater and riding boots, even if she was working with a midday buzz.

My mother shot me a look. "Ray, maybe you should change."

I sighed and slid off the stool, wishing these people would put out some sort of itinerary. "Can you keep an eye on Elara?"

"Of course."

The front door opened, and masculine laughter erupted from the hall. "Shit."

"Shit," Elara repeated, and we all turned to gape at her.

Naomi laughed. "Did she just...?"

"I believe so," my mother answered, also smiling.

"Well, don't smile at her!" What the hell was happening to my well-ordered morning? I had a profane toddler, a murderous husband, and I looked like I stole my wardrobe from a bag lady. This was not how I had planned my day.

Marta carried a charcuterie tray into the dining room. I hung back because I could not sneak upstairs while the men removed their muddy boots in the foyer.

"What happens now?" I asked Phina.

"They eat and brag and fill their bloated egos with old fashioneds until dinner."

It was only ten in the morning, and dinner wasn't until six. Did they honestly plan on drinking for the next eight hours? Why wasn't I told about this back when I could drink? I loved day drinking. Now, it just pissed me off.

I glanced at the back door, figuring that to be the only way to avoid the strangers infiltrating the front of the house. "I'll be back in an hour."

"Okay." Phina uncorked another bottle of champagne.

I glanced at my mom. "Watch her."

My mother waved me away. "We're fine, Ray. Go."

I hadn't even brushed my hair yet. Avoiding the crowd, I slipped out the back door and rounded the house. It was damn cold this early in the morning and I, once again, regretted not grabbing a coat.

"We meet again."

I spun from the car door and came face to face with Alexander Landry. "Xander. I wasn't expecting to see you here."

"Hale invited me last night."

"He did?"

His gaze dropped to my T-shirt and I crossed my arms over my chest. My nipples could cut glass in this weather.

He chuckled bringing his attention back to my face. "You look surprised."

"I guess I am."

"Why? Do you think your husband doesn't like me?"

"That's obviously not the case if he invited you here on Thanksgiving."

"He invited me here in an attempt to intimidate me, Rayne."

Every time he used my name it felt intentional, like he was trying to make a hidden point. "How do you figure?"

"Hale wanted me to see his weapons, generational wealth, and beautiful wife.

Your husband has an undeniably enviable life to flaunt, and he wields it when he has to."

I didn't appreciate being categorized as an asset. If Hale wanted to show off my beauty, he could have at least given me a heads-up. "Are you leaving?"

He chuckled. "What fun would that be? I'm afraid that's not how the game is played. We want to at least give Hale the sense of an upper hand, don't we?"

Was that another gambling reference? "Well, I'm leaving." I popped open the car door and hit the automatic start.

"Will I see you again?"

"Uh, this is my family's Thanksgiving, so yeah, I plan on being with them."

"And your boss's." He winked. "It should be an interesting day. See you later, Rayne." He loped up the front steps, leaving me more confused than ever.

I was going to strangle Hale.

Once I got home I took a bath, in no rush to get back to Remington's house. I really needed to go shopping and considered running out with Phina, but how many stores would be open on Thanksgiving? I needed maternity clothes, which would be even more difficult to find, so I gave up on that idea and stewed in the tub.

My body was expanding by the minute. I was constantly out of breath and forgetting what I was doing. I had to take three breaks just to blow out my hair, and by the time I was finished, I wanted to nap.

Though my wardrobe was limited, I packed a few decent items but nothing suitable for the upper-crust company. Once again, I wished someone had given me a little notice.

Opting for leggings, a white, long-sleeved T-shirt and an orange duster, I made do with what I owned. I had not prepared a designer look for Thanksgiving because, where I came from, Thanksgiving was family, football, turkey farts, and naps.

The mood was lively when I returned to Remington's house, and the testosterone was palpable. One glance into the parlor, and I rolled my eyes. I didn't see Hale, but the rest of the men looked to be on their third or fourth drink.

What an emotional circle jerk. It was one big stroke fest.

Oh, look how big my gun is...

Aren't I powerful?

I can shoot a bird that was bread and fed to think it's safe here...

Oh, that was a bad feeling. I had to watch my inner monologue because pregnancy kept me constantly on the verge of tears. "Stupid men," I mumbled under my breath as I put together a sandwich at the sideboard. "*I don't trust you. Want to come to my house for Thanksgiving...*" I rolled my eyes. "Idiots."

I turned with my plate and came face to face with Hale.

"There you are."

I pursed my lips wondering how much he heard. "Hey."

"How's your morning going?"

"Fine." His easy expression turned unsure. Hale hated when I said I was fine. "Did you kill a bird?"

He chuckled. "No."

My eyes narrowed. "Why did you invite that guy here after I told you how uncomfortable he made me last night?"

"He apologized for anything offensive he might have said and asked for a chance to make it up to you."

"And you're letting him?" Who was this

guy and what did he do with my husband? "A little heads up would've been nice."

"I would have told you, but this is the first we're speaking since last night. You left me there, Rayne."

"You left me on a dance floor, Hale. And no one was dancing."

"I came right back, but you were gone."

I wasn't going to argue semantics. "I don't like him."

"Baby, he's all talk. I made it clear who you belong to."

I scoffed and touched my neck. "That reminds me, where did you put my leash?"

"You know what I mean."

Xander's words came back to me. "Oh my God, he was right. You brought him here to show off."

He stepped closer and lowered his voice, the silver of his eyes darkening to a stormy grey. "Maybe I did. Should we give him a show?"

This was one of those *keep your friends close and your enemies closer* things. I poked my finger in his chest before he could step any closer. "I don't like playing games like this, Hale."

"Some games are fun, Rayne." He pressed the front of his body to mine.

"Right now, my sandwich looks fun."

"Come on, baby. Don't be mad at me." He knew exactly how to push my buttons. One swipe of his fingers along my neck and I was a puddle of goo for him.

"You're such a punk."

He chuckled and set my plate aside, backing me into the wall. When he kissed me, his hands went right into my hair. "Deny it all you want, baby, but you like when I get possessive and stake my claim."

My breath quickened as he pinched my nipple through my shirt. My body's switchboard was a hot mess these days, and I felt too many things at once. Excitement. Fear. Arousal. Longing for my sandwich. "I like it in private."

He dragged his nose along my cheek as if breathing me in, quietly whispering, "I don't want to be private today, Rayne. I want him to see the way you look at me, the way I touch you, the way you make me happier than any man alive. I want him to imagine how hot you are when I'm fucking you, *my* wife. Then I'll make it unmistakably clear that he, or any other man for that matter, will never know you as intimately as I do."

My back bone melted into a puddle in my panties. "Hale..." I whined, completely turned on.

"Rayne," he answered, knowing by the sound of my voice that he was going to get his way—the cocky bastard.

How could I deny him anything when he went all growly-alpha and told me I was pretty? My foremothers would be so disappointed, but my inner slut was reveling in his high-handed dominance.

"I'm not happy about this."

His hand closed around my ass as he loosened the button of his pants. "Are you sure?"

Shutting my eyes, I dragged my knuckles over his swollen length.

"There's my good girl." He kissed my throat and my knees softened. "You spoil me."

Reaching into his clothes, I gripped his length. He groaned when I stroked him.

"Yes." He pushed his hips forward. "Your touch feels incredible."

He knew I couldn't resist him, and he used his potent sexual magnetism to his full advantage. So, I had to deliver at least one dig in defense of feminism. "We better hurry, Hale. I heard the dick-measuring contest starts in ten minutes."

He didn't even flinch. "I've got that one in the bag."

We Like Things Chipper

"**S**noopy!" I cheered as the giant parade float filled the television screen.

Elara's grin widened as she stared at the procession, mesmerized by the production. "'Noopy?"

"Right there?" I pointed to the float when the camera panned out again.

We had been hiding in the den for some time, and the Macy's parade was almost over. Pretty soon, we would have to be with the people again. Back in Oregon, we would be peeling potatoes and snapping green beans right about now.

"Oh, look, Elara!" my mother cheered. "It's Santa!"

Elara was still figuring out the whole

Santa Claus thing. We made every mention exciting enough that she understood the dude in the red suit was a big deal, but for a child who basically had every toy she could want, the Clauses paled in comparison to the powerful Davenport men.

"I can't believe it's almost Christmas again," my mom said. This was her time's flying speech earmarked for fall. She also had a summer speech and one for when the leaves started to turn in October.

"I miss Christmas in Oregon," I confessed, thinking of how basic and chintzy our dollar store decorations were. The Davenports did Christmas very differently than my family, and Thanksgiving, and all the holidays, for that matter. It occurred to me that Elara was only exposed to Davenport traditions. "Mom, do you remember Gran's apple pie recipe?"

"Of course, I do. I made it for the past thirty Thanksgivings, Ray."

I glanced out the window at the changing trees. The world was awash in radiant hues of red and gold. When I was little, we would go on walks to collect leaves and press them in books or color over the ridged veins with crayon.

"Let's go for a walk." Several rows of apple trees grew on the property in a small orchard. "I want to make a Gran's pie. Elara needs to have traditions from our family, too."

"Oh, we would need the ingredients, Rayne. I don't know if stores are open today."

"We probably have everything here, Mom." I stood and set Elara on her feet. "Do you want to have an adventure with Mommy and Grandma Penny?"

"Go bye-bye!" She cheered.

It was settled. I asked Marta for a bag, and she gave me a sturdy tote. Once I bundled Elara up in her jacket, I laced up my boots.

Laughter burst from the parlor. The men were getting louder by the hour. My mom led Elara out the back door and I glanced back, deciding not to interrupt or tell anyone what we were doing. They probably wouldn't even know we were gone.

The estate was beautiful year-round, but in autumn it was radiant. Scarlet maples, golden birches, and amber oaks painted the landscape in fiery hues that contrasted brightly against the clear blue sky. Dry leaves rustled underfoot as the faint scent of chimney smoke drifted through the air.

The orchard was visible from the house, but I'd underestimated the distance. By the time we reached the first apple tree I worried about lugging our harvest back to the kitchen.

"Wow, do you smell that?" my mother asked and Elara scrunched her little nose to sniff the air noisily. The crisp, inviting scent of the apples overtook the earthy aroma of fall.

"Watch your step, Mom." The ground was littered with scattered apples, but once they were on the ground they usually started to rot.

"They're a lot taller than I realized," my mom said, echoing my thoughts.

I looked around and chewed my lip. "Do you think there's a ladder out here?"

"Rayne, you're not climbing a ladder in your condition."

"Mom, I'm pregnant, not made of glass."

"If Hale sees you up on a ladder, he won't be happy."

"Well, Hale's not here, is he?" I scanned the lines of trees. "It doesn't matter anyway. I don't see a ladder."

Elara picked up an apple and threw it, then ran down the path.

"Find the apples, Peanut!" Maybe she could do the work since I was already tired. "We have to fill the bag, but only the good ones."

Once Elara understood the objective, the bag quickly filled. I sorted out the rotten ones and only kept the ones that weren't bruised.

My mom took the bag when it got heavy. By the time we returned to the main house the men were sloshed. They were still in the parlor, but football played on the television in the den.

"Is this all that guys do on holidays, drink and make noise?" I didn't know what men did on Thanksgiving because my dad was never around, but I did have higher expectations than the reality.

"They're just having fun, Ray."

The kitchen was ripe with savory smells. Hugo diced carrots while Marta stirred a large pot of something spicy on the stove. I cleared a space on the old wooden farm table to work. Elara kneeled on a chair and watched as we peeled and cut the apples, eating slices as we went.

Marta located all the ingredients, and my

mom made the cinnamon caramel filling on the stove. I helped Elara dump the dry ingredients into a big bowl to make the dough.

"*Niña*, you need an apron," Marta chided when a dust cloud of flour puffed in my face.

I laughed. "That's okay. It's only flour." I held Elara's hand over an egg and showed her how to crack it against the bowl.

She looked at her hand in horror when a bit of the yoke got on her fingers. I picked the shells out of the batter while she flung the slime off her hand.

"Rayne, there are no eggs in Gran's recipe."

"Of course there's eggs. You used to let me crack them when I was little, Mom."

"That was for the bread pudding, not the pie."

"Shit." I looked down at the broken yoke seeping into the combination of ingredients.

"Shit," Elara repeated, holding out her hand for me to clean.

I wiped her palm with a tea towel. "Hey, don't say that word."

She frowned at the white powder now on her palm. "Shit!"

"Great. Can someone please bring me a spoon?"

Marta handed me a ladle to scoop out the egg.

"There you are." Hale appeared in the kitchen then did a double take. "You're baking?"

"We're making a pie."

"Daddy, shit!" Elara held up her hand to her father.

"Whoa!" He stared wide-eyed at his daughter. "Elara, you do not say that word." He carried her to the sink and rinsed her hand clean.

As soon as he set her down, she said, "Shit!" And ran out of the kitchen yelling profanities.

He looked at me and held out his hands in confusion. "When did that start?"

"Why are you looking at me? You're the one with the dirty mouth."

He raised a brow. "Not according to this morning."

I shot him a look, and he shut up.

Sidestepping Hugo, Marta, and my mother, he rounded the island and stood behind me at the table while I mixed the ingredients. He squeezed my shoulder, massaging gently. "Are you okay?"

"I'm fine."

"Rayne."

I rolled my shoulder, shrugging away his touch.

"Hey, look at me."

I didn't want to. I was mad at him for ignoring us all day and my eyes were starting to water for no particular reason. "I need to mix these ingredients." My vision blurred. It sucked having no control over my reflexes.

He dropped into the chair at my left. "Rayne, what's going on?"

"Nothing. I'm making a pie and you're entertaining company in the parlor. Everything's fine."

"I'm banning that word."

"Like you just banned Elara from saying shit? Good luck with that."

He caught my arm, stilling the whisk. "Penny, Marta, Hugo, can we have a minute?"

The three interlopers quietly left the kitchen and we were alone. I shook my head. "Hale, they're busy and they have stuff going on."

He didn't care. "If you're upset with me, tell me. I don't like games."

I met his stare. "Fine. I'm upset with you. This isn't how Thanksgiving's supposed to go, Hale. You're hanging out with a bunch of strangers and not spending any quality time with us. Holidays are for family. You didn't even watch the parade with Elara."

His hand closed around mine. "I'm sorry."

"Apologizing doesn't fix it. While you're having your little flex fest, I'm trying to show Elara what Thanksgiving means. Is this what you want to show her? Thanksgiving means time with Mommy while Daddy's seducing business deals for the upcoming year?"

He dropped his gaze. "No."

"Then don't. Do better."

"Don't forget, this is my first time parenting, too, Rayne."

"Well, it's Elara's *only* time being a kid, Hale. What we show her, matters." My voice grew tighter the longer I spoke. "I didn't have a dad present for my holidays, and now they only remind me of my mom and Grandmother. If you want to be a part of her memories, you have to be present."

"You're right."

"I know I'm right. I'm a good mom." I didn't mean for my voice to crack but it did.

"Okay, okay. Don't cry." He wrapped his arms around me and kissed my head. His hand went to my stomach, cradling my belly.

"You're right. I need to be there for our children and for you."

I wiped my nose on my shoulder and sniffled. "You can make it up to me tomorrow morning when we hit all the Black Friday sales at six a.m."

He drew back in horror. "Excuse me?"

"We're going shopping." I wiped my eyes, getting flour on my cheek. "Tomorrow. At six a.m. I need maternity clothes."

"You want to go shopping on Black Friday?"

"Yes. Early." I kissed his nose, making sure to get a little flour on his cheek as well. "So don't drink too much at your *bro-orgy.*"

He groaned and stood. "The things I do for love." He pulled a floral apron off the peg in the pantry and tied the ruffled bow at his back. "Let's do this."

"Wait, what?"

"We're making a pie." He peeked into the sauce pans on the stove. "I'm guessing this is us?"

"What about your company?"

"You asked me to be present. I'm present. Let's bake this pie." He looked toward the door. "Elara!"

She came running into the kitchen dragging her baby doll by the ankle and whacking its plastic head on the floor. "Daddy!" She laughed at the sight of him in the apron. "That's Marta's pray-prin."

Hale scooped her up and sat her on the island. "It's mine now." He handed her a wooden spoon. "Hold this."

I called the others back into the kitchen and waved Hale out of their way. Only Marta and my mother returned. Once I showed him how to fold the ingredients, he helped Elara work the dough.

Remington appeared. "What the hell's going on? I have a chef claiming he can't work in these conditions." He did a double take at his son in the apron. "What the hell are you wearing, Hale? Or is it Hazel?"

"Hugo can come back in, Remington. Hale and I just needed a minute."

"To do what? Hale, you're in the middle of a blackjack tournament."

"Deal me out. I've moved on to pie." Hale snagged a spatula from the drawer, determined not to touch the dough with his hands.

Remington scowled as my mother nudged him out of the way. She carried a tray of ice water, shortening, and cubed butter to the table.

"Remington, I'm going to tell you what I used to tell my Rayne when she was little. If you're not going to help, get out of the kitchen."

I hid a laugh as Remington's face darkened. No one had the balls to dismiss Remington Davenport—except for Penny Meyers apparently.

"This is my damn kitchen."

"And it's damn full right now, Remington." My mother steered him toward the door. "Go play with your friends, and we'll call you when supper's ready."

"And send Hugo back in," I yelled as the housemaster was driven into the hall, efficiently exiled from his own kitchen.

Hale and Marta chuckled. As we worked, my mother hummed a familiar tune. Once Hugo returned, she started to sing, *"From now on, our troubles will be miles away..."*

I chimed in, *"Here we are..."*

Hale took over with a deep baritone, *"As in olden days..."*

I smiled up at him as I folded the dough. *"Happy golden days..."*

We looked expectantly at Hugo, who scowled. "I do not sing."

"That just won't work, Hugo," my mother chirped, wiping her hands on a tea towel. "I have an app that shows the lyrics." She propped her phone in front of the grumpy Belgian chef and hit play. "Singing always makes the food taste better."

The recognizable beat of *Jingle Bell Rock* played from her phone and she pointed to the lyrics on the screen. "See here? *Jingle bell, jingle bell, jingle rock.* Go on. You try."

You had to give my mother credit. The woman didn't relent until Hugo finally read the words in the most monotone voice ever. "*What a bright time, it is the right time.*"

Penny and Marta cheered.

"She's persistent," Hale whispered and I smirked.

I lifted the pie crust dough and kneaded it between my hands. "Us Meyers like to keep things chipper. We've never met a grump we couldn't break."

"That's partially true." He kissed my temple.

"Why only partially?"

"You're a Davenport now."

"Ah, yes." I grinned. "And you were once a grump. My record is impeccable."

We sang and danced as we rolled out the dough. Elara giggled and jiggled to the beat. This was what I wanted. I wanted simplicity and chaos. I wanted family time and the stuff of memories.

And damn it, there went the tears again! I blotted my eyes and Hale looked at me with concern. "What is it?"

"I'm just...feeling grateful." Rising on my toes, I kissed his jaw. "Thank you. This is exactly what Thanksgiving should be."

Hale smiled, nodding his understanding. "Thank you for teaching me how to Thanksgiving."

Only then did it occur to me that his mother and sister were nowhere around. Sometimes I forgot how little Hale knew about ordinary things. I gave him a shoulder bump because my hands were full of dough. "Tomorrow, I'll teach you about sales and holiday retail. That's part of Christmasing 101."

He groaned. "Can't wait."

Giddy Up Jingle Horse

"*Pick up your feet!*" I spun Elara, and she squealed as I sang off-key and danced like an escaped lunatic loose from the institution. "*Jingle around the clock!*" I shook my ass and twirled, doing my best pregnancy twerk. "*Mix and a-mingle in the—*" I slammed into a broad chest and my smile fell. "You."

"Am I interrupting?"

I disentangled myself from Xander's arms and protectively held Elara like a shield, back-stepping until I stood next to Hale. The Christmas music continued to play from my mom's phone on the counter.

Hale draped an arm over my shoulder protectively. "Did you need something, Xander?"

His gaze dropped to Hale's apron, and he chuckled. He crossed the room and dropped a load of dirty money on the table. "I won the last hand. I think that about covers your portion."

"I walked away from the tournament. My portion's forfeited. It's all yours."

Xander shook his head. "I don't play that way. I prefer to see things through. That way everyone's clear on the score."

Oh great, more gambling references.

I checked Elara's diaper. The one time I need there to be a poop, there wasn't one. "Let's take a potty break, Peanut."

I excused myself with a tight-lipped smile. No clue how Hale tolerated that guy.

Potty training was intense. But it was probably way more messy with a boy. If the bean turned out to be a son, Hale would tackle that one.

"All done."

I helped her pull up her pants and turned the faucet on so she could clean up. "Mommy's turn." While she rinsed her hands—something Hale's child mastered right away—I tinkled. No matter how often I peed, my bladder seemed to always stay full.

"All done."

"Elara, no, leave the door closed!"

She jiggled the primitive knob and the door opened. Old houses didn't have dependable locks.

"Shit!" I was mid-stream and couldn't reach the door. "You're supposed to be studying my form, brat. You could at least shut the door."

"Shit!" She left me there—ass out, scrambling for toilet paper as she went to find her father.

"Turncoat!" I quickly yanked up my pants, washed my hands, and went after her.

"Where are you rushing off to, Rayne?"

I halted and frowned at Seraphina, who looked...tousled.

Oh, God. I sure hoped she didn't do the nasty with Captain Stubing. He was part of the drunk debauchery in the parlor.

"Elara's on the run." I looked her up and down. "Where have you been?"

She drew back. "What's that look?"

"Were you with that guy?" I whispered, just wanting to get to the tea.

She laughed. "Yes, but nothing happened. Carlisle's an old friend of Daddy's."

Old was the key word. "So, you're not into him?"

"God no!" She laughed again. "I have my eyes on someone else."

"Really?" This I needed to hear. "Who?"

She glanced over her shoulder and lowered her voice. "He's actually here today. Have you met Alexander Landry?"

My curiosity morphed into disappointment. "Oh. Him. Yeah."

"He's so hot. Those dark eyes and that tanned skin." She blew out a breath. "The things I could do to that man."

"He's sort of an odd duck."

"The good ones always are."

"And I think he might have a gambling problem."

"Well, with his net worth, he can afford to."

I forced a fake smile and decided to leave it alone. Plenty of people probably thought I was an odd choice when Hale picked me. "Well, he was in the kitchen if you're looking for him." Maybe she could drag him out of there.

She frowned. "Xander was?"

"Yeah. We were making a pie and—What are you doing?" I was shoved back into the powder room as Seraphina shut the door.

"It's Barrett and McKinsley." She cracked the door and spied on the couple.

"So why are we hiding in the bathroom?" I whispered.

"Because I think he's trying to dump her on someone so he can hang with the guys. I'm not getting wrapped up in babysitting unless it's for Elara."

The couple chatted as they passed the powder room. Well, McKinsley chatted. Barrett seemed to be ignoring her.

"I don't know why he does this," Phina hissed. "Every holiday he brings some bimbo to shield himself from Daddy. Then he gets tired of her by day two."

A shield or a security blanket? These Davenport holidays were exhausting. "I'm guessing you don't like her."

"Last night she talked to me for twenty-five minutes about cuticle care."

I had a hard time judging what self-care topics were green-lit and blackballed in Seraphina's world, so I just nodded like I understood why cuticle care was bad. "I just bite my nails."

"That's disgusting, Rayne."

"Bear," McKinsley mewled, tugging Barrett's hand like a child. "Let's ride into town and see what shops are open."

"Nothing's going to be open this late in the day."

"You don't know that. I saw a few jewelers on the way in."

Both Phina and I rolled our eyes.

I sniffed her head. "What kind of shampoo do you use? Your hair smells like a lollipop."

"It's custom made. I order it from a boutique in Paris."

"So, not something I can pick up at Target?"

"No."

Barrett turned McKinsley's back to the wall, and they kissed. "Well, that's one way to shut her up."

"I'd say."

"Holy crap." I knew I shouldn't be watching but I also couldn't look away. It was like fresh, red district porn. I glanced at Phina. "How are you not grossed out by this?"

"They're just kissing."

No. That was a lot more than a kiss. This was old school, hip gyrating, dry-humping, bump-n-grinding. "Looks French."

"He kisses every woman like that."

McKinsley let out a low, sexual moan.

"That's it." I flushed the toilet and turned the faucet on full blast, alerting the couple that someone was in the bathroom. "I'm out of here."

Barrett sprung away from McKinsley the moment I opened the door. "Meyers."

"Davenport." I kept my head down. "I was just...you know." I left Phina in the bathroom to figure her own way out.

Back in the kitchen, Elara was preoccupied with her father as he took direction from Penny and molded the pie crust onto a beveled pie plate. Xander was still there, standing at Hale's back, bird-dogging the whole display. They both looked up and smiled when I entered.

Weird.

"Hey." I said, sidling up to my mother. The air smelled delicious, and the Christmas music was an instant mood-setter. I peeked at what Marta was concocting. "That smells divine, Marta."

"You will love it, Niña. And I make extra so that you can freeze it for home."

I kissed her sweet head. "Thank you."

Hugo grimaced. "Too many people. You are all in my way."

"Hugo," I said, coming to peek at what he was cooking. "You know, for a guy who literally has the word *hug* in his name, you're about as cuddly as a cactus."

He grumbled something in Dutch.

"A language barrier's not going to stop us from being friends."

"Shit!" Elara yelled, and Xander laughed.

I narrowed my eyes because it was a nice laugh, and I had him pegged for a maniacal one. Then I noticed his apron, and I frowned. "What the...?"

"Here you go, boys," my mother said, carrying the caramel filling to the table. "Layer it slowly so the apples don't tear the crust."

"Yes, Mrs. Meyers."

"Oh, call me Penny."

"Yes, Penny."

Well, wasn't Xander the little ass kisser?

Seraphina walked into the kitchen wearing a fresh face of makeup since the last time I saw her. She'd also applied perfume and fixed her hair.

"Great. More people," Hugo grumbled, slamming a cast iron pan onto the burner.

The man had no problem communicating his feelings.

Seraphina bustled over to the counter and hissed in my ear, "Thanks a lot for abandoning me. I'm going to have to burn out my retinas."

I snickered. "Your friend's over there in the apron."

She looked toward the table and sucked in a breath then frowned. "They're baking?"

"Hale is. I don't know how Xander's involved."

"Hmm." She tapped her lips thoughtfully with one perfectly manicured nail. "Marta, where are the aprons?"

How many Davenports did it take to bake a pie?

As soon as Seraphina had her clothes protected, she joined the men. "How can I help?"

Both Xander and Hale glanced down at her as she intrusively nestled in between them. She smiled up at Xander.

"I think we've got it covered, Phina."

"Nonsense, there's room for everyone," my mother chimed in, handing Seraphina a spoon slathered in caramel. "Have a taste."

They were like three deprived wealthy kids who never had a mommy cook with them before. Didn't anyone ever give them a beater to lick? Only Elara took issue with the sticky caramel. Everyone else gushed over my grandmother's recipe—including Marta. Hugo, not so much, but he did swipe a taste and raise an appraising brow that looked like approval.

My mother coached them in the art of layering pie crust lattice and free-handing autumn cutouts with the leftover dough. I smothered several laughs as they worked like middle schoolers trying to impress the teacher. It was charming and sweet in the most magical sense because the Davenports grew up with maids, butlers, and personal chefs, but never spent this sort of quality time with family in the kitchen. And everyone knew, the kitchen prep was actually the best part of the holidays.

I assumed Xander's upbringing was much the same. None of them were good at what they were doing, but that wasn't the point. The lattice was crooked. The filling wasn't level. The cutout leaves looked like chicken feet. The crust was an absolute disaster. But they were having fun.

Everyone took turns singing as the holiday music continued to play, butchering the lyrics they didn't know. When the kitchen door swung open, and Barrett walked in—a confused expression on his face—his siblings called him over.

Barrett rolled up his sleeves and jumped in. It was really adorable watching them fumble to design the perfect apple pie. Even Xander stepped back, letting the siblings have this moment to themselves. That was the first thing he did that made me actually think he might not be such a bad guy.

He washed his hands at the sink and frowned at his dress shirt. "Well, this shirt's trash." His gaze went to Elara's face, where she rested on my shoulder. "She's precious."

"Thanks."

"It's amazing that she can sleep through all this."

"She's got that work hard, play hard Davenport mentality."

"I bet."

I studied him for a moment. "Are you finished your culinary adventures for the day?"

"I think so. Why? Did you need something?"

I swayed to keep Elara settled long enough for me to transport her to a softer place. "No. I was just curious. How much did you win?"

His smile curled slowly as his gaze darkened. "Thirty-two thousand."

I nearly choked. "In cards?"

"I'm very good."

"I'm sure you're a real Rain Man." Knowing Xander was a betting man, I wondered how much he was willing to risk on a friendly wager. "Think I can sink this in that trash can?" I held up a balled up paper towel.

"One-handed from here?"

"Yup." I swayed, my other arm practically asleep under Elara's squishy butt.

He glanced at my feet then to the trash can. "No moving?"

"Nope."

"Over the island?"

"I won't even move the vase of flowers out of the way."

He laughed. "Nah, you can't make that."

It was my turn to twist a slow grin. "Wanna bet?"

His brow lifted and I knew I had him. "How much?"

I almost said a hundred bucks, but then I remembered who I was dealing with. "How about a thousand?"

It was clear I shocked him. "You know, if you miss, you have to pay up."

"I'm good for it." Actually, the thought of forking out a thousand smackers made me want to vomit, but I wasn't backing down at this point. Besides, Hale would be the one cutting that check.

"All right." He unfolded the wad of money he'd won at cards and counted out ten crisp one hundred dollar bills, laying them out on the island. "Take your best shot."

I stared down at the money, wondering if this was insane.

"Barrett, your leaves are too big. You're crowding my corner of the pie!"

"Who said it's your corner, Phina. You're hogging it."

I glanced over my shoulder. As the two younger Davenports bickered, Hale worked meticulously to carefully braid the dough. I smiled, thinking about how nice it would be to spend Xander's money tomorrow morning at the Black Friday sales.

"It's interesting to watch you two."

I glanced back at Xander. "Why?"

He shrugged. "You actually like each other. He watches you when you're not looking and you do the same to him."

"He's my person." I shifted Elara's weight in my arm. "And baby needs a more manly apron, so I better make this shot."

Xander's gaze dropped to my stomach just as I launched the crumpled paper at the trashcan.

"No way!" he yelled as it swished seamlessly into the bin.

"Ha!" I yelled, startling Elara, but I was too happy to worry about nap time. Swiping up the money, I danced around the island, shaking my ass in a touchdown-worthy victory dance.

"What happened?" Hale asked, suddenly suspicious of his little friend. "Did I miss something?"

"You're wife's a hustler. She just won a grand off of me."

Hale frowned. "You bet a thousand dollars?"

I shrugged. "What, you're allowed to gamble, but I'm not?"

"No, but for someone willing to wake up at the butt crack of dawn to save forty percent at the Pick-N-Save, a thousand dollars is a lot to lose."

"First of all, the Pick-N-Save isn't even around anymore, Hale. We will be hitting respectable retail outlets like Wally World and *Tarjay*. Second, I've been hurling diapers in trashcans since Elara was born. I didn't plan on losing."

"You won a thousand dollars by throwing a diaper?"

"Paper towel, but same difference. A little less weight, but I'm also well versed in the wipey toss." I slapped my wad of winnings against Hale's chest. "Anyway, my arms are about to fall off, so I'm going to take my winnings and lay Elara down. I'm due for a little pre-dinner *nappetizer* myself."

"Here, I can take her," Hale said and Elara whined when he jostled her out of my arms.

"I'm right behind you, babe." I shook my numb arm, trying to get the blood to flow into my fingers again, so I could steal a cookie before heading upstairs.

Xander watched Hale leave then smiled at me. What was his deal?

Tired of guessing, I figured I'd just come out and ask. "Do you not have family to eat with today?"

He laughed at my bluntness. "You don't want me here?"

"No, I—"

"It's okay." He chuckled. "I'm not everybody's cup of tea. But to answer your question, I don't spend holidays with family."

Did he mean he didn't have family, or that they just weren't around today? I decided to be a little nicer to him. "Well, then you came to the right place. The Davenports make enough food to feed an army."

"Damn it, Barrett!" Phina snapped. I looked back at the table just as she smashed whatever Barret was sculpting out of dough. "Now yours is ruined too."

"Oh, boy," Xander mumbled. "We've got a sibling rivalry."

Phina growled and gave up on the pie. "I'm done."

McKinsley entered the kitchen, and Hugo once again grumbled in Dutch about the foot traffic. She immediately started whining in a pitch that would make a basset hound cry. How the hell was Barrett tolerating her?

Maybe he wasn't, because after about thirty seconds of that needy whining he snapped and told her to wait for him in the other room. That quickly, his entire mood changed as he irritably washed his hands.

"Xander, do you want to get some air?"

Phina asked as she removed her apron and fluffed her hair.

"Uh, sure." He glanced back to me and smiled. "Nice chatting with you...*Rayne.*"

Right there! That was the look!

As they left the kitchen, my stare crossed with Barrett's and he frowned. scrunching his nose. "What the hell was that?"

"Did you see it?"

"Yeah, I saw it. Has Hale?"

I scuttled to his side, careful to keep my voice down. "Sort of," I whispered. "Well, I told him about it. I'm getting such a weird vibe from that guy. I can't figure him out."

Barrett looked out the window in the direction Xander had gone with his sister. "Why is he here?"

"Hale invited him after I told him he gave me the ipps!"

"What the fuck are the ipps?"

"You know... not quite the creeps, but something's a little off."

"Sure. The ipps. Got it."

"Barrett!" My shoulders jumped up to my ears when McKinsley returned to see what was taking him so long. "I want to go. You said we could leave, like, twenty minutes ago."

My God, that voice was awful. I hid my

mouth behind a cookie and mumbled, "I've got some allergy medicine in my bag that causes drowsiness if you want it."

He laughed.

"I'm serious. It knocks Elara right out when she's whiny."

"Are you telling me you drug my niece?"

"I'm telling you she has *allergies,* and if your girlfriend keeps whining, I'm afraid my milk's going to come in."

He looked horrified. "Don't talk to me about your boob milk, Meyers."

I rolled my eyes. "Oh, please. Boobs serve a higher purpose than entertaining you, Barrett. Grow up."

"Barrett, I want to go!"

He growled and fished his keys out of his pocket. "Get your coat," he snapped, ushering her out of the kitchen. I wouldn't be surprised if he drove her out to the middle of nowhere and left her there.

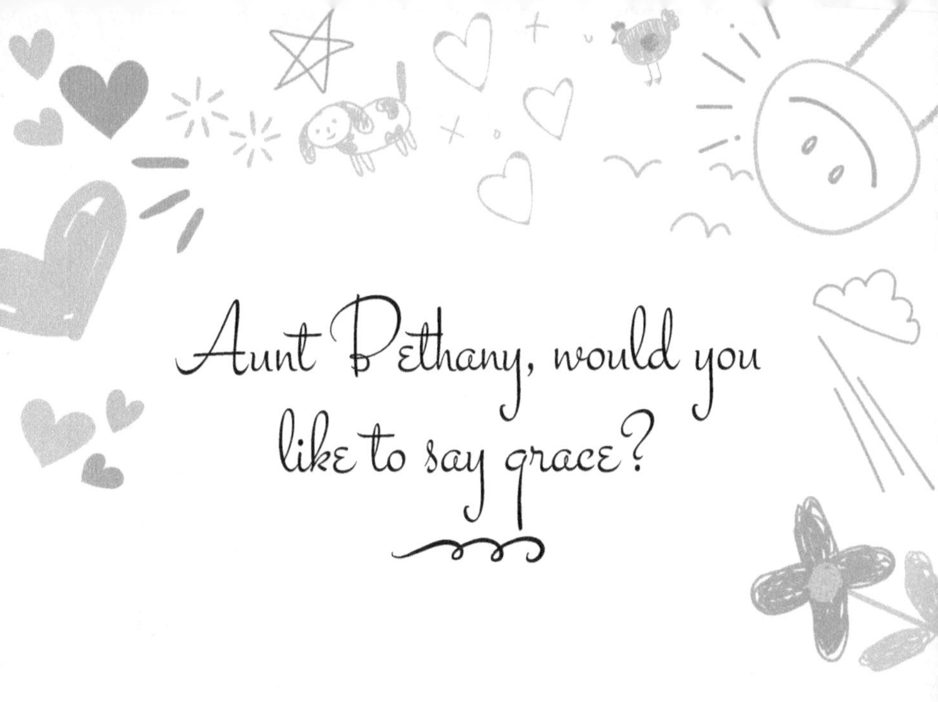

Dinner was a little too somber for my liking. The china was gorgeous, and the tablescape was over the top, but there was a shroud of awkwardness cloaking the festivities. This was probably on account of all the unnecessary formalities and how sleepy some people were from drinking since dawn.

There was no normal chatter. No *pass the potatoes* or *this year I'm grateful for...* Unfamiliar servants served the food in silence. The music was some orchestra crap instead of Judy or Bing or even Mariah. And why the hell did I have five forks at my place setting?

"Where's Marta?" I asked when I realized she wasn't seated at this cold Citizen Cane table.

Remington frowned. "She's eating with her family, Meyers."

But we were her family. "Isn't this table big enough for her and Raoul to join us? They're only two little people."

Some unfamiliar guests glanced up from their plates as another course was butlered about the table. Remington's grip tightened around his spoon. I met his stare head-on, still pissy with him about his behavior the night before.

I glanced at Odette. She wasn't her usual pleasant self today, and I worried she might have figured out what Remington was up to at the party. He was such a fool. The man didn't have a clue how to keep a good woman.

"So," my mother said, trying to break the chill in the room. "Did anyone watch the game today?"

I jumped on the distraction. "I watched the first quarter."

Xander met my stare and smiled. "Do you like football, Rayne?"

"I like big men in tight pants."

Seraphina laughed, and Hale scowled. Barrett glared suspiciously at Xander.

I shrugged and stuffed a sauteed bean in

my mouth. "No other football fans at the table?"

Hale cleared his throat and wiped his mouth. "We have a game planned for tomorrow in the west field." He cleared his throat. "Hopefully, my pants are tight enough for you."

My grin widened. "You guys are playing football?"

"It's tradition," Barrett explained. "The winner gets Leilani Falls."

I frowned. "Who's Leilani, and why is she falling?"

"It's a private island," Hale explained. "The winning team gets it for the year. Sort of like a timeshare."

"Well, that's neat." I liked islands. "Are you any good? I'm assuming the island's nice."

"It's gorgeous," Phina said. "Just outside of Bora Bora. Remember the year we had it? That was the best winter."

"The year you were caught with the Tahitian groundskeeper?"

"Shut up, Barrett." Phina smiled nervously at Xander, but he showed no reaction to Barrett's comment. "You're such a jerk," she hissed at her brother.

My dinner was delicious, but it bothered me that Marta wasn't here for me to thank her. "Excuse me." Like the wave at a baseball game, all the men stood when I stood. "Oh. I, uh…" I hitched a thumb over my shoulder. "I just need to check on something in the kitchen."

"What is it, Meyers? One of the servants will get it for you."

"It's okay." I left my napkin on my seat and left the formal dining room before anyone else could stop me.

When I pushed through the kitchen door I was greeted by laughter that quickly silenced. Raoul looked up and Marta's smile shifted to concern. "Niña, do you need something?"

Hugo was eating with them. So I sat down. "I just wanted to see how you were doing."

"Your dinner is okay?"

"My dinner is flippin' delicious, Marta. I'm already fantasizing about the leftovers."

She hugged me tight and kissed my head. "Good! You're finished already?"

"No, but you guys were in here, and I wanted to say hi."

The three of them looked at me like I was crazy.

"Rayne?" Hale appeared in the doorway and frowned. "What are you doing?"

"I was just checking on Marta and Raoul and Hugo."

Marta dropped her gaze, but the men watched Hale. "Your dinner's getting cold."

The seating arrangement bothered me more than anyone else, including Marta. I sighed. Sometimes, I hated etiquette.

Kissing Marta's dark hair, I hugged her again. "Thank you for cooking for me. The bean is very happy."

She patted a loving hand on my belly. "*De nada, Niña. Me alegro que el bebe este feliz.* Now, go back where you belong."

I followed Hale back to the dinner table. When I entered the dining room, all the men stood again, and I blushed. Getting up sure caused a stir around here.

My mom kept the conversation going at Remington's end of the table while the men mainly discussed social policy and upcoming land interests. By the time I finished eating, I was ready for sweatpants and a blanky, but this group had other plans.

The men went to the parlor for more cordials and cigars. I sent Hale along, because Elara was with his mom and I could tell he wanted some manly time after baking pies all afternoon. The smell of smoke was seeping through the house and making me nauseous, so I took a blanket and moved outside to the front porch, where the air was fresher.

Rocking on the porch swing, I leaned my head back and sighed. The sky was a perfect golden glow at sunset and I was too comfortable to move inside once it got dark.

The glowing cherry of a cigar blazed in the distance, and I sat up, realizing I wasn't alone. A plume of smoke drifted through the air and Xander appeared.

"We have to stop running into each other like this."

I smiled tightly. "I needed some air. The smoke was getting to me."

He glanced at his cigar and pinched off the tip, extinguishing it. "Do you mind if I join you?"

Like there was a polite way to decline. "Not at all."

He settled next to me on the porch swing, using his long legs to rock back and forth slowly.

I lasted about twenty seconds in the awkward silence. "How was your afternoon with Seraphina?"

"Hale's sister is very nice."

"She's single, you know?"

"She made that very clear."

"You don't think she's attractive?"

"I think she's beautiful. But she's not my type."

"What's your type?" Realizing that my question could be misconstrued as interest, I quickly said, "I mean, who do you normally date?" That was no better. "What do you like? Gah, I'm terrible at small talk."

He laughed and glanced down at my stomach. "Let's just say I have very particular taste."

The front door opened, and Odette came out holding a suitcase. I abruptly stood. "Odette, are you leaving?"

"Rayne. I didn't see you there. I'm... Yes. I'm going home."

I had so many questions, like, would I ever see her again? "Are you coming back?"

She laughed, the sound humble and cold. "No. I'm too wise for foolish games at my age." She glanced at Xander. "You are too. Careful of that one."

I didn't look at Xander to see if he took

offense. I crossed the porch and hugged her tightly. "I'm so sorry things didn't work out."

"So am I, but I'm not surprised. He'll never change. I knew that coming into this." She cupped my cheeks. "I wish you and Hale all the happiness in the world. Send me pictures when the baby's born."

"I will."

She kissed my cheek, and then she was gone. I wanted to cry.

"You okay?" Xander asked as her taillights faded in the distance.

I sighed, my heart heavy with disappointment. "She was one of the good ones."

"If that were true, he never would have kissed someone else. Men like Remington know how to hold onto a good thing."

"Men like Remington—*ooh*." My hand went to my stomach, and I gasped when the baby kicked. "Oh, my God."

Xander stood. "Should I get Hale?"

"Yes." It happened again and I gasped louder. "No. I'll go." As soon as I stepped inside, Hale stepped out of the parlor in a cloud of stale smoke.

"I was about to get some air—"

I grabbed his hand and pressed it to my belly. "Feel!"

His breath caught. "Oh, my gosh!" He laughed, then brought his other hand to my stomach, his smile stretching across his beaming face. "Incredible."

"It must be all the spicy food I ate at dinner."

"It's something. What does it feel like to you?"

"Sort of twitchy and tumbling, soft like butterflies, but somehow more. Kind of like I'm driving over a steep hill."

He met my stare, and we shared a smile, our expressions one of complete awe. "I love you," he said leaning in for a kiss.

"I love you too." I covered his mouth with my hand. "Did you smoke?"

"No."

"Okay then. Kiss away!"

He gathered me in his arms and pressed his lips to mine. "Mmm." He was such a good kisser. As soon as he let me go, I asked, "Is your father smoking?"

"We're not doing this now, Rayne. It's Thanksgiving. You're off the clock."

But Remington's heart was on the clock. "Hale—"

"No, Rayne."

I huffed. "Fine. I'll kill him tomorrow."

"Come on." He took my hand. "I'm taking you home to bed."

"I need my coat."

"I'll get it. You warm up the car." He handed me the keys and went to find our coats.

When I turned, the dark cherry of a cigar glowed on the other side of the window that framed the door. Xander watched form the shadows. How long had he been staring at us? He had to know I saw him.

Refusing to be intimidated, I walked back outside. "Goodnight, Xander."

"Good night, Rayne. I'll see you in the morning," he said as if purposely ensuring I thought about him after this.

Blue Forty-Two! Rover Sit! Hut, Hut!

"I think we just walked onto the set of Downton Abby."

My mother and I stopped several yards from the field where the men were warming up. "Who plays football in white?"

"Rich people."

They looked like a bunch of ice cream cones. On the sidelines, lawn furniture had been set out. Not those collapsible stadium chairs soccer moms dragged to the edge of a field. These were natural wicker and teak pieces.

"I feel underdressed."

I was still in my shopping clothes from that morning. My leggings were built for speed and thriftiness and my sweater was the furthest thing from a fashion statement. Hale could have warned me this was a semi-formal affair. Everyone was dressed New England casual, which looked like they basically raided the set wardrobe of *Succession*.

"Rayne, there you are!" Seraphina called, holding a wide-brimmed hat on her head as she marched over to greet us in a flowy linen dress. "The game's about to start." She bent over the stroller and tickled Elara. "Hello, beautiful."

My eyes searched for Hale. He paced what I assumed was a goal line as he strategized with several men about their plays. "How do they tell who's on which team?"

"They wear designated sweater vests. You'll see."

Remington sat at a round table shaded by a canvas umbrella. A brunch buffet of refreshments and fruit sat beneath a canopy several feet away. Hugo operated an omelet station to its right. I was definitely getting an omelet.

"So I guess you guys don't do soft pretzels and hot dogs."

"No, but we have beer," Phina joked, honestly believing those fancy German bottles represented some version of roughing it.

"Oh, a beer sounds nice," my mom said, pushing the stroller toward the refreshments.

I sat beside Remington, offering a cold, "Good morning."

"It's past eleven, Meyers. Morning's over."

"I was merely reporting that I had a good morning." I lifted my nose. "I'm guessing you can't say the same."

His head remained straight, his gaze focused on the field and hidden behind his Cartier glasses. "You have something you want to say to me?"

"Not particularly." I drew my cardigan over my chest and stared at the field. "I saw Odette leave last night."

"Leave it alone, Meyers."

I looked at him and slouched. "I really liked her, Remington."

"So did I. But a smart man knows when it's time to move on."

"Well, aren't you just a rolling stone."

"Moss is overrated."

A whistle blew, and Alphonse walked to the middle of the field. "Is he the ref?"

"Yes. Pay attention."

I watched the field as the men lined up. Argyle sweaters were passed out, some in navy blue with green diamonds, others in brown with burnt orange stripes. As the men suited up and adjusted their old driving hats, I laughed. "They look adorable."

"I'm sure they'd thrill at hearing themselves described in such a way."

If bean was a boy, I could totally see him wearing something similar for his first portraits. "How come you don't play?"

"I host. Besides, I can't run like I used to."

"Oh, I don't know. You seem to run around pretty well at parties, Remington."

"Don't make me fire you on vacation, Meyers."

Naomi sat down on the other side of Remington. "Here, Remy. So your stomach doesn't get upset from the vitamins."

I frowned as Hale's mom placed a plate of fruit and toast in front of Remington and lovingly draped a napkin over his lap. What in Satan's fresh hell was this?

"I can always tell when you're hungover." She set two capsules beside his plate.

"What are you giving him?" I oversaw all of Remington's medication, and he didn't need anything interacting with his prescriptions.

"It's just a little vitamin C and an immunity booster." She stole a strawberry off his plate and took a bite. "Mmm. The berries are so fresh. Taste."

I gaped in horror as she fed him the other half of her strawberry. He ate it right from her fingers, and then she sucked off a dribble of juice. Was no one else seeing this?

I banged my knee against Phina's as she shaded her eyes and watched the men line up. "Ouch!"

Angling my head toward her father and Naomi, I shot her a wide-eyed look.

"What's wrong with you, Rayne? Are you having some sort of fit?"

"Look at your dad and Naomi," I whispered through clenched teeth, and she glanced past me.

"So? They're always like that."

"*What?* No, they're not."

"Yes, they are." She looked back at the men.

"I've never seen them act like this together. They're being...gross."

She chuckled. "This is nothing. You've probably never noticed because Odette's always around. She's gone now. Just wait. It gets way worse. They'll end up in the same bed tonight."

"*What?*" Did Hale know about this?

"Relax, Rayne. He does this with all of them."

"What *all of them*? Who?"

"The moms."

"You mean he does this with your mom too?"

"And Barrett's. Ooh, they're about to start." She stood and clapped.

I also stood and threw out a two-fingered whistle that earned me several scowls from the older folks. I was so confused. How had I suddenly become Julia Roberts at the polo match in *Pretty Woman?* This was a football game, right?

A more refined whistle blew, and the men got into formation. Hale jogged over to the table and gave me a quick kiss. "Where's Elara?"

"She's getting a beer with her grandmother. Shouldn't you be out there?"

"I'm on the bench for now."

"Oh." I tugged at his sweater. "You look so dapper."

I glanced at the bulge below his belt. "They'll do."

"Good." He smacked my ass, and not discreetly.

"Ooh!" I corralled him away from the table. "I have to tell you something."

"What is it?"

I moved far enough away from the table that he could see what I was talking about without being overheard. "I just thought you should know your mom and dad are doing some pretty hardcore flirting."

He glanced over my shoulder and shook his head. "I'm not surprised. Odette left last night. Be grateful it's my mom and not Barrett's girlfriend."

"Hale!" I laughed, because that was pretty funny—and plausible.

"What? You going to pretend that's below him?"

"Well, I doubt she'd blow him."

"I said *be-low* him."

"Or that." I snorted. "Actually, I haven't seen McKinsley since last night." I sure hoped Barrett knew I was joking about drugging her.

"Just follow the money." He lifted his chin, and I followed his gaze to a group of older men. Barret's girlfriend was practically spoon-feeding that Captain Stubing dude.

"Does Barrett see this?"

"I think he's hoping one of them will take her off his hands."

"Oh, well, in that case, I'm in full support."

Two men careened into the dirt at our feet, and Hale ushered me back a few steps. My eyes widened.

"This is *tackle* football?"

"We're fashionable, Rayne, not fragile. I gotta get back." He kissed my cheek and jogged across the field while the ball wasn't in play.

I looked down at the two men wobbling to their feet. They laughed and patted each other on the back, then returned to their teams. Those grass stains were never coming out of those white pants.

The first half of the game was entertaining—until it wasn't. Football involved a lot of stopping and starting. Hale was a faster runner than I realized, and he'd scored two touchdowns. I cheered, as did Elara, but everyone else seemed content to ignore the game and sip tea.

"Come on, Xander!" Seraphina cheered, rising to her feet. "*Run! Run!*" The whistle blew, and she threw her hands in frustration. "He had that."

"So," I said as she returned to her seat.

"What did you two do yesterday when you left the house?"

She twisted her lips. "Nothing. We walked for a while, but he never even tried to hold my hand."

"Now that you had a chance to get to know him, do you like him?"

"Rayne, he's gorgeous. And Daddy seems impressed with him."

I pitied how desperately she wanted her father's approval. "Your dad wants to buy out his company, Phina. That's why he's interested in him."

"Oh, well, Xander's not selling. He told me so yesterday."

"Everything's for sale."

She laughed. "You're starting to sound like Hale."

I was actually quoting Remington, but Hale would agree with me.

There was a commotion, and Remington was on his feet. "Go! Run!"

Barrett had the ball and was closing in on the mark when another man charged him out of nowhere. He threw the ball, and Hale caught it. I was up and screaming for him to move when a body flew through the air and toppled him into the dirt.

I gasped. "Oh, my God."

Remington caught my arm. "He's okay."

Hale wasn't moving. The other guy pushed himself off Hale, and I recognized Xander's dark hair. "What the fuck?" I waited for Hale to sit up, but he didn't move. "I have to go to him."

Remington's hold tightened. "He's a big boy, Meyers. And you're pregnant. Sit down."

I looked back at the field, my lip trembling as the men huddled around Hale's sprawled body, making it hard to see. If he didn't get up in five seconds I was going out there.

Barrett walked over to his brother and laughed. Then he held out a hand and plucked him off the ground as if nothing happened. My heart spiked with relief, and I exhaled as Hale brushed the dirt off his pants and blew me a kiss.

Was he laughing? He could have broken his neck or worse.

Xander patted a hand on his back and pulled him into a headlock, swatting his wool cap against his chest. It must have been knocked off his head when he savagely tackled him to the ground.

I sat at the table and chewed my lip. I wanted to punch Xander right in the dick.

Hale returned to the table at half-time, but my nerves still hadn't settled and I didn't trust myself to talk without getting overly upset.

"What the hell were you thinking, letting him come at your blind spot like that?" Remington snapped. "Your wife doesn't need to see that in her condition."

Rather than tell his father to butt out, Hale's attention turned to me and laughed off my concern. "I'm fine."

I shoved him away when he tried to hug me. "I thought you were really hurt, Hale. What the hell's wrong with Xander? He didn't have to come at you that hard."

"It's how the game's played, baby. Believe me, I'm completely fine."

I scowled. How dare he minimize this to make me feel like I was overreacting? "There's mud on your shoes."

"It happens."

Who was this man?

Xander wandered over and Phina greeted him with a lemonade. When he smiled at me I scowled and turned my back on him.

"Rayne's upset with you," Hale explained.

"I couldn't tell." Xander winked when I gaped at him. "She gets annoyed with me so much I'm beginning to think she has a crush on me."

I nearly choked on my virgin julip. "Hardly."

Hale moved closer and put his hands on my shoulders, massaging the tension from my neck. I allowed it.

Xander watched us as Hale knelt in the grass behind my chair and whispered in my ear. "I keep thinking about last night. I want more."

I laughed because he was tickling my neck, but my stare never broke from Xander's. I swear, his nostrils flared before he abruptly turned and walked away.

"Whoa, get a room, you two," Phina said.

After the game, everyone lingered on the lawn, enjoying the fall foliage. When the sun started to fade, hot cider was served, and one by one, the guests wandered back to the houses to change for dinner.

I glanced at my phone, and Hale noted the time. "Has he landed yet?"

"I haven't gotten a text."

Tyler was supposed to be there for dinner, but his flight had been delayed so I wasn't sure when he would arrive. Hale arranged for Alphonse to pick him up whenever he landed.

"What do you say we grab a shower before he gets here?"

I was starting to get cold, so a shower sounded great. "Mom, can you stay with Elara for a while?"

"Of course."

We weren't far from the house, so it was an easy walk, but we only made it halfway there. "Come here." Hale pulled me behind one of the outbuildings that faced the woods.

"Hale, it's getting too cold."

"Just five minutes." He opened his pants and stroked his length. "Show me."

"Are you kidding? Here?"

"Baby, it's all I've thought about all day."

I looked left then right, making sure we were completely isolated. Then, I dropped the picnic blanket to the ground as he helped me lower to my knees. "You're so spoiled, it's ridiculous."

"I know, baby, but I can't help it." He cupped the back of my head, guiding my mouth to his cock. "You're the one addiction

I'll never give up." He fisted my hair, sliding to the back of my throat. "Fuck."

The scent of his body mingled with the grassy scent of earth that clung to his clothes and the sweet smell of chimney smoke nearby.

"That's it, baby. Nice and deep. Let me see those eyes while you take care of me."

I looked up at him, mouth full, hands balanced on his thighs.

"Fuck. That's it. That's my good wife." He rocked his hips forward, thrusting deeper. "You like my cock down your throat, don't you, baby?"

I moaned, and he pumped his hips faster.

"Show me how much you like it." His hand tightened in my hair, his hips thrusting as he cursed and sucked in a sharp breath, finishing faster than I expected. "Yes. Swallow it."

My throat was still working as he pulled me off the ground and pressed my back into the wooden building. "You're the sexiest fucking woman alive, Rayne. Do you know that?"

His tongue swept into my mouth, where I was sure he could taste his release. His fingers shoved into my cotton leggings, dipping into my panties to rub my clit. He pressed a finger inside of me, and I gasped. His tongue licked deeper as he turned his wrist, finding the perfect angle.

He pushed my shirt upward, exposing my round belly and full breasts. Shoving the lace cups of my bra to my ribs, he crouched and sucked my nipple into his mouth.

I cried out at the sharp bite of pleasure, my body more sensitive than usual. There hadn't been any more embarrassing nipple leaks since that first time, but he was sucking hard enough to possibly cause one.

"Hale..."

"Let it out, baby. I want you to come all over my hand."

Shutting my eyes, I tried not to think about the little control I had over my body and focused on the pleasure he delivered. My head tipped back, and I gasped. He sucked my engorged nipples into dark points and rubbed his palm along my clit until my legs trembled.

I clung to him as my knees went out. "Fuck, fuck, fuck, Hale, I'm coming!"

"I've got you, baby."

He fucked his fingers inside of me as I clutched his shoulders and bit my own hand to stop from screaming. He dropped to his knees, yanking my pants below my hips, and sucked my clit as hard as he'd sucked my nipples.

"Hale!" My fingers knotted in his hair as he pushed one climax into another. I was losing my grip on reality as much as I was losing the ability to stand.

"One more, baby."

"I can't."

"Please. Show me what a good wife you are. Show me how much you love it when I touch you." He looked up at me with those devastatingly dark, gunmetal eyes and dragged his tongue along my slit.

My hips reflexively cocked forward and I squeezed my eyes shut. He had me so sensitized it only took one lick. He successfully found the fucking center of my Tootsie Pop.

Everyone's Two-Faced

"Wait, so, you're sleeping with her?"

"Don't look so shocked, Ray."

But I was shocked. And, for the first time in a long time, I missed our old friend Elle, because she would have been shocked too. "Tyler, I thought you liked..."

He frowned. "Blondes?"

"Sure." We could go with that. If it was code for dick.

He shrugged. "I guess I don't have a preference." He scrolled to the next picture on his phone. "Here we are at the cliffs. Can you believe how blue the sky is in Colorado?"

"Wow." I took his phone and zoomed in on the girl. She was dressed from head to toe in earth tones, and her boots looked more masculine than anything I'd ever seen Tyler wear. I handed him back his phone. "So, where did you meet her."

"An app. Nothing interesting to report there." He passed me the fries, and I traded him the jalapeno poppers.

Hale was back at the main house with the plethora of guests who still had nowhere better to be. I told him I was spending the night on the couch catching up with Tyler. We started the night ordering takeout and looking for something to watch, but our attention span never got further than the Netflix menu.

Once the food arrived, we gave up and just started catching up. It had been three hours of updates, couch cuddles, and memories—a perfect BFF night in my opinion.

Lights trailed across the back wall. "Hale's back."

"Already? That was fast."

"Remington's place is literally on the property. Nothing's more than a four minute drive around here."

"Quaint."

"Or crowded."

Tyler couldn't believe how many people were here when I explained our strange

Thanksgiving with him. It felt more like a business retreat than a family holiday at times.

Hale's laughter carried up the steps with the sound of his footfalls and I frowned, because it didn't sound like he was alone.

"Incoming," I warned just as the front door opened.

Hale entered with Xander and Barrett on his tail. I adjusted my blanket for privacy. Not that I cared how Barrett saw me, but Xander was an outsider.

"Hey, Tyler!" Barrett greeted, crossing the room to shake Ty's hand. "Good to see you."

"You too." Tyler looked up at Xander and cleared his throat. "Hi. I'm Tyler, Rayne's friend."

"Nice to meet you. I'm Xander, Rayne's current chosen adversary."

Tyler laughed in a strangely enchanted way. "I haven't heard Rayne mention you before."

I waved away his words. "He's new and unimportant."

"Ouch." Xander placed a hand on his chest and feigned pain. "And here I thought we were making progress."

I popped a fry in my mouth. "What would give you that idea?"

He shrugged and rubbed his jaw thoughtfully. "After the game today, I was walking back to the house, having a peaceful moment of reflection, and I said, *God, does she hate me?* Then I heard the faintest echo of a woman—and, you know, she even sounded like you."

My mouth snapped shut. What was he getting at? My gaze drifted to Hale and back to Xander. "You're lying."

He held up his hand like a Boy Scout. "God's honest truth. I said, *God, give me a sign. Does Rayne hate me?* Then I heard the echoing reply cry out *yes, yes, yes.* So I asked, *God, will she ever grow to like me?* And I heard the same reply, *yes, yes, yes.*"

My eyes widened. That was the last time I did it with Hale outdoors. "I hate you."

"See, I know that. But I've seen signs from above that it won't always be that way between us...Rayne."

Barrett cleared his throat, and Tyler gaped at me. "Ray, did you and Hale get busy in the woods?"

"No," I lied. "Not according to Clinton's definition." I scowled at Xander.

"Come on, Barrett, I'll get you that suit jacket," Hale said, leaving us there with intrusive Xander. I had never met a man with worse timing.

"So, where are you from, Xander?"

"Brookline, Massachusetts."

Tyler raised a brow. "Where the Kennedys are from?"

Xander grinned, impressed by Ty's trivial recall. "Correct. Not a lot of people know that."

"I went through a minor obsession with the Kennedys."

He laughed. "Then you'll get a kick out of this. My great grandparents came from Wexford."

"No way!" When I looked at Tyler confused, he explained, "JFK's paternal lineage comes from Wexford, Ireland."

This was why I had a hard time imagining him dating a woman. What straight man knew stuff like that?

"As a matter of fact," Xander continued, "my mom's parents and the eldest Kennedys used to play bridge together."

I frowned. "I thought you didn't have family."

"I don't." He glanced at Tyler. "We had a falling out several years ago."

"I'm sorry."

Xander waved away his apology as he lowered to sit on the arm of the loveseat, making himself right at home. "Don't be. I'm not."

Hale and Barrett returned, suit jacket in hand. "What did you guys end up watching?" Hale asked.

"Nothing. We just talked and ate."

Hale glanced at Tyler. "Did she give you her list of baby names?"

"You have names?" Tyler's face beamed with curiosity—not the straightest response to possible baby names, but whatever. "Spill!"

I tucked my feet under my legs and cradled the basket of fries. "Nothing's set in stone yet. But for a boy, I like River or Quest, and for a girl, I like Sage or Harlow."

He looked back at Hale. "I'm scared."

I shoved him. "Why are you scared, dork?"

"Because those are names that you'd typically make fun of."

"I would not."

He looked at Barrett. "What's your girlfriend's name?"

"McKinsley. And she's not my girlfriend."

"Yeah, okay," I mumbled.

Tyler held up a silencing finger. "Did Ray make fun of her name?"

"What's your point?" I snapped.

"My point is, those names are a little more *new age* than I expected. But I really like Sage."

"It's cute, right?"

"Very."

"Do you have kids, Tyler?" Xander's question caught me off guard, but didn't surprise me. I often caught him staring at my stomach. Maybe procreation confused him.

"Me? God, no." Tyler laughed and I frowned at his look of repulsion.

"But you like kids."

"I like *your* kid. I can handle kids in small increments, but I'm not interested in long term investments."

"Charming. And to think I was going to ask you to be godfather."

"Hey!" Barret objected. "I'm the godfather."

"You're already an uncle and Elara's godfather."

"So? I can be both."

A horn beeped, and Xander looked out the window. "Your girl's here."

"Shit." Barrett slipped into Hale's jacket.

"See you guys later." He pointed at me and Tyler. "I'm the godfather."

When I looked back at Tyler, I shook my head.

Hale dropped onto the cushion beside me and stole a fry from the basket in my lap. "Let's put something on. Xander, you want some fries?"

What was he doing? Those were my fries and this was mine and Tyler's night. There was no Xander space here.

"Sure." He slid fully onto the loveseat and took my fries. He just took the whole basket as if he paid for them.

Hale looped an arm around my shoulder and pulled me closer as I stared in stunned silence.

When he adjusted the blanket, I asked, "Can I talk to you for a moment?"

Hale finally read the confusion on my face. "Sure."

I handed Tyler the remote. "Put something on." Hale followed me into the kitchen, and I turned on him the moment we were alone. "What are you doing?"

"What do you mean?"

"You're crashing my couch time with Tyler."

"Is that a problem?"

"For you, no. For Xander, yes."

"Rayne, he's not that bad."

"Hale, he's been hitting on me since the moment I met him." Hale usually had a jealous temper, but this guy kept evading his radar. I didn't get it. "You didn't even say anything when he claimed to hear us having sex earlier!"

He laughed. "He was teasing you."

"He's flirting!"

"No, he's not."

I scoffed. "You should hear the shit he says when you're not around."

"What's he saying?"

I scoffed again. "You know.... *Rayne*....and... *See you tomorrow...*"

"I'll fucking kill him," he said sarcastically.

"You don't get it! It's the way he says things!"

"With words?"

"Oh, forget it. And, B-T-dubs, he didn't just hear us fooling around today. He also watched us kissing on Thanksgiving."

"The nerve!" He laughed. "Did you ever consider he might just be envious, Rayne? We're happy, and he's single. There's nothing wrong with looking when you see a happy couple."

"I'm telling you, Hale, something's different about him."

"You're absolutely right, but I'm one hundred percent certain he's not hitting on you."

I rolled my eyes. "Because you know and see all?"

"No, because Xander is gay."

"You men are so—I'm sorry, he's what now?"

"Xander is gay."

I blinked, my brain a little slow on the computing part. "It sounded like you said he was gay."

"Exactly."

"How do you know?"

"Because he told me."

"He told you he's gay? When? How?"

"We were having a drink, and the other guys weren't around, so he told me."

"He just blurted out, *I'm gay*?"

"Pretty much."

I thought about Tyler, who had a million different opportunities to come out to me, but never did. "Well, I guess you just get everything then, don't you?"

"I'm sorry. Are you upset that he's not hitting on you?"

"No. I'm just..." I didn't know what I was, so I threw up my hands in frustration. "This pregnancy has my instincts all messed up." Then it finally occurred to me. "Oh my God, wait! He's into *you!*" I knew I sensed a red flag! I was just reading it wrong.

Hale shrugged. "Maybe, but he realizes I'm straight and happily married."

"He gives me *Hand That Rocks The Cradle Vibes.*" I protectively rubbed my belly. "I don't trust him."

"Xander's a good guy, Rayne. He's not trying to steal me or our baby from you. We're working on a few business ideas together. That's all."

Another red flag. "Hale, you can't."

"Sure, I can. His company's in trouble and I can help."

"But the only reason you know his company's in trouble is because I told you."

"It's not like you had confidential information, Rayne. I asked, and he confirmed. He's never going to sell to my dad."

"Why not?"

"Because he's a prick."

"Which one?"

Hale laughed.

"It's not funny, Hale. I work for your dad. You might think you're screwing him over, but I'm a part of this."

"Baby, Xander already told my father he's not interested. Their meeting's been postponed indefinitely."

"I can't believe you."

"Rayne, there is nothing underhanded here. This is how these things work out."

"Don't patronize me, Hale. You used Thanksgiving to schmooze a business deal, because it was one more way to stick it to your dad. I thought we were past this."

"Rayne—"

"No." I evaded his touch when he reached for me. "You know you did something wrong, and you did it knowing I was involved. I'm mad at you and you gave him my fries." I pulled open the door to walk out on him then immediately closed it, deciding to stay in the kitchen a while longer.

"What's the matter?"

"They're making out."

I Hate Goodbyes

"**W**hat do we do?" I pressed my back to the kitchen door and looked up at Hale.

Holy shit, they move fast. One second Tyler's on the couch and Xander's on the love seat. Next minute they're sitting together, groping man chest, with their tongues down each other's throats. He really was gay!

I was more shocked about Xander than Tyler. I always suspected Ty liked men, but he never came out and said it.

"Oh, my God." I covered my mouth. "Ty has a girlfriend!"

Hale's face was comical as he blew out a breath. "We could make popcorn."

"Huh?"

"Popcorn has a strong smell and it's noisy. It'll remind them we're here."

I cracked the door and squeaked, quickly shutting it. "They are all over each other!"

Hale went to the cabinet and pulled out a pot. Then he loudly dumped kernels into it and turned on the burner. "That should only take a minute."

"They're on my blanket." I cracked the door again and gasped. "Hale, look at this!"

"I'm good."

"You're missing out. They're really going to town. Guys just get right to it, don't they?"

He peeked over my head. "So much for Ty's girlfriend."

"I know!" I let the door close. "This means he'll finally come out of the closet. Thank God, because the secrecy was killing me."

"It was *his* secret, Rayne."

"Yes, but I've felt the weight of it since tenth grade. This is huge!"

The kernels started to pop and the scent of buttery popcorn soon filled the air. Once we had it in a bowl and ready to go, we carried everything to the door, making as much noise as possible.

"Act casual," I said, looking back at Hale.

I pushed open the door and yelled behind me, "Babe, grab me a water."

Tyler sat stiffly on the couch and Xander paced as he fumbled with his shirt as if trying to hide whatever was going on in his pants. I hid a smile because this was so much better than the creepy vibes I'd been getting all week from him.

"Did you figure out something to watch?" I asked Tyler as I plopped onto the sofa next to him.

He cleared his throat. "That Will Ferrell movie looks okay."

I looked at Xander, but he still wasn't facing us. Hale came out with a few bottles of water.

I put the popcorn on the coffee table. "Oh, shoot," I said unconvincingly. "I forgot my ginger ale. Tyler, will you come help me find it."

He frowned. "You need help finding your —*ah!*" I pinched him and he got my message. Rubbing his arm, he scowled. "Let's go find your ginger ale, you maniac."

I left Hale to deal with Xander. The

second we reached the kitchen I turned on Tyler. "You're gay!"

"What?"

"Enough already with the denying," I moaned. "You're gay. You like boys. I saw you kissing Xander!"

"You saw us?"

"It's not like you were hiding."

He flushed and scrubbed his hands over his face, groaning.

I frowned, wondering why this was so stressful for him. "Are you upset about the girlfriend?"

He stilled then winced. "Fuck!" Pacing to the island, he forked his fingers through his hair. "I don't know what happened."

"I do. You made out with a boy."

He glared at me.

"What? There's nothing wrong with that."

"I know. It's just..." He blew out a breath. "We were sitting there talking about the Kennedys then the next thing I knew, he was looking at me in this strange way. I got all flustered. He moved closer."

I grinned and nodded. "Then he stuck his tongue down your throat."

"Don't be crass, Ray."

"You were just dry-humping a random dude on my couch, Ty. Are we going to pretend either of us is demure?"

He pinched the bridge of his nose. "So not cutesy."

"Aw, you are gay! This is wonderful!"

He frowned at me. "What do you mean *some random dude.* He's Hale's friend."

"Not really."

"He's here."

"So are twenty other strangers. The Davenports do Thanksgiving all wrong."

"So, you don't know him?"

"Five minutes ago I didn't even like him."

"Great."

"Ty, it's fine. He might be a bit of a prick, but anyone with eyes can see he's good looking. You get your jollies! You deserve this!"

"I have a girlfriend."

"Your girlfriend looks like a lesbian."

"Rude."

I shrugged. "As a beard, you should be able to recognize another beard. You told me you liked her hiking boots. That's the only thing you mentioned about her appearance. What does that say to you, Ty?"

"It says she has good taste in boots."

"Have you kissed her."

"Yes. I'm not a monk, Ray."

I went to the fridge and grabbed a can of ginger ale. Popping the top, I said, "I honestly believed it was this big secret you've been hiding your entire life, but you still seem confused."

"It's called fluidity, Rayne. It's not as simple as you think."

"It's also not that complicated."

"What do you mean?"

I shrugged. "I'm straight. I know I'm straight. I like Hale, and I like having a monogamous marriage. Can you claim the same?"

He met my stare. "No."

"Then why stress over it? Be gay or be bi or pan or whatever you want to label yourself. The label doesn't matter, Ty. I love you any way you come. And I never want you to feel like you have to hide your true self from me."

He reached across the counter and squeezed my hand. "Thank you."

I smiled. "Now, we can finally talk about it."

"What do you mean, *finally*?"

"Ty, I suspected you liked guys since we were kids. You were obsessed with Jimmy Ferguson and made us go to all the football games."

He blushed then his expression turned apologetic. "Part of me was scared—not of you or what you'd say, but of what my life would become once I admitted who I actually was. The world's easy for straight guys. I wasn't ready to give that up."

"It doesn't have to be difficult, Ty."

"I know. But you also can't guarantee me it'll be easy, Rayne."

I squeezed his hand. "No matter what it is, I'm here for you."

"Thank you."

I glanced at the door. "So...is Xander, like...the first guy you kissed?"

He blew out a long breath and laughed to himself. Then he met my stare. "He's fucking hot."

"Yeah, the assholes usually are."

"Is he an asshole?"

I shrugged. "Hale says no, but I'm not so sure. I might have been misreading him."

"Fuck, Ray, what am I doing?" He rubbed his forehead. "This is so unlike me. I don't even know that guy. I don't just go around kissing people. I went out with Carla four times before I kissed her."

"Who's Carla?"

"My girlfriend!"

"Oh. Right. I keep forgetting about her."

"Tell me about it."

We both glanced at the door, and I sighed. "We should probably go back out there."

Tyler hesitated. "How am I supposed to act, now? I've never been in a situation like this before."

I laughed. "Act normal, you weirdo. Just go out there and be cool."

"It's pretty bad when you're the one giving me behavioral advice."

"Yeah, well, I've had a lot of experience with awkwardness. I know how these things go. Just walk out there and act like nothing happened. Let him take the lead."

He nodded. "Okay. I can do that. Let him take the lead."

"Ready?" When he nodded again, I pushed the door open. Hale and Xander looked up at us and I waved up my ginger ale can. "Found my soda."

We settled onto the couch—me beside Hale and Tyler to my left. Xander sat alone on the loveseat, his stare glued to the television.

Hale's phone pinged, and he glanced at it, but went back to selecting the movie.

"Who's texting you?"

"It's Phina."

My eyes widened. Someone was going to have to break the news to Hale's sister.

The movie started, and Hale lowered the lights. The sexual tension completely distracted me. I kept watching to see if Xander looked at Tyler. Then Tyler would look at me as if I was doing something wrong. At this pace, he was never going to get the guy.

I decided to meddle. Stretching my arms over my head, I yawned loudly. "Wow, I'm exhausted."

Xander looked at me, and Tyler glared. Hale fixed the blanket and pulled me closer to make me more comfortable. I waited about thirty minutes—just enough time to get the boys thoroughly invested in the movie plot—then I announced I was going to bed.

My plan went swimmingly. Tyler was staying the night, so there was no reason for Xander to leave before the movie was over. Hale was following me to bed, and I purposefully dimmed the lamps on our way up the steps.

The following morning, Tyler's room was

empty the next morning, and there was no sign of him or Xander. I had s

amed when I found Tyler making coffee in yesterday's clothes! "Sooooo?" I sidled up to him with my empty mug as we watched Hale's fancy machine percolate.

"I need coffee first." He smelled like Xander.

"Oh my God, the suspense is killing me, Ty! I need details. Did you sleep with him? Was it good? Are you pregnant?"

He ignored me and stared at the kettle as the coffee slowly dripped. I tapped my foot, impatiently waiting. The second it finished brewing, I yanked the pot free and filled his mug.

"There. Talk."

He poured in some cream and slowly stirred, hiding a smirk as he brought the cup to his mouth at a glacial pace and sipped. "Mmm. Coffee's good."

"I will burn you."

"Fine." He set down his cup and sighed. "It was incredible."

"Did you have the sex?"

"It was better than sex. We stayed up all night talking and drinking wine." He laughed. "I think I'm still drunk."

"You just...talked?"

"Well, we did other stuff, but we mostly talked. He's a fascinating guy, Ray. And he's cool with taking things slow." Tyler blushed and dropped his gaze to blow into his coffee.

My eyes narrowed. "What aren't you telling me?"

"Nothing."

That was clearly a lie. "Did you give him a handy?"

"No." But the flush on his cheeks said otherwise.

"Ah-ha! You got one, though, didn't you?"

"Fine. Yes. But could you not make a thing of it? He's coming here to take me to breakfast in an hour."

I melted. "You guys are going on a date."

"It's just breakfast," he said, his tone the complete opposite of my swoony one. "You and Hale and Elara can come."

"No, I don't want to intrude. Besides, we have the family photo shoot later today."

"Cute."

"I know. We're adorable." I set my mug in the sink because I wasn't supposed to drink caffeine anyway. "You're still able to photograph us, right."

"Of course."

"Okay, then I need to shower. Hale's mom said she'd do my hair and makeup. But you two have fun, and I'll get all the details when you come back."

"Ray," he called, before I left kitchen.

I paused and looked back, but he didn't say anything. We both smiled, and I read the joy in his eyes. "I know, Ty. I know."

He bit his lip, looking happier than I'd seen him in long time. "Yeah. Okay, go get ready for your pictures."

I wasn't thrilled about my clothing options so I asked Seraphina to come over and help me put something together for the shoot that afternoon.

"I really should design a maternity line," she commented, also frustrated with my options.

"I don't think that's the solution. I'm only pregnant for a few more months."

"You might have other kids." She flipped through my closet. "Or I might have one."

I stilled. "What are you talking about?"

"Oh, I don't know. Things can move fast when you find the right guy. You know how it goes. You and Hale got married in a New York Minute."

Was she implying that Xander might be the right guy? Because he wasn't. But I wasn't going to be the one to break that news to Seraphina.

Elara and Hale were picture perfect by the time Tyler returned from breakfast. I, on the other hand, looked bloated and puffy and tired.

"You look great," Ty argued. "Naomi did an amazing job with your hair and makeup.

"I'll just hold Elara to hide my clothes."

"Isn't the whole point to show off the baby bump?"

"Who knows what the point is with these things? Like we're ever just wandering through an autumn field dressed in our Sunday best."

"Would you be in a better mood if I gave you my leftovers from breakfast?"

"Maybe. What'd you have?"

"French toast—"

"Ooh, yes, please!" I took the box from him.

"Don't get it on your clothes or mess up your lipstick!"

The photoshoot was adorable. It had all the autumn flare a family could ask for, and Tyler knew exactly what we wanted. Afterwards, he took his laptop to a local coffee shop where I couldn't hover, and worked on the edits. That evening, when he showed me the proofs, I was obsessed.

"Look at this one!"

"You look *fabulous*," Tyler gushed.

I laughed. "You hook up with one guy and you're using words like *fabulous*?"

"Is it too much?"

I patted his hand. "Not at all. Don't let anyone ever make you second guess yourself, Ty. And if some people think you're 'too much,' then they just aren't your person or your people."

He sighed. "Is it just me, or has pregnancy made you wiser?"

"It's not pregnancy. It's being with someone who loves and accepts me just the way I am."

I selected all the proofs and moved them into the cart. "Done. What do I owe you?"

"Nothing."

"Don't be a jerk."

"I'm not. A jerk would make you pay."

"Tyler, if you don't let us pay for your work I'm not accepting a single portrait. And then I'm going to be sad, because some of those pictures of Elara are amazing and I need them on my desk at work. Do you wanna make a pregnant woman cry?"

He sighed. "You were easier to control when you were broke."

"I know. No discounts, either. You charge us full price."

Another formal dinner was scheduled at Remington's that night and it would be the last of the trip. Sunday would consist of packing and goodbyes, but to be honest, I missed home, so I was okay with how things were wrapping up.

As we bundled up to drive over to Remington's I could tell Tyler was nervous. He fussed with his hair and obsessively worried if his clothes were wrinkled.

"I should have ironed. I'm never satisfied when I steam my shirts."

"For the love of God, you look fine, Tyler. Hale! If you don't feed me soon I'm going to get cranky!"

Hale came down the steps empty handed. "Elara's staying home."

"What? Why?"

"She said shit again and she's never going to learn if there aren't consequences."

That made sense. "Is she staying with my mom or yours?"

"Yours."

"I'm sure she'll really feel Daddy's wrath when Grandma Penny's giving her ice cream and letting her stay up late to watch Frozen for the thousandth time," I mumbled.

"What?"

"I said I love you."

"Oh, you're ready." I gave him a cheeky smile.

Tyler returned to the foyer in a different shirt. "I went with the brown one."

"Great. Let's go." I handed Hale the keys. "Xander's probably waiting."

Hale stilled, so we all stopped and looked at him expectantly. Sometimes getting out of the house was so much more complicated than it needed to be.

"What are we doing?"

Regret flashed in Hale's eyes as he looked at Tyler. "Xander left."

Tyler's expression fell. "What?"

"He had an early meeting tomorrow and a long flight."

My jaw gaped. "Are you kidding me? He didn't even say goodbye! Gah! I knew he was an asshole! What a dick!"

"Dick!" Elara's voice echoed from the

stairs as she scooched down step by step after my mom.

"Nice, Rayne." Hale picked up Elara. "What did we say about repeating bad words?"

She immediately looked repentant. "It's bad."

"Good girls don't say bad words."

Man, did I get a different speech from him...

"This is why you aren't coming with us tonight. I don't want to hear that kind of language from you again, Elara. Understand?"

"Yes, Daddy." She grabbed his nose, and he handed her off to my mother.

I looked at Tyler. "You okay?"

"Fine." There had never been a more unconvincing fine.

I gave him a sad smile, wishing there was more I could do. "For what it's worth, I'm sorry."

"Yeah. Me too." He walked out the door, which was code for not wanting to talk about it.

When we arrived at Remington's, Tyler was somber. I could tell he was second-guessing everything, and I wanted to punch Xander in the dick for hurting my friend.

How did you have a talk-all-night connection, breakfast in the morning, and then ghost without a goodbye? I was glad we weren't doing business with him next week because I didn't want to see him ever again.

I wasn't even sure if Hale should work with him now. He was obviously undependable.

As predicted, Naomi took a time machine right back into Remington's bed. It was weird, especially because no one acknowledged the weirdness.

"Are they getting back together? Don't you think it's a bad idea? They got a divorce for a reason."

Hale didn't want to talk about it. "It's a holiday weekend, Rayne. They're grown adults. They probably just wanted something easy to get through Thanksgiving."

"Your father is the last person I'd call easy."

"My mom's not easy, either, Rayne. Let them figure it out."

Tyler and my mother left for the airport before breakfast the following day, so we headed to Remington's, where Marta was most likely preparing something to eat. I didn't know what Naomi was doing, but she lived only in New Jersey, so technically, she could drive home if she missed her flight. I had a feeling Remington was going to ask her to stay.

I was just sipping my morning decaf and considering what a mostly peaceful family-ish getaway this had been when all hell broke out. Remington's voice boomed from the study, and Hale snapped back in an irritated tone.

I took a deep breath and exhaled, looking up at the ceiling as if some supernatural force up there might send me strength. "Well," I said to Elara, "It's been a while since we've had a good ol' family brawl."

"Shit," she said.

I twisted my lips. "My thoughts exactly."

Right on cue, Marta appeared with Elara's coat. "I thought I should take *Princesa* for a walk."

"Good idea." I lifted her from the high chair and dusted the cheerios off her clothes.

As soon as they were gone, I went to investigate the situation. Those two could fight about the most ridiculous things. It was anyone's guess what triggered this argument. Unfortunately, I had a hunch about the cause.

"He was my target!" Remington blared.

"You knew that, and you worked him over anyway."

"I didn't work him over. I listened to him. Something you never learned to do!"

"You listened to him," Remington muttered disparagingly, swatting his words away. "You saw an opportunity, and you took it, knowing full well that I had my eye on his company first."

"What if I did?"

Uh-oh. I stepped into the room hoping if they saw me they'd act more civilized toward each other.

"Are you going to tell me you would have done differently if the shoe was on the other foot?" Hale challenged.

"When are you going to let this rivalry go?"

"My disapproval of how you live your life and conduct your business is not a rivalry. It's a direct result of your selfish behavior!"

"Everything I did, I did for my family."

"Is that what you told yourself when you fucked over your own son, *Dad.*"

"I made a mistake but your life is still better for it!"

Hale scoffed. "You're unbelievable. The way you twist your shitty behavior so you can take credit for any positive outcomes..." He threw up his hands. "Sometimes I think even you believe your own lies."

"It's not a lie if it's true."

"And I did nothing, right?" Hale stormed. "It was all you? You hired her. You brought her into my life."

Remington held up his hands in surrender. "Do you expect me to argue? I did hire her."

"All right, you two, that's enough," I said, knowing the next accusation would likely involve Elara and that would not go over well.

"*You,*" Remington said in a tone he'd never taken with me before, "betrayed me."

I drew back. "Excuse me?"

"I had you research a potential buyout, and you told a known competitor what we had planned."

"I told Hale, your son."

"You told him, knowing full well he'd take the first opportunity to fuck me over!"

"Hey, take it easy," Hale snapped.

"Remington, I did no such thing."

"Did you tell him about Xander Landry?"

"Yes, but only because we talk about our day—"

"And did you share that I wanted to buy out his company?"

"I mentioned that his company was in trouble—"

"Then you betrayed me!"

The lash of his temper was so sharp tears pricked my eyes.

"Hey! Take it down a notch," Hale growled, coming to stand protectively in front of me. "Xander was at the dinner party on Wednesday night. *I* approached *him* after he approached Rayne. This had nothing to do with you."

"This is my house!" Remington bellowed, slamming his fist on the desk. "It has everything to do with me!"

"Remington, settle down—"

"Do not tell me to settle down, Meyers!"

I drew back again, shocked he would speak to me that way. My chin trembled as I stared at his red face. My main concern was for his heart and his blood pressure. "Don't yell at me."

He shook his head and dropped his volume. "I always knew this would happen."

My vision blurred. "What are you talking about?"

"Your interests are divided. I can't trust you."

I gaped at him. I would have been less shocked if he'd slapped me. "Remington, stop. You're being ridiculous."

"Ridiculous? That buyout would have made this family millions, but you and your husband—"

"Enough!" Hale stormed. "Rayne had nothing to do with my actions. I approached Xander. I heard him out, and he and I came to an understanding. Rayne wasn't even there. She's blameless in this."

A tear fell past my lashes as I stared at Remington in shock. "How could you?" I rasped. My chin trembled, but I said what I needed to say. "Is that what you honestly believe, Remington? That you can't trust me?"

He knocked a box of tissues forward with his knuckles and turned away from me. "Pull yourself together, Meyers."

"No, you look at me and answer me. Is that what you believe?"

Remington slowly met my stare but didn't have the guts to answer. Hale stood protectively by my side but didn't interrupt.

I took a step closer to his desk. "I would never knowingly betray you or do anything to hurt you, Remington. I have put you before my husband and child more times than I can count. The fact that you can make such an accusation—" My throat closed around my words, and my heart seemed to shake in my chest. "I just can't believe you."

"It's okay, baby." Hale touched my back when I could barely get the words past the lump in my throat. "You don't have to do this."

"No, it's not okay." I straightened my spine and lifted my chin. "Remington, I quit."

Screw Santa

"Is that another one?" I asked, as I grunted and stretched, pulling the wrapping paper over the gift.

Hale read the card. "Looks like it."

"Send it back."

It had been four weeks, and Remington still hadn't apologized or tried to make things right. He had, however, sent numerous gifts to Elara, posed as Christmas presents, but she hadn't accepted a single one. If he wanted to play the doting grandfather card, he could bring his mean ass to our front door and act like a decent human being.

I whined when I realized I left the tape out of reach.

"I don't know why you insist on wrapping everything yourself. We have people for—"

"I am not going to let *people* wrap my daughter's Christmas presents, Hale. It's the parents' job. Now, hand me the fucking tape."

My sciatica was killing me, despite my ass going numb an hour ago. I would have moved to a more comfortable position, but I couldn't get up.

Snatching the tape from his hand, I snapped, "You could help."

"I am helping. I did all the little things in her stocking."

The paper ripped as I tightened it around the corner of the box. "Son of a!" I flopped back in defeat. "I give up!"

Hale chuckled and crawled across the carpet to me, shoving the gift away. "The magic of Christmas is coming down the stairs and finding everything done, baby. Let me take care of all of this for you."

My body slid down the sofa until my back was on the floor. I needed a hug, yet I was being as approachable as a cactus. "I'm sorry."

"It's okay. Holidays are stressful."

"But I don't want them to be. Christmas is supposed to be fun."

"And it will be."

"Gah! You have an answer for everything."

"And you talk too much." He leaned over my swollen body and kissed me.

"Mmm, you taste like merlot." I missed wine. Especially when wrapping presents. Maybe that was what was wrong with this picture.

"You should take another sip." He lowered his mouth to mine, making slow, sensual dips with his tongue and teasing a laugh out of me.

"Flirt." I arched my back and it pinched. "Ah!"

"You okay?"

"Yeah—" I coughed as acid rushed up my esophagus. "Wait." I pushed his mouth away and rolled to my side with the grace of a beached whale. "I can't do this on the floor."

Hale sat up and pulled me with him. I was like one of those untippable punching bags that wobbled into position. "Couch?"

I scrunched my nose. "I think bed."

He looked disappointed. Probably because every time we went to bed all I wanted to do was sleep. But he pulled me to my feet anyway.

"Ah! Leg cramp!"

Hale looked at me with concern. "What do you need?"

"I need to not be pregnant anymore!" Cradling my back, I wobbled to the stairs. "Can you clean that up so Elara doesn't see it?"

"I...I thought..." He glanced back at the unwrapped presents and wrapping paper and sighed. "Sure."

"Thanks, babe."

I was conked out when Hale came to bed. I vaguely recalled him kissing my temple and trying to cop a feel, but he gave up when it felt like necrophilia.

The following day, he had to fly to Chicago. I finished my fall semester, and with no current employment, my schedule was wide open.

We kept Andrew on full-time because I was exhausted, and we didn't want to lose him, but he mostly hung out in the guest house until I called him in to take over.

As Christmas approached, my emotions gained on me. Why couldn't Remington just apologize? Miles and Marta both told me he was miserable since I'd quit. I missed my job. I missed him—the stubborn butt face. And I missed having an outside purpose. But Hale was right. I needed to stick to my boundaries, and Remington had crossed a line.

It wasn't just about him trusting me. It was about him respecting my life and my personal time the same way I respected his. It was difficult standing up to him. But the hardest part of all of this seemed to be my pregnancy. Remington was like a father to me. Pregnancy was a major milestone and I wanted him to be a part of the process. Every time I thought of something I wanted to tell him or ask him, I was reminded that he wasn't there and it was hard not to cry.

"Let's check the advent calendar, Peanut."

When I was little, my mom always bought me one of those paper calendars that hid a piece of chocolate behind a tiny paper door. The candy was never good, but that wasn't the point. It was the tradition of opening it each morning and counting down the days until Christmas with my mom.

"Let's count. How many more days?" I pointed and Elara repeated my words. "One, two, three, four, five." I helped her pull open the door.

Of course, Elara's advent calendar wasn't

made of paper. When I explained the tradition to Hale, he had a local woodworker custom-build a Victorian dollhouse for his daughter. It had shutters, interior lighting, and even a mechanism that made the chimney puff when a button was pressed. And there was no crappy chocolate in hers. He had every little box stuffed with a small prize.

"What is it?"

She popped open the small door and pulled a small, plush dog from the box and held it out to me. "Doggy."

"Ooh! What's the doggy say?"

"*Woof-woof!*" she barked, racing into Hale's empty office to show her father what she found. "Daddy?"

I wobbled after her. "Daddy's not here, Peanut."

"Daddy gone?"

"Daddy's gone. He'll be back tomorrow." My hand cradled my back, and I frowned. The kink in my back returned and I massaged the area.

The doorbell rang, and I sighed, pulling the door to Hale's office shut. "Come on." I corralled Elara to the front door. When I opened it, there was another pile of boxes, and the brown delivery truck was driving away. "Hey! Wait!"

"Wait!" my mini-me echoed.

"Damn it."

"Damn it."

I looked at her sharply, but she only flashed me a cheeky smile.

With a sigh, I checked the labels. As expected, they were all from Remington. "Your grandfather's a coward."

I spent the next hour stewing on the couch. Elara played with her doggy while The Backyardigans sang on the television. The longer I sat there, the angrier I became, until I finally texted Andrew, requesting him to come watch Elara.

I backed my Jeep up to the front porch and loaded all the boxes into the back.

"Rayne, should you be lifting them?"

"They're not that heavy."

Andrew rushed to pick up the last few and loaded them into the Jeep. "What are they?"

"Gifts from Remington. I'm taking them back." I wiped the sweat off my brow and tried to remember where I put my keys. They were still in the ignition.

When I reached Remington's house, I

burst in without knocking and dumped three boxes onto the foyer floor.

Marta appeared in a rush with a dust rag in her hands. "Niña, what are you doing?"

"Is he here?"

"Mr. Davenport is in the den."

"Good." I walked back out to the car and grabbed another armful of packages.

"Meyers, what the hell is this?" Remington barked when I dumped the next armful onto his floor.

"Stop sending presents to our house, Remington."

"Those aren't for you. They're for Elara."

"If you want to give your granddaughter gifts, have the decency to deliver them in person. You live one mile from her."

"God damn it, Meyers, this can't be good for you." He followed me out to the Jeep where I proceeded to gather more packages. "You're as stubborn as a goat. Put them down!" He followed me back inside, and I let the boxes fall.

"You're as stubborn as a coward."

Miles appeared, and Marta quickly tidied the boxes into piles so they weren't all over the foyer.

I shook off a dizzy spell as I bent over to

drop another box onto the floor. "You can't even bring yourself to apologize or admit when you're wrong. Well, guess what? We're a package deal. You can't buy her off! If you want to be in her life, you need to treat her parents right—including your son. I'm sick and tired of this petty rivalry between you two. There are other people impacted by your childishness, and some people just want to live a normal life with normal—" I sucked in a sharp breath.

Remington stilled. "What is it?" He yelled for the housekeeper, "Marta!"

Marta appeared as Remington ushered me to a bench.

"I'm fine." I massaged the pinched nerve in my back. Tightness stitched across my abdomen, and I winced.

"She's not fine. Something's wrong. Where's Hale?"

"He's in Chicago." My face tensed as another cramp contracted around my abdomen. Something wasn't right. I looked up at Remington, too afraid to be angry anymore. "Call a doctor."

He flew into action. The next thing I knew, I was sitting in the emergency room getting a lecture about something called prodromal labor, similar to Braxton Hicks, but more painful.

"It's all that damn spicy food you've been eating."

"Actually," the doctor corrected Remington, "Prodromal labor isn't caused by diet. It can, however, be triggered by stress or anxiety."

I glared at my father-in-law. "Are you happy now?"

"I haven't seen you in a month!"

"And look what's happened!"

My phone buzzed, and I looked at the doctor apologetically. Hale was going to implode if I didn't answer. "Go ahead," she said.

"Hale?" I brought the phone to my ear. "I'm on my way. Have you talked to the doctor? Did they find anything—"

"Hale, Hale, calm down. I'm fine. The baby's fine. It was false labor." I quickly informed him of everything I'd been told over the last hour, but he insisted on coming home anyway.

Unfortunately, prodromal labor could last several days. The doctor recommended reducing stress and distracting myself with music, television, or a warm bath if the contractions started again.

When Hale returned home, he was a mess. I was certain he spent the entire flight home researching false labor. He kept stuffing pillows around me like I might break, and he made me drink copious amounts of water to stay hydrated.

"Why were you at my dad's?" he finally asked.

"I was returning his packages."

He held back his words because he didn't want to stress me out, but I knew he had plenty to say by the twitch in his jaw.

"It's not your father's fault, Hale. It was mine. I shouldn't have gotten myself all worked up. And I shouldn't have lifted so many boxes."

His expression could have been carved from stone. "Quitting was supposed to lower your stress."

"Well, what can I say? I work best under pressure."

"This isn't funny, Rayne. What if you went into actual labor? You're only in your sixth month."

"Prodromal labor doesn't lead to real labor."

"That's not the point."

"Then what is the point?"

"You shouldn't have been over there."

"Avoiding him forever is not the solution, Hale. Your dad—"

"My dad is a chronic source of stress in our life!"

I sighed. It frustrated Hale to no end that, after everything, I still defended Remington. "Hale, we can't stay mad at your father for the rest of his life. I miss him. Elara needs a grandfather. And I want things to go back to normal."

"Normal." He scoffed. "That word doesn't exist in this family."

"Well, it does in mine. We Meyers might be weird and quirky and a little scatterbrained at times, but at our core we're just boring, normal people. Christmas is next week, and I want us all together at one table. No strangers. No business colleagues. Just family—and that includes Marta, Raoul, and Alphonse."

"Rayne, the staff—"

"The staff is family, Hale. We did Thanksgiving the Davenport way, but I'm claiming Christmas. I want cranberries from a can and green beans with those crispy fried onions and a basic bitch honey-baked ham. The.

End." I shoved myself off the couch because I had to pee.

"I'm fine with that. But I can't guarantee the guestlist."

I shot him a threatening look. "Then figure out a way to fix it. I'm off stress. This has officially become your problem—doctor's orders." I waddled to the bathroom.

That's Not a Red Rider BB Gun

My mom and I did all the Christmas cooking, which meant the food would be mediocre at best. But dinner tasted like childhood and brought back memories. And, for that, I was happy.

I wasn't sure what Hale said to Remington, but he was there. He came over Christmas morning with a reasonable amount of gifts that didn't outshine Santa, and managed to keep his commentary to a minimum.

I wanted to avoid a tit-for-tat gift-off in which the men tried to outdo each other. I would not let my daughter's personality pay the price for their competitive spoiling. She already lived the life of a toddler princess in extreme privilege. As her mother, I felt it was my job to set boundaries and keep her grounded.

Hale didn't hold the same concern I did about things like that. He simply accepted that it was the top one percent's right to live a life built entirely around excessive luxury. But I stood my ground because I didn't want my kids to grow up as an entitled little assholes.

Some privilege I'd allow, but I still wanted Elara's upbringing to resemble mine. There could be a car when they turned sixteen, but nothing over the top. She would only need something dependable and safe to get her to work, because my kid was going to have a job. I didn't care how big her trust fund was. Employment gave a person a greater purpose, and I wanted her to learn the value of a hard day's work.

Birthdays would be reserved for the family unless it was a milestone year—double digits, turning into a teen, sweet sixteen, eighteen, and of course, twenty-one. Filler years would be reserved for classroom cupcakes, random sleepovers, and casual picnics around the pool. There would be no private chefs, yacht galas, island excursions, or ski resorts in Aspen. Not for my babies.

These were not pressing concerns of Hale's, but they were the thoughts that kept me up at night while I was growing a human in my womb. Other mothers in Davenport's social circle were already whispering about waiting lists for private pre-K academies and middle-grade prep-schools.

One woman at a function mentioned her son's private tutor. She expected him to be multilingual in four languages and fluent before age five. I told her that Elara figured out Blue's clue almost every single time.

She wasn't impressed. But I was.

As I carried out a tray of mangled sugar cookies Elara and I made, I walked them around the table to each guest so Elara could hand them out. She was so proud of her work and happy to share her cookies with those she loved.

"Did you make these, Meyers?" Remington frowned at the lopsided confection

"Elara and I did."

He smiled at his granddaughter. "Thank you, angel."

"Eat it, Pop-Pop." She pushed his hand toward his mouth, forcing him to take a bite.

"Mmm," he said, looking up at me with concern. "Is there milk?"

My mom carried out a tray of milk and coffee. Marta served a red velvet cake she made, which—I'm not gonna lie—totally overshadowed our cookies.

After supper, we moved to the den and watched *A Christmas Story*. The Davenports didn't understand our affinity with the movie, and Barrett earned the stink eye when he called it stupid.

I survived countless fundraisers, balls, auctions, elaborate dinner parties, and mind-numbing business functions for these people. They would stomach my cheesy Christmas traditions -- even if they had to choke them down one dry swallow at a time.

Hale lifted my socked feet onto his lap and massaged my swollen ankles as I watched Ralphie suck on a bar of soap. To this day, the movie made me laugh.

Marta fussed over Elara's new toys, as she showed them off to her. Remington and my mother chatted quietly in the dining room while Seraphina texted friends and updated her social media with holiday selfies.

There were no outsiders. Only us. And, for once, things seemed imperfectly perfect.

When the movie ended, everyone said goodnight. I forced leftovers on Remington, which confused him, so he handed them off to Marta with a mumble about being mistaken for a food bank.

"Thank you, *Niña,*" Marta said, accepting the doggy bag of cookies and ham then kissing me on my cheek. "You did a beautiful job. And," she pinched my cheek, "everyone was civil."

I smiled. Small victories shaped big changes.

My mother took Elara up for a bath and when the house was finally empty and silent, I collapsed on the couch with a satisfied sigh. I was exhausted.

"Do you regret not letting me hire a chef?"

"No," I said stubbornly grateful for the ache in my back and the soreness of my feet. "This was perfect."

Hale gathered up some plates and cups and carried them to the kitchen. He returned with a long, Tiffany blue gift box. "I have one more gift for you."

"Hale..."

He sat beside me and placed it on my lap. "Open it."

I pulled the satin ribbon, and he lifted the lid. "Oh my gosh."

A vine of diamonds twinkled from a bed of black velvet. He pulled the necklace from the box and draped it around my neck, closing the clasp and sending shivers down my spine. I ran my hand over the diamonds and looked up at him lovingly.

"Thank you."

He kissed my temple and hugged me close. "Merry Christmas, baby."

After Christmas, things were quiet. That lingering magic slowly faded as the cookies disappeared and the garland yellowed, but I refused to pack up the holiday until after the New Year.

We watched the fireworks over Times Square from the penthouse of The Plaza as the ball dropped. Elara loved the sparkles and cheered every time one exploded in the sky. By twelve o'five, I was in bed and half asleep.

When we returned to the Keys, the holiday décor was packed away, and the house felt empty.

"What's that smell?" I sniffed the air. Pregnancy had given me a bloodhound's sense of smell.

Hale set down our bags and sniffed the air. "I don't smell anything."

"It's like…" I sniffed again. "Paint."

"Hmm. Where's it coming from?"

I waddled to the staircase, following my nose as the scent grew stronger. "Upstairs, I think. Did you have painters come to the house while we were gone?"

He followed me up the steps. The smell was coming from the spare room. Elara ran ahead and disappeared into her playroom. I pushed open the guestroom door and stilled.

"Hale... What did you do?"

He watched my response cautiously. "Do you like it?"

The room had been transformed into a baby boho sanctuary. Natural wood furniture blended perfectly with the neutral walls painted in white and beige. Tropical plants formed an awning in the corner over a bamboo glider with a big cushion and ottoman. Darling designer clothing items hung from the bar in the closet, and wooden baskets overflowed with rattles and bottles.

It was a haven. "I love it."

"Here, Mommy."

I looked down at Elara and frowned as she held out a cupcake. "Oh, careful, Peanut. You can't have food in here." I took the cupcake out of her little hand. "Wait. Where did she get a cupcake?"

"Aunt Phina!" She pointed to the door.

I looked up at Hale suspiciously. "Is your sister here?" We had just left her in New York, so that didn't make sense. I followed Elara into the hall when Hale stayed silent.

"Surprise!"

I staggered back into Hale's chest. Andrew, my mother, Hale's mother, Seraphina, Marta, and Tyler clustered outside of the new nursery. "What are you guys doing here?"

"It's your baby shower, silly," Phina announced.

I looked down the hall, but the house seemed otherwise empty. I'd been expecting some over-the-top nightmare for a baby shower, but these were my people. "It's just you guys?"

"Just us. Well, there's one other person, but we think you'll be happy to see her."

Her? My stomach knotted, and I shot Tyler a paranoid glance, fearful they might have invited Elle. It had been a difficult but healthy choice to cut her out of my life, and I wasn't looking for a reunion.

Tyler shook his head and looped his arm through mine. "Trust me, you'll be happy."

We walked into the guestroom, which had been transformed with flowers and balloons. The sight brought tears to my eyes. "You guys!"

Baked goods spread across a dressed table like a scene in Alice in Wonderland, and the bed had been adorned with piles of ruffly pillows to resemble a throne.

"Hello, Rayne." Willow crossed the room with angelic grace and hugged me. "You look wonderful."

"Was this why I couldn't get an appointment with you yesterday when we were in New York?"

She laughed. "I knew I'd see you soon enough."

I was truly surprised. "I can't believe you're here! I can't believe any of you are here." I laughed and wiped my eyes. "Mom, you just left!"

"No, I didn't. Hale sent me to a spa for a few days." She preened. "I've been dipped and waxed in places that haven't seen the light of day in decades. You should feel how smooth I am—"

"I'm good." I held up my hands when she pulled at a button on her dress. I grinned at Hale. "Sneaky. I'm totally surprised."

He bent to kiss me. "You deserve it."

"That's enough smooching, you two. Let

her sit down, Hale." Phina ushered me toward the bed where I noticed several crystals on the end tables. "Later, Willow is going to do a private Reiki session with you."

"Oh, I can't wait."

My mom handed me a frosted mini cake. "Chef Dubois sends his love."

I took the confection, and my eyes welled. I lifted it like a champagne toast. "To all my favorite people."

"To Rayne and Hale and the new baby," Tyler said holding up a mimosa. "Cheers."

"The real shower's next week with a hundred and fifty women from your wedding."

The blood rushed from my face and Hale's sister laughed. "Not funny, Phina."

"You're so easy. We wouldn't put you through that in your condition, Rayne."

I sighed, grateful that we had reached a point where the Davenports were truly getting to know me and what kind of shindigs I enjoyed. "This is perfect."

We spent the afternoon relaxing, eating, and telling stories that had me laughing until my bladder was about to explode. I opened a few presents, but nothing overwhelming. Hale had taken care of everything, and the gifts we received were incredibly heartfelt.

My mother gave us a blanket, and Naomi gifted us with couture Christmas stockings, one for each of us with our names embroidered on the cuff. Phina gave us a silver-plated baby brush to be engraved when little Conley or Keeley was born.

Tyler had canvas prints made of animals he'd photographed at the Washington Park Zoo. Marta made my favorite meal for dinner and told me to expect enough frozen suppers to fill an industrial fridge when the baby was born.

"You guys are the best." I blew my nose and mopped the tears of gratitude from my face. "I'm sorry. I just cry all the time now."

After dinner, I returned alone to the guestroom, where Willow did her magic.

"Your heart chakra's no longer as closed off as it once was, Rayne."

I sensed as much. "I've been doing the affirmations we discussed, and I try to meditate a few times a week."

"Good." She placed crystals over my protruding stomach and walked me through several breathing practices.

"I'd like to help you cleanse the house of negative energy while I'm here."

"That would be great." Then I had an

idea. "How do you feel about coming out again when I'm due?"

"I could do that."

"Good. You can be my spiritual doula." Willow had such a calming effect on me.

"As long as you understand I'm not an actual doula. I have no medical expertise where babies are concerned."

"I know. But you're good for the mommy, and what's good for the mommy is good for the baby. I'll tell Hale to arrange your flights. We'll take care of everything."

That night, when I told Hale my plan to fly Willow in for the birth he was confused. "You want me to what?"

"Fly her in. She calms me down, Hale."

He frowned. "That's my job."

"This is different. What's the big deal?"

"You're talking about the hippy who works underground in New York, right?"

"Don't be disrespectful. She's my spiritual doula."

"That's not a thing, Rayne."

"It is now." I rubbed cocoa butter on my belly. "Don't you want me to be happy?"

"You know I do. But what happened to keeping things *normal*?"

I paused. This was a little excessive, but

the thought of having Willow's calming presence nearby for the birth really relieved some of my fear. I was terrified of labor pain and worried my vagina would be ruined after passing a human through it. Honestly, a C-section and heavy drugs seemed like the Cadillac way to go, but that wasn't an option right now.

"I want this one bougie thing. I'm giving you a child, so I think you can give me this." It wasn't like Hale didn't give me everything I wanted anyway. We all knew he'd say yes. He was just having a hard time understanding that Reiki was more than an energetic scam job.

"Fine. I'll make the arrangements."

"Thank you."

The following day, Hale arranged brunch for our guests. I insisted on inviting Remington, Miles, Alphonse, and Raoul since they weren't included in the baby shower.

Willow fluttered to Remington like a moth drawn to a flame, and plucked at the air around his head. "Your aura has some darkness to it."

He shot me a look and growled, "Meyers."

"Willow, I don't think he likes that."

"Negative energy pollutes the soul. You should let me help you unblock your chakra."

"For pity's sake, where do you pick up these strays?" He glared at Willow. "I like my aura just as it is. Put back anything you took." Taking his fruit plate to the table, he grumbled, "Worse than a Roman pickpocket."

I chuckled and ate my French toast.

After brunch, Alphonse drove Tyler and Willow to the airport. My mom stuck around to spend the day with me. We watched some of our favorite movies like *Overboard* and *The Princess Bride,* then topped off the day with some trashy reality television—the kind Hale hated but was secretly invested in.

Every time he entered the living room, he stared at the screen, watching the drama unfold until he caught himself watching. Then he would shake his head and mumble how ridiculous our shows were. Yet he always conveniently needed something from the living room whenever there was drama with the characters.

"You've got yourself a good one there, Ray," my mom said, after Hale brought me a cup of tea. "You're very lucky."

My mom never complained about raising me as a single parent. My dad had been around when she was pregnant, but I couldn't imagine him being anywhere near as supportive as Hale.

"I guess Dad was nothing like Hale."

"No, but I'm not just thinking about your father. Hale's special. He truly cares about your well-being."

We rarely spoke about my father, mostly at my request. After the wedding, I wanted to forget my Dad existed—much like he'd forgotten I'd existed for most of my life. But becoming a parent changed my perspective about a lot of things.

"I was scared at first." I kept my voice low so Hale wouldn't overhear me.

My mom frowned. "Of what, sweetie?"

This wasn't an easy confession for me, but it felt good to get it off my chest. "I sometimes think that's why I didn't get pregnant immediately. I was afraid of doing it alone. You made it look so easy, Mom. Even when we were barely making it, you made sure I always had everything I needed."

"Oh, honey, Hale would never abandon you."

I believed that too, but there was still that deep seated fear that no man could tolerate me forever. "Sometimes dads leave."

She squeezed my hand. "And sometimes they stay and break the cycle. Hale loves you and Elara with all of his heart. He'll love this new baby just as much. You'll see."

"I hate that his abandonment left such a prominent scar."

She paused the television and turned to fully face me. "Honey, your father didn't abandon you. He left because I threw him out."

"What?"

She wrung her hands. "You have to understand. I only wanted to protect you. I always tried to make the right choices, but you see now there's no one-size-fits-all playbook for parenting."

My mind was reeling. "Hold on. You're saying Dad never actually left?"

She scoffed. "Believe it or not, getting him out was quite the chore. But I knew it would be for the best."

"How was that for the best?"

"Rayne, a mother's love is so overwhelming and all-encompassing, I don't know if men can fully grasp what we feel as mothers. Fathers are different. You were precious and perfect and I would have done anything to protect you. Even if that meant protecting you from a lousy father."

A few years ago, I would have questioned my mom's assessment of the man who shared my DNA. But today I was wiser. My father would have continuously let me down and hurt me. I believed she protected me from that, even if it was sometimes lonely and confusing not to have a dad around. "You did a good job, Mom."

"I did my best."

I never thought of my mom as tough, but it took a strong backbone to throw a man out, knowing life would be hard in other ways without him. "Was it because of Laura?"

"Laura, and the others. Your father has always been an extraordinarily selfish man. Ray was always worrying about Ray. The funny thing is, our life actually got easier without him. There were no more surprise collection notices, no more missing paychecks. What we had, we earned, and I made sure we kept everything that was ours."

My hands rested on my belly. "I think you made the right choice."

"I hope so." She pressed play and the drama on the screen continued.

That night, when I went to bed, I was still

thinking about the things my mother said. Unlike my father, my mother had kept her word. She did her best to raise and protect me, always putting my needs before her own.

When I was younger and he'd stand me up, I'd cry and she'd say, "You don't need him, Rayne." It took me more than thirty years to realize she was right.

I never told my mom that I met Laura or that I had two half-sisters. Just like she wanted to protect me, I wanted to protect her.

As I lay in bed, I wondered how she managed. I was a frantic mess the first time Elara got sick, but Hale was always there to calm me down and help with the decisions, the way a true partner should. We had the financial stability to give our children everything they could possibly need. My mother had no such security, yet she still made sure my needs were always met.

I wondered how much she had to sacrifice to make that happen. I couldn't recall her ever having her nails done at a salon or splurging on a pretty piece of clothing simply because she liked it. As a matter of fact, my mother was still wearing clothes she'd owned since my childhood.

Unable to sleep, I put on Hale's robe and tiptoed down to his office. I logged onto the laptop and opened a search engine. An hour later and I had a list of addresses and names.

"There you are." Hale appeared at the door, bare-chested and holding a bottle of water.

"I couldn't sleep."

He came into the office and glanced at the computer screen. "What are you doing?"

"You know how you're always telling me not to feel bad that we have money?"

"Yes." He chuckled nervously. "Are you impulse shopping?"

"I haven't bought anything yet, but I've decided you're right."

"Is that so?"

"Yup. I'm about to cost you a ton of money, sir." I clicked open a tab and turned the screen so he could see what I found. "We're buying my mom this house."

By the time March rolled in, I was roughly the size of a planet. My cravings consisted of antacids, key lime popsicles, and the saltiest olives I could find. My weight was not to be discussed—at least not by anyone who valued their life.

I'd found the perfect gem for my mom, about twenty minutes from our house, in the center of the iconic Old Town. She loved to people-watch and talk to strangers, so this seemed like the perfect place. It was quaint and buttercream yellow, with a balcony on the front and a big porch for sitting and taking in the tourists.

The house also had a super cute attic loft. My plan was to get my mother settled then convince her to rent the loft to Tyler. Of course, I'd also have to convince him to uproot his entire life, find a new job, and move to the other side of the country, but those were minor details.

We had the property completely renovated, inspected, and furnished without my mom's knowledge. She was set to fly out this Friday and stay until the baby was born. Little did she know that she could now stay as long as she liked.

"Don't forget you have your ultrasound today." Hale placed a plate of toast in front of me.

"I know. You're picking me up at two, right?"

"Yes." He sipped his coffee. "Andrew has Elara for the day, and I have a meeting with Xander in Miami."

"Miami? He can't fly out to meet you here?"

"I suppose he could, but I offered."

I buttered my toast with obvious disapproval. "Seems to me that would be the thoughtful thing to do since you have a pregnant wife at home who could pop at any minute, and Xander's perpetually single and living a less complicated life on account of being a prick."

"You're not due for three weeks, Rayne."

"Says you. I could blow at any second, Hale." I took a bite of my toast. "Which reminds me. We have to book Willow's flight."

"Are we still doing that?"

"Of course, we're still doing that. I want her here for the birth."

"Reiki is not a calculated science. This woman has no experience with childbirth, yet you act as though she's a midwife."

"She's my spiritual doula, Hale. Are you trying to make me cry?"

"How long are we putting her up?"

Considering that I often performed like a prized pedigree for formal affairs that helped Hale's business connections, I didn't see this as a huge ask. Not to mention that I had to stomach Xander's presence more than a few times since he and Hale started collaborating on projects. The man gave me agita worse than Marta's spiciest *birria*.

"I don't know, Hale. How long will I have to smile and be nice to your friend who F-U-C-K'd over my friend?"

We had started spelling out profanities to stop Elara from repeating bad words. It didn't matter that Elara was already out with Andrew. We got in the habit of doing it so much that we did it whether she was there or not.

"This again? You promised to keep an open mind."

"Keeping an open mind and liking someone are two different things."

"He didn't F-U-C-K over your friend. They had a one-night stand. Tyler's an adult. It happens."

"Tyler's in a delicate state! He just figured out he likes D-I-C-K, and boys are complicated. You wouldn't understand what it is like to date one. Lucky for you, I'm incredibly easy when it comes to partners."

"You're right, I wouldn't." He stood and dumped his coffee into the sink. I hadn't had caffeine in months, so it felt a little like showing off.

"You're just P-I-S-S-Y because I don't like your friend."

"No, I'm P-I-S-S-Y for my own reasons."

I stilled then wiped the breadcrumbs from my lips. "Wait, you're really P-I-S-S-Y?"

He rolled his neck to release the tension in his shoulders. "No. I'm fine. Forget I said anything."

"Hale."

"Rayne," he held up his hands in a calming gesture. "I misspoke. Let's move on."

I scoffed. "You're totally lying right now. If you're upset with me, say so."

Yes, I was pregnant and delicate and cried at the drop of a hat. But we never kept secrets from each other. If Hale was mad at me, I wanted to know why.

He sighed. "It's just frustrating when you're more concerned about your friend's S-E-X-L-I-F-E than ours."

"No, I'm not. I care about your D-I-C-K just as much as I care about Tyler's."

His lips formed a straight line. "Not the answer I want, Rayne."

"Well, what do you want?"

"I don't know. You're pregnant, and I want you to be comfortable, but it's been weeks, Rayne. I'm allowed to be a little on edge."

I tried to remember the last time we had sex. I couldn't. My nightlife had been consumed by pillow propping, snacks, and guilty pleasure shows. Hale was right. My husband's dick was a thing of the past.

"Well...it's a little hard." I stood with a groan and waddled to the sink, my belly now hard as a rock and hanging over the waistband of my pajama pants.

"Tell me about it."

My gaze snapped to his, and he lifted a brow.

"Oh, please. Like you really want to F-U-C-K this."

He leaned across the counter, pressing his weight into his fists as he growled through clenched teeth. "I not only want to F-U-C-K you, I want to eat your P-U-S-S-Y and F-U-C-K that filthy M-O-U-T-H of yours, too."

I blinked at him, shocked. Nothing about my body felt remotely sexy at the moment. I hadn't even shaved my legs in weeks. He had to be lying. "You don't have to spell the non-dirty words, Hale."

"Well, I'm frustrated!"

Maybe he wasn't lying. "You think I'm not H-O-R-N-Y? I have needs too, you know! But I get winded pulling up my pants these days, and I have to pee every ten minutes, so it's not like investing all this sexual energy somewhere else. You act as if I'm plotting some sort of revenge to neglect you. Look at me!" I held out my arms, my swollen boobs looking like two Goodyear blimps hiding under a hanky. "If anything, I'm saving you from myself."

"Saving me?"

I sniffed. "Yes. I'm harboring a human being in my belly, and I wasn't the most coordinated person to start. I'd probably end up hurting you, because my weight is..." My voice broke and I looked away.

"Sweetheart, don't cry. This is why I didn't want to say anything."

"I'm not crying because of this. I'm crying because..." I wiped my nose. "Gah! Do I need a reason? This is just what I do now! I cry all the time! So fucking sexy, right?" I wailed.

"Hey." He pulled me into a hug and I wiped my nose on his shirt. "I know your body's changing, but you're still my little Rayne. You could never crush me, baby. And, whether you believe me or not, I will always find you sexy."

"Really? Even knowing that I sometimes pee my pants a little when I sneeze?"

He laughed. "Even then."

I blotted my eyes. "Well...then I guess we can have sex."

"It's fine, Rayne. I can wait."

"No. I want you to be happy. Your penis is my priority. I'm sorry I've been a slacker."

He pinched the bridge of his nose and chuckled. "My dick is not your job, Rayne."

"Yes, it is. I'm your wife and I want you to be satisfied. Tell me what you want and I'll do it."

He arched a brow. "You mean it?"

I nodded. "I miss it too."

"Okay." He checked his watch. "I have to send a quick email. Go upstairs and take off your clothes. I'll meet you up there in five minutes."

I bit my lip. He wanted *naked* sex? In broad daylight?

"You're not moving."

"I'm nine months pregnant! How fast do you think I can move?" I shuffled to the steps, hand on my stomach as I warned little Elodie or Gideon, "Mommy and Daddy are going to have some grown-up time. Shut your eyes and cover your ears."

I figured it was easiest to just take a shower. I shaved one leg before I lost interest. When Hale came upstairs, I was sitting on the bed in a towel, trying to remember what I was supposed to do.

"You okay?"

"Yeah, just having a moment of pregnancy brain.

He crossed the room and traced a finger down my cheek. "Did you change your mind?"

"No. But I think I lost my mojo."

He gave a silent laugh. "No, you didn't." He pulled my hand to the bulge in his pants. "Feel that, Rayne. That's how much I want to fuck you. Your mojo's just fine."

I looked down at my boobs and stomach then I held out my hands in defeat. "Well, here I am. Have at it."

It wasn't that I didn't want to have sex with him. I did. Desperately. But it had been months since I saw my feet, I was too fat to shave, and my agility had disintegrated to that of a tug boat, and I was pretty sure I had to burp or fart, or maybe the baby was just sitting on a vital organ.

"I can see I have my work cut out for me." Hale pointed to the bed and removed his suit jacket. "Lie down."

I fell back on the mattress like a starfish. "Oh, hold on. Little Clementine's right on my bladder."

"I thought it was Kiernan."

"That name's so yesterday." I shifted.

"*Oomph.* That's no good either. I need a pillow."

Hale grabbed several pillows and hoisted me up, stuffing one behind my back and one under my knees. "Better."

"A little." I caught my breath.

He tugged my towel open and smiled. It amazed me that he could see me like this and still want me.

"You're beautiful."

"Don't stretch it—"

"Hey." He caught my jaw and forced me to look him in the eye. "You're *beautiful.*"

I blushed. Maybe I was being a little hard on myself. I reached for his hip. "Thank you."

He bent forward and kissed me slowly, his hands gently roving over my curves and reminding me how good his touch felt. He climbed onto the bed, careful not to crush me, and pulled my hand to his cock. My fingers curled around his thick length and stroked slowly as he kissed my neck.

"Careful with that thing," I warned. "You don't want to poke poor little Alaric or Aurelia in the eye."

"That's not possible." He massaged my breasts softly. "Does it hurt when I touch you here?"

I moaned and shut my eyes. "No, actually, it feels really nice."

He kissed my neck and shoulders, trailing his touch over my belly until I anxiously parted my thighs for him. I was ready to get to the good stuff. His stroking fingers teased my folds until I was writhing and begging for more.

Hale pulled me to the edge of the bed and dropped to his knees. I tried to cover myself but he pulled my hand away.

"Sorry."

"What are you sorry for?"

"I haven't...groomed down there in a while."

"Knock it off." His mouth closed over my clit and I gasped as he pressed his fingers inside of me. The first stroke of his tongue had me fisting the sheets and soon enough I was panting and gasping his name. "Hale..."

"I'm right here, baby. Let me take care of you."

I sobbed with relief as he drove me to climax. "I really missed sex."

He kissed my inner thigh and dragged his tongue slowly through my slit where his fingers teased. "We haven't gotten to the sex yet."

That was true. On account of little Shiloh

or Skye weighing me down, I really couldn't do much more than lay there. But so far that was working out just fine.

"Don't fight it," he said, curving his touch to reach that magical spot. "I know you're good for one more."

I didn't doubt it. As long as he kept touching me the way he was now, there would be no stopping it. I cried out as he kissed my clit as his fingers delved deep. I cupped my breasts, massaging slowly as my muscles tightened and my legs trembled.

"Mmm, that's a good girl." With one final lick, he slowly rose. "I think, on your side would be best."

He helped me reposition as he aligned his body with mine. It wasn't the most ergonomic position, but he was able to make it work. Luckily, Hale had the right tools to make just about anything work. But I couldn't say I loved the position, two minutes later we were trying something else.

And then something else. And then something else. It seemed nothing was comfortable when we had a beach ball separating us.

"Maybe this way's better." I draped my

knee over his thigh so our bodies formed a sort of V on the bed.

He thrust a few times and I frowned. "How's that feel?"

"Meh."

"What's wrong with doggy style?"

"I don't think it's a good idea to have my stomach down. We could crush little Banks or Clover."

"Sometimes I wonder how many babies you have in there with all these names."

"Really, Hale? A reference to me possibly carrying twins or quintuplets? Now?"

"No, no, no. That had nothing to do with your body." He panicked then took a calming breath. "Never mind. How about missionary?"

I flopped to my back. "Try."

He repositioned himself and pressed forward. "And we're not naming my son Banks."

I couldn't meet his eyes. My boobs were suffocating me and the weight of my stomach left me winded. "Maybe we should just wait—"

"No, we're figuring this out."

"My belly's in the way, Hale. I'm too big."

"Your belly's a part of you, Rayne."

"Well, my boobs look gross like this. I don't like it."

He withdrew and rubbed his jaw. "Try getting on top."

"I'll crush you."

"Knock it off." He moved to his back and guided me over him, but I hesitated. "Go ahead." He helped me seat myself. "See, you fit perfectly." His hands cupped my stomach as he slowly flexed his hips.

Okay, this way was actually pretty good. "Don't look at me."

"Are you kidding? I love looking at you. You're gorgeous."

"Err," I growled, because I didn't feel gorgeous.

"Don't growl at me. You're a fucking goddess, Rayne."

A goddess? That was a new one. And I kind of liked where this was going. "Tell me more."

"You're radiating life. Knowing you're carrying my child in there...It's a total fucking turn-on."

"Ooh, I'm picking up on some big daddy energy." I rocked my hips as he held my hands.

"Fucking right I got big daddy energy.

That's my baby in there." He bucked his hips and I gasped. "And you're my sexy little wife."

"Ha. Not really little anymore."

"To me you are. You're fucking adorable, Rayne. When I see you wobbling around, I get an instant hard-on. The other day, when you were flopping around trying to find the remote, I nearly came in my pants."

"You saw that?" I snicked my tongue against my teeth. "You could have helped me."

"No way. It was like live wife-porn. I think I've been hard for you ever since."

I laughed and clenched around him. "I can tell."

He groaned. "And when you walk around in those little shorts with the waistband rolled down and your belly sticking out... God, I just want to bend you over and fuck you into next week."

"All right, take it easy."

"I'm serious. Your body is a thing of raw beauty. I look at you, and I'm awed by every inch of you."

"Hale, if you wanted a blowjob, there are easier ways to get one."

He cupped the back of my neck and pulled me down for a kiss. "I'm not trying to get a blowjob, baby. I'm just trying to get through to you. I love you—every single part of you. I don't care about your size or how you dress. I just want to be close to you."

And those were the magic words I needed to hear. Brick by brick, he broke my inhibitions down as he always did. Sex might be a physical act, but sometimes it was more emotional than anything else. Hale loved me, and I loved him. I knew then that we could go through anything together, including the unflattering beauty of childbirth.

We were ready.

I Should Have Suspected...

"I don't understand." My mother said as I handed her the key. "You rented a place for me to stay? I thought I was staying with you to help out."

"No, Mom, we didn't rent it. We bought it."

"You're moving? This seems like an inopportune time, Rayne. Shouldn't you have waited until after the baby's born?"

Oh, my Gosh. I mentally counted to ten.

Maybe I was saying it wrong.

"We bought you a house, Mom. It's yours. To live in."

She just stared at me. "You... You bought me a house?"

"Yes!"

Hale cleared his throat. "Rayne wanted to do something special for you, Penny, since you've done so much for her. We also liked the idea of having you close by so you could see your grandchildren more often.

"You... But... I don't..." She blinked rapidly and looked up at the large, ornate door. "You bought me a house?"

"Yes, Mom." I opened the door and waved her inside. "Go in and check it out."

"But...I have a house."

I rolled my eyes and nudged her over the threshold. "This one's nicer. And you can sell the other house and live off the money. You can retire."

"Oh, would you look at those moldings?" She crossed the foyer and peeked at the furnished living room. She gaped at the dressed dining room, her hand rushing to her mouth. "This is all mine?"

"All yours."

She laughed as if she couldn't believe it. "I never imagined anything like it. Will you look at the size of that kitchen!"

"And she's off." Hale chuckled.

We followed her throughout the house as she *oohed* and *ahhed* at every little fixture and detail. By the time she toured the entire property, she was flabbergasted.

I plopped into an overstuffed chair in the living room, and she sat on the edge of the couch. "Who's furniture is this?"

"It's yours, Mom. It's all yours."

"Oh, Mylanta." She reached for the tissue box. "I don't know what to say. I'm touched and overwhelmed and…well, shocked!" She laughed through tears and blew her nose. "I can't believe I own a house like this."

She thought we were the ones who gave her something, but her joy at owning such a property was the greatest gift of all. I could never articulate how much I loved her for putting me first all those years. She never once complained of loneliness or bitched that the man who fathered me had also broken her heart and let her down. She just handled everything stoically, like any good mom would.

"I love you, Mom. I'm glad you like it."

"Oh, sweetie, I love you too. Both of you. And I don't like it—I *love* it!" She pulled Hale into a hug then bent to hug me because I was stuck in the chair. "Thank you."

When we drove home, I smiled at Hale. "Thank you for letting me do that for her."

"You don't have to thank me, Rayne. I'm glad Penny's going to be close by. I was happy to help you do it for her."

"Our lives are so different now."

"In a good way, I hope."

"In a great way. My mother never dreamed of owning a home like that. And me —ha—I never even dreamed of owning a decent car. But it's not just the money. Look at me. I'm a mom and I'm about to have a baby."

He took my hand and brought it to his lips, kissing my fingers. "You changed my life for the better, too."

After that, mom stopped by on a daily basis. She raved about how much she loved her house and bragged to anyone who would listen about how her daughter and son-in-law spoiled her. She put in her notice at work, and we arranged to have a moving company pack up all of her things so they could be shipped from Oregon.

Remington had once told me that Hale wouldn't put down roots. He warned me that his son would eventually become so successful he'd move overseas or to a more metropolitan area like New York.

He was wrong.

Hale loved the idea of home. He loved marriage and family and all the things his father could never fully appreciate. Remington had multiple houses, as did Hale, but Remington could never claim the level of contentment Hale found through family. He once told me, wherever Elara and I were, that was home.

I was in no rush to return to work and unsure if I'd ever go back to working for Remington. I wanted to take my time and enjoy my children. Not every mother had the option to stay home, so I never lost sight of how lucky I was to choose.

Willow flew in three days before my due date. The doctor said I was progressing right on schedule and things looked good. That made me hopeful that this was going to be a smooth birth.

I had a few random contractions but no real signs of labor yet. Things were actually pretty peaceful. So much so, that I wasn't stress eating or having any sort of anxiety whatsoever.

Willow definitely helped as she filled the house with tranquil music and diffused aromatherapy to release any negative tension. My stress levels were lower than ever before, and I started to think Hale was right. I was a fucking goddess.

My husband had one last trip out of town, then he was homebound for the next two months. I was relieved to start this next chapter of our lives, so I planned on making a nice dinner to kick things off when he returned home that evening.

But first, Marta's *Chiles En Nogada.* "Hello, lover," I said as I opened the Tupperware and breathed in the fiery poblano peppers and ground picadillo. I was just about to take my first bite when the doorbell rang.

"Damn it." I hoisted myself out of the chair and waddled to the door, disappointed and a little surprised to see Xander on the other side. "Oh, it's you," I greeted. "Hale's not here."

"Rayne." Why did my name always bother me when he said it? "You're looking... uncomfortable. Hale told me to meet him here. He's on his way."

"Come on in." Buttressing a hand at my back, I waddled back to the kitchen, leaving Xander in the foyer.

"He has some papers he wanted me to sign before he goes on baby leave. Which, by the looks of things, should have already started. Are you overdue?"

I sat down and glared at him over my stuffed pepper. "You're very funny."

"I try." He sat across from me, always making himself right at home. "What is that?"

"It's mine." On second thought, I slid the spicy dish closer to him. "Did you want to try?"

He leaned forward and sniffed. "I'm set."

Great. So he was just going to sit there and watch me eat. Awesome...

"How's Tyler?"

I chewed slowly, narrowing my eyes. "Why do you care?"

He shrugged. "Just being polite."

"How courteous of you. Tyler's great. He's dating this fabulous architect he met in Malibu last month." That was a lie. Tyler was stuck in boring Oregon, reading a book a day and doing the same old stuff he usually did, but I wasn't about to tell Xander that. "The new guy's a real hottie."

"Good for him."

"It's great for him. He's not a man-child like the first guy he slept with, and he doesn't play games. Rumor on the street is, he's so hung he could make a Clydesdale blush. Also good, because I heard the first guy also had a micro-penis."

"I know for a fact that's not true."

I shrugged and scraped up the last bite of peppers and sauce. "I can only go by what I hear." I wiggled my pinkie. "Hung like a light switch."

He narrowed his eyes and inhaled slowly. "Any idea how far away Hale is?"

I hoisted myself out of my chair and carried my plate to the sink. My stomach tightened and I grunted. "I haven't talked to him."

"Maybe I'll come back later."

As I turned, a strange sensation pulled low in my abdomen. I was just about to tell him I thought that was a great idea when a rush of fluid spilled down my legs. I looked at the floor then up at Xander in shock. The plate I'd been holding shattered on the floor.

"Oh, fuck. Is that what I think it is?"

"Um..." I looked again at the puddle by my feet, my mind blanking on what I was supposed to do.

"Rayne?" Xander was in front of me. "Call Hale." He shoved his phone in my hand. "Where's your broom?"

"Um... " There was glass everywhere.

"The broom's…" I pointed toward the pantry. "Where's my phone?"

"I don't know. Just use mine. It's already ringing."

I brought it to my ear as I started to hyperventilate.

"Xander, I just landed."

"Hale?"

"*Rayne?*"

Panic welled-up inside of me. Hale was my always in charge, always punctual, and always logical person, and he wasn't here! "Honey, my water broke."

"Shit! Where are you?"

"Standing in the kitchen. Xander's here. Willow went for a walk with Andrew and Elara. I don't know what to do."

"Okay, listen to me, baby. You're going to get into Xander's car and let him drive you to the hospital."

"No, I don't want to do that."

"What do you mean, no? Baby, your water broke."

"The books say sometimes that can happen days before the birth."

"That may be true, but I still think you should get checked out. You were having contractions this morning. Have you had any more?"

"No..." I lied.

"Rayne, are you lying?"

"Maybe..."

"Baby, please just get in the car with Xander and let him drive you to the hospital. Either that or call my dad or your mom and have them take you. I can meet you there."

"I'll call Remington."

"Okay, but you need to leave in the next ten minutes, Rayne. Promise me."

"All right. I promise." As soon as I hung up the phone another contraction hit, this one long and painful enough to make me grip the counter.

"Rayne? What can I do?"

"Son of a mother-fucker!" I blew out a breath and met Xander's wide-eyed stare. Something told me there wasn't time to call Remington. "I need you to drive me to the hospital."

"No, no, no, no. I'm not trained for this. There has to be someone else."

"God, you truly suck." I held out the phone to him. "Do you have Remington's number in here?"

"Yes, but I doubt he'll take my call."

"Just dial!" I blew out a hard breath as another contraction cinched my insides.

He handed me the phone and I brought it to my sweaty ear. It rang twice then went to voicemail.

"Damn it. I need my phone so I can call my mom."

"You don't know your mom's phone number?"

"No, I don't know my mom's phone number! It's the twenty-first century. Who remembers phone numbers anymore?"

"But your mom's number's probably something—"

"Shut the fuck up and call my phone so I can find it!"

"God, you're scary." He took the phone and paused. "Do you know your phone number?"

"Yes, I know my phone number," I snapped, rattling off the number to him as I panted through the pain. "Why are the contractions coming so fast?"

"I don't know but I'm really praying it's just gas."

"Shh, it's ringing." I held up a hand, silencing him. "Hush!"

"I'm not saying anything."

"I said *shush*."

"God, you're terrifying."

I sent him a scathing glare as my ears tracked the ringing. "Where the hell is it?" I waddled into the living room, flinging cushions off the couch until the call went to voice mail. I dialed again.

"Look, why don't we just get into my car and take you to Hale?"

"I'm not going to the hospital with you!"

"Why not?"

"Because I don't like you!"

"Well, I'm not a huge fan of yours right now either, but you have goop and people coming out of you, so I really think we should find a doctor."

"I need my spiritual doula."

"Your what?"

"My—*Woahaaaaaaaaaaoweee—oooh*, fucking butt-fucking fuck! *What?*" Okay, that one really hurt.

"Jesus Christ. How did I get here?"

I swallowed, almost positive I was going to vomit from the pain. "I need water."

"Are you allowed to drink during labor?"

"Just get me some fucking water!"

"Okay, okay!" He rushed to the fridge, slipping and sliding across the floor until he caught the counter and glared at me. "You're so lucky I didn't fall in that shit."

"That *shit* is the miracle of life, you insensitive prick!"

He shoved a bottle of water into my hands. "We're going to the car."

My face pinched as tears rushed to my eyes. "I don't want to go without Hale."

"Rayne, Hale's going to meet us there. I'm going to get you to him as fast as humanly possible. Believe me! But you have to get into the car. The sooner you get into the car, the sooner we get to Hale."

"Okay." I sniffled and leaned into him as he helped me to the door. "I'm sorry I yelled at you."

"Don't worry about it." He led me out the front door to a tiny black Lamborghini. "Not to be a dick, but could you try not to leak anything on my seats."

"Oh, my God, you're such an asshole."

"I'm sorry! But I just had the upholstery redone."

Stifling a sob, my chin quivered as a low hum whistled out of me. Where was Hale? Where was Willow? I wanted my Mom. This was not my birthing plan. And this prick of a man was not going to make me cry.

"No, no, no, no!" He held up his hands like I was a fragile vase about to fall. "Never mind. Fuck the seats. Get in. Everything's fine. Don't cry."

Shaken and terrified, I lowered onto the seat as my insides twisted like a vise. How the hell I was ever getting out of such a low car?

Xander's phone rang the moment I buckled the seat belt. I looked up at him with desperate hope in my eyes. "Is that Hale?"

"Yes. Here." He shoved the phone into my hands and raced around to the driver's side.

I brought the phone to my ear. "Hale?"

"Baby, are you okay? You sound upset."

The driver's door slammed. "Wait! I have a bag."

Xander looked at me like I was asking him to leap out of an airplane. Then slouched and sighed. "Where?"

"It's under the table in the foyer." He rushed back into the house. "Hale?"

"I'm here, baby. I'm driving as fast as I can to get to you."

"I don't want to do this without you."

"You won't. I'm on my way. Tell me what's happening."

"Xander's getting the bag."

"Okay, good. And what about you? Any more contractions?"

Oh, there were contractions. As I tried to answer, one tore through me, and I gasped. "Hale," I said, my voice laden with fear.

"Shit." He heard my worry and sensed I was in pain. "Remember everything we learned, Rayne. Deep, calming breaths."

I inhaled and blew out a jagged breath. Small whimpers were all I could manage to let him know I was still there as my stomach tightened again.

"I'm about ten minutes from the hospital," he said. "I called your mom, and she's going to meet us there."

"What about Andrew and Willow? I can't find my phone and I didn't leave a note."

"They know what's going on. I spoke to Andrew. Willow is walking back from the park and she's going to be right behind you. Andrew's got Elara covered. You just have to worry about you and the baby."

My lips formed a small O as I panted out rapid breaths. "What about your dad?"

"My mom's calling him. And I texted Barrett and Seraphina."

He did all of that, and I barely made it

twenty feet from the door. "I hate that you're not here."

"I know, baby. I hate it, too. But I'll be with you when you get to the hospital."

"Here comes Xander. Hale, I need you."

"You have me. I'm coming as fast as I can."

The car door opened and Xander flung my bag behind the seat. "Okay, found the bag." The car roared to life.

"I love you, Hale."

"I love you, Rayne. I'll see you soon."

I ended the call and held my stomach as Xander flew out of the driveway. It would be amazing if I didn't puke on this trip. Swallowing back the urge, I said, "Hale called everyone."

"Great, where are we going?"

"Lower Keys Medical Center."

He plugged the name into his GPS as we sped toward to the bridge. "That's twenty-two minutes away."

I sucked in a breath and fisted my hands as another contraction cinched tight. "Then drive faster!"

His wide, dark eyes bounced between the road, my face, and my stomach. We only made it one block before we stopped at a traffic light, trapped in midday traffic.

Sweat trickled down my cheek as I panted like Zuul in Ghostbusters.

"You doing okay?"

I bared my teeth because that somehow eased the pain ripping through my abdomen. "Just peachy."

"Does it hurt?"

Was he dropped as a child? "Yes, it fucking hurts! Why else would I be breathing like I'm in an aerobics class?"

The light turned green and he raced ahead of traffic, mumbling, "It's amazing you got pregnant at all."

My scowl snapped from the road to him. "What's that supposed to mean?"

"You're not very nice."

He had balls! "I happen to be a lovely person. Hale thinks I'm a goddess!"

"I'm sure."

I scoffed. "You just don't know a unicorn when you see one."

"It's not a unicorn when there are two horns."

I growled at him because it was hard to breathe and talk. "How about you just drive and don't talk anymore."

"Fine by me."

The silence only lasted a few minutes. I moaned and cursed, "Fuuuuuuck." The contractions were getting sharper and closer. We still had a ways to go to get to Hale.

"Shit. Should I pull over?"

"No! Just keep going!" I could not have my baby on the front seat of some asshole's Lamborghini.

"This is probably because you ate that spicy burrito thing. What were you thinking?"

It was just like a man to put all the blame on a woman. "This is because Hale's put a giant baby—*owwwwwwwwdrivedrivedrive!*"

He whipped around the corner and I scooted low. There was no comfortable position and his driving was making me motion sick. Pressure built at my hips as a web of fire burned from my back to my uterus.

"Should we call someone?"

"*Ahhhhfuckfuckfuckaduck! Why the fuck does this have to be so painful?*" When the contractions got so intense that my screams silenced, I knew something was truly wrong.

"Call Hale. Tell him we're not going to make it."

"The fuck we aren't." Xander pressed the

gas pedal to the floor, but there was no dri-ving through the midday traffic.

"Xander, call my husband right fucking now!" I shrieked.

He navigated the controls on his dash-board, and the car veered into oncoming traffic.

"Watch out!"

"Stop yelling at me!" He exited the GPS and fumbled with Bluetooth.

"Hello?"

"Hale. The baby. It's coming."

"Shit. Okay, Rayne, listen to me. I want you to use Xander's phone and ping me your location. I'll come to you." The contractions were taking all of my focus and I didn't see his actual phone.

"Rayne, baby, give the phone to Xander."

"You're on Bluetooth."

"Hale!" Xander shrieked. "Man, your wife is about to give birth in my car! I did not sign up for this."

I squeezed my eyes shut. This could not be happening. I did not manifest giving birth on the shoulder of the fucking road.

Xander quickly told Hale where we were. I moaned and turned, trying to find any position that made this more bearable. I needed to get out of this car!

When I realized he was talking to the good people taking calls at Emergency 9-11, I wondered how I missed my husband saying goodbye. That was when I knew this wasn't about Hale anymore. This was about survival —mine and the baby's.

"I don't want to die."

"You're not going to die! Everyone is going to be fine! I have a woman in labor!" he shouted. Any attempt at maintaining his cool façade was now long gone.

"Tell them to bring drugs!"

He sped into the parking lot of a strip mall as the operator recorded his responses. "Sir, are there any immediate complications or signs of distress?"

"She's breathing really hard and she doesn't look good."

"Fuck you," I hissed between breaths.

The operator realized I was right there. "Ma'am, have you had any prior complications?"

"No."

"Sir, are you pulled over at a safe location and out of harm's way?"

"Yes. We're at a strip mall." As Xander

described landmarks, I reclined my seat and propped my feet up on the dashboard.

"What are you doing? Why are you lying like that?"

"Why isn't Hale here yet?"

"Sir, do you have any blankets or towels? If the contractions are that close, now's the time to prepare the environment as best you can."

"Where's the freaking ambulance?"

"The ambulance is on its way, sir. Try to stay calm."

"This woman doesn't even like me!"

I started to cry. It was true. I hated him. I hated this car. I hated how my ass felt like it was going to explode at any second. And I hated that this abso-freaking-lutely wasn't a bad dream. Loud sobs poured out of me as I threw my head back in pain.

"I think it's getting worse."

"This is your chance to win her over," the operator said with encouraging calm neither of us felt. "Help her get as comfortable as possible. Use any clean blankets you have on hand to prepare the area. You'll need something to support the baby when it comes."

"I can't have my baby in a Lamborghini at a strip mall!"

"Ma'am, try to stay calm and keep breathing. Sir, keep her head supported, and her body reclined."

"I'm in a car!" Xander panicked. "Where the hell am I supposed to find blankets?"

"I want my doctor," I cried.

My door opened, and Xander looked down at me, the horror on his face mimicking mine. "Well, you've only got me right now. Fuck!" He shrugged out of his jacket. "This is a nine-hundred-dollar jacket."

"Could you be any more pretentious? I'm in labor, you prick."

"I'm just making sure you note my sacrifice."

"Oh, my God." I dropped my head back and unbuckled the seatbelt.

"Her head's elevated, and she's lying back," he told the operator as he shoved the jacket under me as if it were a fitted sheet. "Do you think you can aim toward the door?"

"I think if you stuff that jacket any further under my ass, I'm going to hurt you."

"I'm just trying to protect the upholstery."

"I don't give a fuck about your fucking upholstery! *Ahhhhhowyowyowyow!*"

"Sir? Sir, are you there?"

"I'm here!"

"Sir, do either of you have a string or shoelace?"

We both frowned. "For what?" Xander asked.

"To tie off the umbilical cord."

Xander's face paled and he pressed a fist to his mouth, his skin now a sallow shade of green. "I'm wearing loafers."

"I'm wearing flip-flops."

"We're so fucked." He looked at the dashboard. "How far is that ambulance?"

"Help is on the way, but we want to be ready in case the baby comes first. Ma'am are you hanging in there?"

"I'm...trying." Pressure pushed and I wanted to run outside of my body but there was no getting away from it. I kicked my leg, nearly kicking Xander in the face. "Sorry!" I squirmed, but no matter what position I tried, there was no relief.

"Have you been timing the contractions?"

"No." I was doing everything wrong. "But they're close. I don't know how close." Hale would know. He'd done so well at all of our birthing classes. He was supposed to be here, holding my hand and encouraging me and ordering drugs to make the pain go away.

"Would you say they're less than five minutes apart?"

"Yes," both Xander and I answered at once.

"Then we need to check if the baby's head is visible."

Everything stilled.

"Sir, are you there?"

Xander held my stare, his expression one of absolute horror. "I'm here."

"Can you check if the baby's head is visible?"

Mother Earth, swallow me now. The only person allowed to see my unmanicured nine-month pregnant hoo-ha was my husband and my doctor. "Absolutely not."

Xander nodded in agreement and told the 9-11 operator, "I'd rather wait for the professionals."

"Ma'am are you having the urge to push?"

"No," I lied, then admitted, "Mostly because I don't want to."

Tyler would be proud if I ruined Xander's car. But even that wasn't enough to make me push.

"Ma'am, for your safety and the baby's, I

need you to get into position and let him take a look to see if the head is visible."

I closed my eyes and whimpered. I should have expected catastrophic level calamities. Things had been too good, too easy. I was happy. I knew better. I should have anticipated my worst nightmare coming to life.

A hand squeezed mine and I opened my eyes. Xander was there, fear clear on his face, but something had changed. Was that compassion in his stare?

"It's okay," he assured. "We can do this."

With a shaky breath, I nodded and turned my body so my legs hung out the door. "You make one snide comment, and I swear I'll kick you right in the nose." I lifted to pull down my underwear. They only made it to my thighs before I was bowing backward in pain.

"Shit. The contractions are getting worse," Xander snapped at the 9-11 operator. "Where the hell's this ambulance?"

I howled. "Something's wrong! What do I do?"

He yanked my underwear off and pushed up my dress. "Holy shit."

"What? What is it?"

"It's a brunette."

"Don't tell me that!"

"What should I do?" Xander yelled. "I see a head!"

"Place your hands under her and support the baby's head, sir. Ma'am, once he's in position, you have to push."

"I want Hale!" I wailed. Wheels squealed in the distance as sirens blared, blending into a roar with my own screams as I had no choice but to start pushing as the pressure took on a life of its own. *"I can't do thisssss!"*

"Rayne!"

My breath hitched as I tried to see past Xander's sweaty head, but tears blurred my vision. *"Hale?"*

"I'm here!"

"Oh, thank fucking God." Xander disappeared and Hale was there, kissing me and taking my hand as he checked the situation.

"Hale, it's happening!" A demon-like guttural growl bellowed from my lungs.

"You got this, baby! Keep pushing! Keep pushing!"

White light burst behind my eyes as the pain made me momentarily deaf and the world slowed in its orbit. There was Hale, smiling and cheering me on with his sleeves rolled up and his hair a mess as my body seemed to split in two. I couldn't hear over the pain. My life flashed behind my eyes, and all my focus turned to survival. I pushed harder than I ever pushed. Then...

Sound came back with the whooshing sound of a gas igniting into flames. A battle cry ripped from me, loud and deep. And then there was a smaller sound, fragile, like the delicate squawk of a bird, and tiny, like the voices of the little Whos of Whoville.

"You did it!" Hale cried and laughed in awe, his compulsion for cleanliness gone as he pulled our newborn to his chest.

Then...there was peace. Hot, searing, sit-me-in-an-ice-bath peace. I sagged back in relief and caught my breath as those tiny squawks filled the air.

"Oh, Rayne, she's perfect."

She? I closed my eyes and smiled victoriously. We had a girl. Elara had a sister.

Tipping my head, I weakly watched as he used a pristine pocket square to wipe her mouth and nose. Of course, Hale would know exactly what to do.

He gathered her little body in a pure white towel, and I frowned. "Where did you get that?"

He winked at me. "My beautiful wife gave her to me."

My laughter was a mix of tears and euphoria. "I meant the towel."

He smiled. "I always have a clean towel in my car in case of emergencies."

Of course, he did.

The 9-11 operator instructed Hale to place her on my chest, skin-to-skin, so she stayed warm until the ambulance arrived.

"She's so tiny." It was hard to believe Elara was also once this small.

Lights flashed against the windshield, and Hale kissed his fingers and pressed them to my lips. "The EMTs are here."

The paramedics rushed into action, and I was moved onto a stretcher. As soon as I was transported to the back of the ambulance, the cord was cut.

"You're doing great, Mom."

I smiled into my daughter's squinting, silver eyes. "Hello, angel."

"She has your hair," Hale said, crouching by my side, staring in awe.

"And your eyes."

"What should we call her?"

There were so many beautiful names that I honestly didn't know which one I would choose until the moment I met her. "What do you think of Avalyn?"

"Elara and Avalyn," he said, testing the names together. "I like it."

"It means *breath of life*." That was what Hale did for me. He breathed life into my soul and from our love a family bloomed.

"I think that's the perfect name for her," he whispered, gently tucking the tip of his pinky into her little curled fist. "She's our little breath of life. Plus, it sounds a lot like Avalon."

"Oh, where you were born."

He smiled. "That, yes, but it's also where we first met."

"Aw, now I love her name even more!"

We looked into our daughter's eyes, both of us blinking back tears of joy. Hale kissed my head and traced a finger over Avalyn's tiny eyebrow.

The irony of childbirth was that it was absolute hell, and then it was heaven. All the pain and fear and heartburn and morning sickness was worth it in the end.

Hale's phone rang, and in a matter of minutes, we were *en route* to the hospital. As soon as we arrived, we were swarmed by nurses and family. It took a while for everything to calm down, and I was so tired that I was somehow wired.

My mom hovered close by, adjusting my blankets and tracing gentle touches over Avalyn's soft hair and tiny fingers. "She's a little you, Ray."

"Oh, boy," Remington said, entering the crowded room with an armful of balloons. "That's just what the world needs, another Meyers running around." He handed off the balloons to Barrett and stepped close to my mom, looking down at his granddaughter. His gruff expression softened. "That's a Davenport if I've ever seen one." He turned and faced Hale. "Congratulations."

Hale held his father's stare, then stepped forward and hugged the man. My heart stopped as Remington tensed in surprise. Then I melted as he wrapped his arms around his son.

"Thanks, Dad."

"Do you want to hold her, Remington?"

His stare met mine and I felt life correct itself. Despite how perfect the Davenports appeared to the outside world, on the inside they were like everyone else—a little broken and living for the first time. They didn't always get things right on the first try, especially the emotional stuff. But Remington did know how to love, and I felt his love now.

He stepped closer and gruffly cleared his throat. "She sure is a pretty thing—like her momma."

I smiled up at him and turned Avalyn for the pass-off. He carefully lifted her slight weight out of my arms, and I blinked back tears as he lowered his face close to hers and whispered, "Spit up on whoever you want while you can. Later, it'll cost you in lawsuits."

"Nice, Remington."

"What? It's true. Someone has to teach her these things." He nuzzled her with his nose. "And don't you worry about the ABCs. Davenports only focus on ROIs."

"Okay, that's enough advice from Grandpa," Seraphina said, taking Avalyn from her father. "Let Aunt Phina teach you about shopping."

"How about we worry about her tycoon training later?" Hale said, retrieving our daughter. Then he smiled and changed his voice to the playful tone he used with Elara. "Because we're only a few hours old. Yes, we are."

Love filled my heart as I watched him.

Them. Elara also watched curiously, and Hale lowered Avalyn so she could see her new sister.

"Can you say Avalyn?"

"Ab-lyn?"

Oh boy, that sounded a little like goblin when she said it. We'd work on that.

Amid the chaos, I looked over Hale's shoulder and met Xander's stare, surprised that he lingered. He'd been so anxious to escape the situation earlier, yet he stuck around for what was clearly an intimate family moment.

Although he didn't fully enter the room, he watched the scene unfold with a look of longing in his eyes. I took pity on him. Today had been rough on everyone.

Looking back at me, he smiled and gave a subtle nod. My earlier frustration disappeared. In a way, Xander saved me today. If he hadn't stopped by the house when he had, I would have been all alone, unable to find my phone, and terrified for my life and Avalyn's.

"Thank you," I mouthed.

His lips curved in a subtle grin. Then his expression turned to one of surprise and his expression shuttered. I frowned as he stepped aside but soon understood.

"Tyler," he said, with flustered shock.

Tyler paused in the doorway, also surprised to find him there. "Xander." He frowned but then thought better of making small talk with the man who emotionally screwed him over. "Excuse me. I'm here to see my friends," he said, making it clear that Xander didn't fit that category.

Tyler entered the room and Xander took that as his sign to leave. He quietly left with little notice. My gaze turned to Ty. "Hey, you."

"Hey." He bent to kiss my head. "How was it?"

"Oh, it was lovely, like passing a watermelon through a keyhole."

"I'm sure you weren't at all dramatic," he teased.

"Drama's not my style, Ty. You know I'm all sophistication."

He laughed then greeted Hale.

"Meet Avalyn," Hale said as he placed her in Tyler's arms.

Tyler cradled her gently and smiled. "Wow, Rayne. She's beautiful."

I wiped a tear from my eye because, apparently, the crying thing didn't stop for something like eighteen years once a person became a parent.

"You okay?" Hale asked softly, kissing my head.

"Oh, yeah." I sniffled. "These are happy tears." Despite all the unpredictable calamities, today had turned out to be a perfect day —one I'd never forget.

The family stuck around for a few hours, but when I started nodding off, they left so I could rest. Tyler left with my mother and Elara, promising to return in the morning. Seraphina promised the same.

The nurses tried to take Avalyn to the nursery, but Hale wouldn't have it. He slept in the chair beside the bassinet while I slept in the bed, waking only to nurse when Avalyn started to cry.

I awoke the following day to daylight flooding through the curtains and Avalyn being wheeled out of the room. "Where are they taking her?"

"For some routine tests. Nothing's wrong."

My sudden panic shifted to relief, and I sat up. Breakfast had been delivered, so I perused the bed tray. The eggs looked rubbery.

"Don't eat that," Hale said. "Phina's bringing real food."

"Thank God. How long have you been up?"

"A few hours. Avalyn and I returned a few emails and checked some accounts."

"She's only a day old, Hale. The rule is they have to be at least a month old before prepping for their MBA."

I was moving slower than usual, and my body was sore, so Hale helped me shuffle to the bathroom. While I peed, he tidied up the bedding and sanitized the bed rails.

My rubber-treaded hospital socks stopped at the bathroom threshold as I watched him. "I leave you alone for two minutes, and the whole place smells like disinfectant."

"Germs are dangerous for newborns."

"I'm sure that's why you bleached the bed." He helped me get comfortable and situated under the sheets. He looked at me in a strange way that made me frown. "What? Why do you look like you have bad news?"

"Not bad."

"But something. What is it?"

He sat back and sighed, which did

nothing to ease my sudden anxiety. "I wanted to wait until you were—"

"Just say it, Hale. Whatever it is, I'll handle it." He knew I didn't do well with suspense and could make a mountain out of a molehill.

"It's about Xander."

Ugh. That could go either way. I still didn't trust the guy, but since giving birth in his very fancy car, I sort of decided to give him a mulligan. "What about Xander? Did he say something to Tyler?"

"No, this has nothing to do with Tyler."

"Then what?"

He leaned forward, bracing his elbows on his knees as he interlaced his fingers. "You know I like to do thorough research whenever I go into business with anyone."

"Yes," I said slowly.

"Well, when I look into any company, I also look into the shareholders' personal lives."

"Okay."

"I never meant to cause problems between you and my dad, Rayne."

"I know."

"But Xander was never going to sell to him."

I knew that too. "We've been over this."

He sat back and scratched his jaw where stubble had grown. "Xander's mom passed away last year."

"He told me he didn't have family."

"That's not exactly true."

"Oh." As someone who had no contact with a parent, I understood how complicated family situations could get. "Well, he strikes me as a bit of a loner, so maybe that's by choice."

"Rayne, he has family. Quite a bit. It turns out he has two brothers and a sister."

"Okay." I didn't know what he was getting at. "Are they not close?"

"Not yet."

I frowned. "Why are you being so cryptic? Just say whatever you're trying to say." Honestly, who cared what Xander did in his personal life?

"Rayne, I'm trying to tell you that Xander and I have more in common than our business interests."

The hair on my arms stood up and I slowly sat back. "Wait. What do you mean? Are you saying...?"

"It turns out we also share a father."

I stared, slack-jawed. "*He's your brother?*"

"Who?"

My wide eyes jerked to Seraphina as she stood in the doorway holding a caddy of coffee. I looked back to Hale with wide eyes. "You're joking."

"I'm not. I didn't want to tell you until after the baby was born because I didn't want to stress you out."

"How long have you known?"

"Known what?" Seraphina demanded, setting the food and coffee on the counter by the sink.

My heart pounded. Did we tell her? She had a right to know. As did Barrett. *Holy shit!* "Does Remington know?

"My dad doesn't know. I've only known for a week. I wanted to make sure it was absolutely certain."

"Jesus Christ, your dad will have to buy another yacht." It was common knowledge that he bought one to represent the mother of each of his children.

"Will someone please tell me what the hell you two are talking about!" Phina demanded.

I looked at her, shock making my brain slow, then I covered my mouth. "Oh, my God. You almost hooked up with him!"

"Who?"

Hale's lips firmed. It was clear he hadn't expected an audience for this conversation, but he was getting one as Barrett also walked in.

"Good morning, parents!" He greeted, carrying a beautiful bouquet. "Where's my goddaughter?"

I frowned. We already made it clear that Tyler would be the godfather. "Those flowers are beautiful."

"Thanks. They're for Hale."

Hale rolled his eyes. "Maybe it's good that you're both here. I have some news."

The room sobered, and Barrett crossed his arms. "What's going on?"

"It's about Xander Landry."

Seraphina perked up, and Barrett glanced at me in question. I was staying out of it. "What about him?"

"As it turns out..." Hale cleared his throat. "He's our brother."

Both of their jaws nearly hit the floor.

"*What?*" Seraphina snapped in a high pitch voice. "That's impossible."

"Come on, Phina. Nothing's impossible with Dad."

"No," she argued. "We..." She shook her

head. "I... There has to be some kind of mistake. Who told you this?"

"A doctor."

"Does Xander know?" Barret asked, on an entirely different train of thought, one that likely had to do with math and word problems revolving around inheritances and fractions that just got a lot smaller.

"He does now. We saw a specialist to confirm everything last week. I wanted to be sure before I told you guys."

"What would make you even suspect that?" Phina demanded. "He looks nothing like a Davenport."

"He brought his suspicions to me after we returned home from New England. His mom passed away a few months back, and he had been sorting out her assets. He came across some old pictures of her and Dad. Apparently, they dated somewhere between my mom and yours, Barrett."

"Does Dad know?"

"No. And Xander asked that we keep it that way until he's ready to tell him. He'd like to break the news himself."

"I don't like that," Barrett said. "Why the prolonged secrecy?"

I was with him on that. Secrets only complicated matters, and the Davenports were complicated enough.

"He wants a chance to make things right with Dad after the dispute last fall. Xander made it clear he's not after money or any sort of compensation."

Barrett scoffed. "Oh, please. I don't trust that guy as far as I could throw him."

"He has his own money, Barrett," Phina said defensively.

"Everyone thinks they have money until they see Davenport money. And why are you sticking up for him, brother lover?"

She gasped. "Don't call me that!"

Barrett shrugged. "You're the one who tried to sleep with him."

"We went for one walk!"

"Nothing would have happened anyway," I jumped in before they broke into full-on juvenile bickering. "Xander's gay."

"*What?*" Phina's eyes bulged. "He likes men? What the hell is going on with my instincts?"

"You're upset your half-brother *didn't* have a crush on you?" Barrett asked.

"Shut. Up," Phina growled through bared teeth.

Barrett looked back at Hale. "What do you think of all this?"

Hale, the ever-patient, pragmatic one, drew in a slow breath. "I think it is what it is. He's our brother. We should probably get to know him."

I smiled, proud of how accepting my husband was. "I like that idea."

"Me too," Phina said.

"You already know him well enough," Barret joked, and she shoved him.

I looked at Hale, and my grin widened. Our eccentric, little, dysfunctional family grew by two in only one day. Color me surprised! I had foolishly assumed this was the part of the story that got boring. But, apparently, we Davenports had a whole world of fresh drama to look forward to. And I was here for it...

As I'm sure you will be too.

THE END
...for now.

Want Gran Meyer's Apple Pie recipe?
CLICK HERE to get it along with a personal
letter from Lydia Michaels.

Also by Lydia Michaels

BOOKS BY SERIES

Many First in series books are FREE

Grab them here!

Free Books Here

MCCULLOUGH MOUNTAIN

Almost Priest *

Beautiful Distraction

Irish Rogue

British Professor

Broken Man

Controlled Chaos

Hard Fix

Intentional Risk

JASPER FALLS

Wake My Heart *

The Best Man

Love Me Nots

Pining For You

My Funny Valentine

Side Squeeze

CALAMITY RAYNE

Calamity Rayne Gets a Life *

Calamity Rayne Back Again

Calamity Rayne Gets Hitched

BONUS: Calamity Rayne Veiled & Railed

Calamity Rayne Over the Moon

Calamity Rayne Knocked Up

THE SURRENDER TRILOGY

Falling In

BreakingOut

Coming Home

Ruthless Billionaires

One Billion Secrets *

Two Billion Enemies

MASTERMIND

Blind

Untied

NEW CASTLE

First Comes Love *

If I Fall

Shattered Vows

ADDICTED TO YOU

Crush *

Bang

Throb

THE ORDER OF VAMPIRES

Original Sin *

Dark Exodus

Prodigal Son

Immortal Bastard

Primal Kill

Blood Moon

STAND ALONES

La Vie en Rose

Simple Man

Sugar

Breaking Perfect

Hurt

Protege

About the Author

To receive Lydia's Newsletter and 7 FREE Books
CLICK HERE!

Lydia Michaels is the bestselling and award-winning author of more than forty novels. She writes heart-clenching, unpredictable romance with dark elements and high heat. Her work is character-driven and bursting with broken heroes and badass females. With a sweet spot for overbearing, territorial types, her deeply emotional books are spicy, emotionally satisfying, and guaranteed to leave readers with many book hangovers.

Lydia is the consecutive winner of the *2018 & 2019 Author of the Year Award* from *Happenings Media* and the recipient of the *2014 Best Author Award* from the Courier Times. She has been featured by *USA Today*, *Romantic Times Magazine*, the *Women in Publishing Summit*, and more.

Michaels started her author career in 2007, becoming a recognized presence and advocate within the publishing industry. She is the CEO of LMC Consulting, a certified author coach specializing in character and plot development, and the founder of the *East Coast Author Convention*, the *Behind the Keys Author Retreat*, and www.LydiaMichaelsBooks.com.

She is happily married to her childhood sweetheart. Her favorite things include cooking Italian cuisine, hosting extravagant dinner parties, sipping espresso martinis, listening to her husband play piano, and escaping to her coastal home on the Jersey Shore. She's an LGBTQ ally, a BLM supporter, a firm believer that the patriarchy

must end (women's rights are human rights),
and an advocate for pediatric cancer research.

L Y D I A

Follow Lydia Michaels on social media!
Facebook | Instagram | TikTok

Thank you for your review!

Reviews help authors so much!
If you left a review for this
book, I greatly appreciate it!
Thank you,
Lydia

Click HERE to return to Amazon.